About the author

Nick Kenefick is forty-seven-years old and lives with his wife and three children in Devon on the south coast of England. For the last twenty years, he has worked as a surgeon in emergency and general surgery. This is his first fiction novel.

"Writing this book has brought me incredible joy and my sincere hope is that some of that enjoyment is passed on to its readers."

THE SCENT

Nick Kenefick

THE SCENT

Vanguard Press

A CIP catalogue record for this title is
available from the British Library.

ISBN 9781784656461

*Vanguard Press is an imprint of
Pegasus Elliot MacKenzie Publishers Ltd.*
www.pegasuspublishers.com

First Published in 2020

Vanguard Press
Sheraton House Castle Park
Cambridge England
Printed & Bound in Great Britain

Dedication

For my children, they are my everything.

CHAPTER ONE

The scent. It came to him first.

Perhaps it was because of his position; perhaps it was because of the direction of the gentle breeze that barely cooled them in the harsh tropical heat; perhaps it was because the seven others were behind him, precisely positioned, as they had been trained to be. He knew none of these reasons were correct. He knew the truth. He knew the reason that he alone had detected that unmistakable scent was that it was sadly all too familiar to him. It was the scent of his first memory. One that he had tried so hard to bury deep in the past, a scent that belonged to a previous life. He had tried to forget, to relinquish his former existence, but he knew he would never succeed. He knew all too well the significance of that unique scent. He knew what it meant and what they would find. It was the scent of destruction, devastation, despair and death.

PRESENT DAY, CAMEROON, WEST AFRICA

His name was Will James and he was twenty-seven years old. Although from his appearance he looked older, weathered and hardened by life. He was on point, at the front centre of his unit of eight men. They were a single tight unit of the special air service infantry, the SAS. Will had been put in front for several reasons. The first was due to his knowledge of the local language; there were not many members of the British special forces who were fluent in the various dialects of this forgotten war-torn part of the world. The second was so that his team leader could keep him under constant surveillance, both for his protection and for his assessment. Will was a Marine, the special forces limb of the United Kingdom's navy. He had been placed with this SAS unit for this mission partly for his ever-evolving training but mainly due to his unique knowledge of this broken country. The third reason that he was on point was more basic. If they came under fire it was likely that he, Major W. James would be the first point of contact, and as such the most vulnerable. However the simple harsh reality was that he was a visitor in this unit and as such quite simply he was the least valuable member of the team. As far as the UK armed forces knew, based on his file, Will had been born in the French-speaking part of Cameroon on the West Coast of Africa and then had left shortly after the start of the civil war at the age of fifteen to live in England as a British citizen. This was all the detail they had and was all the detail they required. This explained his appearance, his almost unique knowledge of the local area and his multiple language abilities. There was no record of the real, bitterly harsh life he had once been forced to lead. There was only one living soul who knew of his real upbringing at the hands of, and as an active part of, the guerrilla forces of this vicious region. That individual would never reveal the truth.

They were in the Ekop district, a little-known region in the south west tip of Cameroon. Officially Ekop was part of the Reserve de Campo, one of the National parks of Cameroon supposedly dedicated to the protection of the natural flora and wildlife that flourished in this vast unpopulated country. The real value of the Ekop district however lies in its geographical location and its functional infrastructure. To the east it was within striking distance of the border with the oil-rich Republic of Congo and, to the south the even more valuable mineral-rich Equatorial Guinea. Also unusually for an isolated West African country Cameroon and Ekop had a functional network of passable roads that linked Ekop with the nearby working deepwater port of Kribi. Will and his eight-man unit were part of an advisory and peace-keeping force nominally under the authority of the United Nations. In reality however they were an independent elite cell, tasked with assessing the stability of the area and reporting back to their superiors. They did not know the specific reasons for their mission, nor did they care, they were professional soldiers with a job to complete, that was enough for them. The real reason they had been sent was that this war-torn region, now completely destroyed by years of conflict, robbed of any financial worth, was of interest solely because of its geographical position. This wasted country had a coastline and with this came the once functional port of Kribi. This small town on the southern part of the coast at the head of the river Kineke was unusual in that it had a deepwater port capable of taking large tankers. This vanishingly rare combination of functioning infrastructure, a useable deepwater port and the geographical location gave this otherwise unknown region significant value. Its importance was to the major multinational business conglomerates that transferred vast quantities of oil and other mineral resources out of the Congo and Central Africa and onto the unquenchable thirst of the Western economy. Recent political upheavals and regime change in central Africa, a not unusual event, had necessitated alterations of previously well-established and agreed export routes so that now they had to pay for more expensive, longer land-based or even more costly air-based transport routes. Gaining access to this small, otherwise insignificant, region could potentially re-establish a direct and crucially economically viable export route, unlocking the valuable exports and potentially saving millions. This was the real reason for Will and his team's current deployment. They knew none of this, nor did they wish to know, completing their mission, getting home alive, was their only focus.

Four days previously they had been dropped from *HMS Dauntless*, a Type-45 class destroyer, officially on joint tripartite Anglo-American-European exercises, belonging to the Royal Navy. They had arrived by Zodiac under the cover of darkness and had been patrolling on foot, completely independent, for the last four days. There had as yet been no single human contact, no trace of the indigenous local population nor any signs of the guerrilla forces that had seized control of this remote and unknown part of West Africa three decades previously. Over the last few years the LPT, as they were called, had grown in strength by a combination of ruthless violence and the enforced abject poverty of the downtrodden population creating a total dependence. Their pre-deployment briefing had informed them that the "Liberte Pour Tous" organisation, or LPT, had started originally thirty years previously as a freedom group, formed from the local population rebelling against strict controls imposed by the central government, mainly around the growing of marijuana and cocaine. In response to international pressure and in exchange for certain amounts of Western aid the national government had agreed to make the production of such drug crops illegal. However to these locals they were simply the staple crops that had been grown in this region for many generations. Over the last thirty years however, the LPT had evolved into a far more sinister organisation and they now had absolute control over the entire region, particularly now dominating the only two active trades that were flourishing currently in this part of the world: drugs and human trafficking. Through complete dominance of these two illegal trades they had defiled the region, depleting it of all its wealth, both material and human, and had created a virtual state within a country. Very few in the outside world had even heard of the LPT and even fewer cared, they had learned the lessons of the past decade when they had grown too large, too obvious. They were currently not considered a terrorist organisation as they remained within their own borders. While they were totally ruthless, and not shy of using force when required, they were sensible enough to remain within their own country. They had no misguided belief that the rest of the world should follow their idealism, they had never placed bombs to target the innocent, never taken Western hostages or demanded ransoms, never made ridiculous demands or performed senseless acts of violence in other countries and, as a consequence, were of no real interest to the outside world. Even in Cameroon they were tolerated as in reality the action that would be required to eradicate them was simply not worth the effort. The sole reason for the current interest in this particular part of the world was purely geographical and financially driven, purely due to the possible trade routes. Recent political changes in neighbouring countries had meant that the normal land- or air-based routes to the east were now becoming more and more expensive to maintain and as such Kribi, the previously functioning deepwater port on the south-west coast of Cameroon, was now of significant interest. The minor problem however was that within this area the LPT was the ruling power.

They were well organised, affluent and totally ruthless in their dealings with both the outside world and their own people and they had little interest in the vagaries of international trade. Currently there were no official or unofficial lines of communication between the LPT and any of the other interested corporations or governments. The lack of any contact with either the downtrodden people of this region, or any of the LPT, over the last four days had perturbed them. That had suddenly all changed. Will knew what they would soon find. He had seen it before, inhaled it before, lived through it before.

The officer in charge of their eight-man squad was thirty-two-year-old Captain Jonathan Jenkins, JJ to his friends. He was a career army officer and in Will's opinion a good one at that. As they advanced slowly another fifty metres through the thick jungle the acrid scent became obvious to the others. Their period of isolation was at an end. JJ tapped his neck-mounted radio mike twice, two distinct static hits, and issued a single two-word command.

"On me." It was all that was required and was inaudible to anyone else not equipped with their advanced comms gear. They assembled rapidly, silently, crouched and took cover. They had been together as a unit for three months and had trained hard. It was now time for business. The situation was succinctly discussed; it was now obvious that contact was imminent. Their remit as a so-called peace keeping and advisory force was clearly defined, in essence no engagement unless first engaged and in imminent danger. The rules were clear; no one liked them, all understood them, they were professionals. Will was put back on point, the seven others fanning out as they had been trained to do; each controlling a specific arc of vision, a specific arc of potential danger and a specific arc of fire that would overlap and protect each other. No further words were required. They were highly trained.

As they moved slowly, cautiously, forwards as a unit Will could feel his senses heightened. Despite the adrenaline beginning to surge through his veins he could feel his heart rate slow. He was returning to the basic instincts that he had known for so long, instincts that had served him so well over the years, instincts that had allowed him to survive where many had perished. As they reached the junction of the thick tropical jungle with the open clearing marking the start of the village they stopped as a single unit, moving any further forward would expose them. They froze, immobile and almost impossible to detect, hidden in the dark impenetrable tropical forest in their patterned combat camouflage gear.

"Wait three," was the succinct command and all eight stopped, silently surveying the area ahead of them. As the seconds ticked by in virtual slow motion there was no movement, no signs of life or of any threat. Two stray dogs meandered through the thick black smoke that now billowed towards them. A domestic pig squealed as the flames crept towards it. Naked panic at its impending doom took over control of all its other instincts and it crashed blindly through its enclosure and fled to safety. Two minutes had passed and still no significant movement. The flames from the burning village huts crackled and leapt upwards towards the cloudless blue sky, the intense heat was palpable on their exposed faces. The dark, acrid smoke fanned by the gentle tropical breeze caught in their throats. The bodies of the dead villagers lay where they had fallen. Rigor mortis had not yet set in and their postures, although grotesque in death could almost be as though they were simply sleeping. The hard sun-baked dusty ground of the central square, once smooth and dark brown in colour, had been turned crimson red and was now damp and muddied. There had been no rain! Three minutes had now passed. Still no movement.

Three clicks came over their comms gear, a pre-programmed request for a situation report. In practised order the two-word reply returned.

"No contact," came back from each of the seven other men of their unit.

"Wait one further," was the command. The cautiousness and slow dogged progress of the SAS was one of the most admired aspects of their abilities. Their lack of arousal in stressful conditions and supreme control was one of the many exceptional parts of their creed that Will admired and one of the reasons they were arguably the best in the world. Three clicks came again.

Seven "No contact" replies. They were still within the protection of the jungle and as yet remained undetected. If they were to leave, now was the time. The decision was taken, not by committee but by their leader. Now in a potential combat situation each member of the team was referred to as a number. JJ was the alpha, Will point, the others one to six. Despite the fact that they had been together for over three months and knew most things about each other's lives, in a combat situation it was purely professional. They operated in this manner so that if one individual had to be replaced another could be parachuted in and all would understand the same language, there would be no confusion. It was how they had been trained. Staccato commands were issued, inaudible to others:

"One right flank, Six left flank, Two eyes high, rifle support, one minute." Sixty seconds passed and three replies rang in.

"In position." JJ did not hesitate, the command was issued, there was no room for confusion.

"Slow advance". They moved forward as one, creeping out of the protective shadows of the jungle into the harsh, bright light of the African sun. They were now visible, now vulnerable. For seven of the eight men it was their first experience of so-called ethnic cleansing; the incomprehensible process where one group destroys another for an almost always inexplicable reason. Almost always this was perpetuated by the strong and armed, preying on the weak, straightforward normal people just trying to simply carve out a peaceful life for themselves and their families. No one who experienced this process first-hand, could remain untouched. No one can avoid being forever altered by such sights and sounds. For Will however this was not his first time, this was a living memory from his previous life, one that would never dwindle in intensity. Unlike his team members he had been here before, in a different place and from a very different angle. The scent, however, was always the same!

CHAPTER TWO

They moved purposefully forward as one, a tight unit, each arc of fire and vision controlled and contained, overlapping each other as they were meant to be. Their pupils constricted, almost to pinpoints as their eyes adjusted to the blinding light of the exposed village after the dappled shadows of the canopy. As they advanced the team was now out in the open, visible, vulnerable. Each individual had their own private thoughts as they ghosted forwards through the human carnage surrounding them. For Will it was as though he had come full circle, returning to his first childhood memory. For the others it was a macabre baptism. There was no need to check the prostate bodies for any signs of life; it was obvious that none had been spared. Whichever inhumane group had carried out this atrocity it was clear that they had been efficient in their task; it was not the first time that this terror had occurred in this forgotten region. They continued to move forward, slowly, cautiously, yet secure in their ability as a team and in their purpose. As the distance between Will, in the lead, and the support sniper, "Two", increased the first communication came through their comms.

"Two losing line of sight on point." All understood, particularly Will that as they moved further into the village their thin veil of protection was ever decreasing. They were soldiers after all and this was their day job.

"Continue," was the single word issued from JJ, they continued. Another 300 metres and five minutes had passed. At this range the sniper's support, hampered by the billowing smoke, was becoming less and less effective. As Will moved into the central square of the village he felt the terrain change. Up to now the ground underfoot had been concrete-hard, sun-baked mud smoothed by the passage of countless feet. Now however here, in the principled killing zone the ground beneath him had become a soft, reddened mud.

Suddenly through the shimmering heat haze, mixed with waves of blinding black smoke, a group of guerrilla fighters appeared. There were five of them, confidently sauntering forwards, laughing and joking among themselves, totally oblivious to the devastation that surrounded them, the devastation that they had delivered. Why they had returned would never be known, it was irrelevant, what mattered now was that as the group of five turned the corner and entered the village square they saw Will, isolated, alone in front of them. They froze. Clearly they were not expecting to find anyone alive in the village, definitely not a fully armed Western soldier in full tactical combat gear. Will on the other hand was not frozen, he was calm, rapidly calculating the possible outcomes of this unplanned encounter. It came down to two options. Either this splinter group remained calm and slowly walked away, or they would not. He figured the former was seriously unlikely. His only sign of recognition was to utter two words through his neck mounted comms,

"Contact forwards." Then he stood, apparently alone, ready and faced them. With these two words the unit reacted instantly; the centrally placed soldiers moved closer and those out on the flanks advanced to cover the threat. As yet the group of five had not had time to react. Will watched them as they watched him; both were in open ground with no cover or shelter. Perhaps it was overconfidence instilled by their superior numbers, five against one seemed good odds. Perhaps it was the fact that they were still intoxicated from a lethal combination of the adrenaline-fuelled atrocities that they had delivered earlier in the day combined with the marijuana they had been incessantly smoking. Whatever the reason they began to do the one single action that would end their miserable lives. The taller man, at the front of the group, was the first to react and he began to swing his arm upwards and attached to that arm, as it had been for several years was his weapon, an ugly short-barrelled, black AK-47. This automatic rifle, the AK-47, was without doubt the most successful weapon ever built. It was originally designed in the later years of the Second World War by Mikhail Kalashnikov for use by the Soviet Army. It is virtually indestructible, required almost no maintenance and is still unequalled in its reliability and simplicity, requiring almost no skill or training to use. Testament to its success is that there were currently over seventy-five million in circulation throughout the world. At any significant distance it is worse than inaccurate, however up close, at less than twenty metres, the length of a tennis court, as it was now from Will, it was one of the most deadly hand-held weapons in the world.

As the fastest of the five continued to raise his weapon two things happened in very rapid succession. The first was that Will moved, faster than them. The second was the command "Engage, engage, engage! now shouted out loud, was issued, the time for remaining unobserved had passed. Will moved in a blur of speed born out of years of survival. This was not the conscious movement of one who saw an action, digested the consequence and then reacted, that would have been too slow. This was the feral fluid motion of one whose entire life had revolved around similar situations, of one whose inbred instincts for survival had now taken over considered reason. As the guerrilla fighter's index finger tightened on the trigger of his AK-47 a volley of lethal bullets ripped through the now vacant space where Will had been moments before. In less than a single heartbeat he had dived out of the killing zone, rolled and in a single fluid motion had come forwards to a crouching firing position, his own automatic rifle now nestled firmly to his shoulder, his cheek snug to the barrel, his eyes clear, open and searching for his target. The weapon appeared to be a part of him, almost as an extra limb, integral to his body. Before anyone else present had even acknowledged his rapidity of movement three precisely aimed bullets struck the lead guerrilla squarely in the chest. There was no sound on impact, just three small puffs of dust erupting from his torso as they hit, penetrated and then exited through his back. The man fell, instantly dead. As his body struck the ground the shattering sound of gunfire galvanised the others into action. They were not as fast as their now dead comrade but the current situation had encouraged them. Will had nowhere to go, he was exposed, out in the open, he had no option and so he reacted without hesitation, as he had been trained to do. He engaged them directly, with the speed and aggression that had always served him so well in the past. Two of the remaining four fell under Will's accurate fire before they had time to react. Will knew however that this situation could not last for much longer. While three assailants had gone down, two remained and they were now training their weapons directly at him. He was less than the distance of a tennis court away and there was no time left, no space for manoeuvre, nowhere to hide. He realised that very shortly his twenty-seven years was about to come to an end. Then through his comms gear hope arrived, "Engage, engage, engage! was repeated and before the third word was complete the immediate area around them erupted. The deafening sound of six automatic weapons opening up in a confined space could only really be appreciated by those who have experienced it up close. They created a roar like no other as they literally ripped the air apart. The physical space of the village square was now shattered by the supersonic passage of a fusillade of bullets crossing from different vertices. The ground was violently torn apart with puffs of pink dust as the lethal projectiles slammed into the dirt and the bodies of the remaining two guerrillas convulsed with each impact like epileptic fits. They had not been aware of the other members of the unit, as they were not meant to be. With the initial dialogue "Contact forwards the remaining members of the team had moved up and taken the positions that they had practised many times before. Six professional marksmen had zeroed in on the killing ground. There was no competition, it was not a fair fight and it was not meant to be. The contact lasted less than twenty seconds and then silence fell like a blanket over the village. Will was left still crouching in a firing position with five dead men sprawled out in front of him, in a village that few cared about in a nowhere location in a conflict-torn state. In the exaggerated post-contact silence mixed with the unmistakable scent of burning cordite fumes JJ broke their brief reverie.

"Contact terminated, rapid retreat.

CHAPTER THREE

They were on a so-called peacekeeping and advisory mission. This would be seen as a right royal fuck-up and they knew it. At the debrief all would agree that there had been no other viable option, however the outcome could not be altered or denied. It was a peacekeeping mission and it had resulted in lethal contact, the polar opposite. While this was the grey reality of their world the end-points were always more black and white in the world of politics and retrospective analysis. This was not a good outcome!

"Rapid retreat," was the command issued once again and they moved as one, remaining in formation they retraced their path back to the cover of the jungle, not hurried but at a fast, controlled pace. Once they were one hundred metres into the relative protection of the dense canopy of the jungle Will allowed himself to breathe more slowly, more regularly. Once again he had come close to his own death yet had somehow survived. He had been saved by the considerable ability and rapid actions of his team and he knew it. The extreme arousal of such decisive contact flowed through all of them, their senses raised to supernormal levels. They were professional soldiers but part of them enjoyed this adrenaline-fuelled sensation, if they were honest with themselves it was one of the reasons they did what they did.

They regrouped, took cover and appraised the situation. It was less than ideal. They were eight men in a foreign country and they were pretty sure that they had now seriously outstayed their welcome. JJ was a good officer but inexperienced, he was good enough however to realise this, another one of the better British qualities.

"Suggestions?" he asked. There were no immediate replies and he looked to Will. They all knew that he was far more experienced in such circumstances and the only one of the eight who knew the terrain and the enemy. Will thought for a second before replying:

"That was a small group of unskilled stragglers. They alone could not possibly have caused the devastation we just saw. My guess is that they were returning looking for leftovers. The main group must be close by and they will have heard us. They will either ignore it, which is un-fucking-likely or they will come for us. Any show of strength or defiance against them is unacceptable and a potential threat, they will not allow it and will want us gone, permanently. We need to call this in, request immediate extraction and get the fuck out of here, fast." There were nods of agreement all round and JJ fired up the satphone. The reception via satellite link was as clear as any mobile phone and the chilly reception of their news was predictable. There was no tacit approval of the outcome despite the lack of any loss of life to their own team. It was clear however that the region remained unstable, that much was obvious and one of the main reasons for their mission was to answer that precise question. The nearest extraction point was four kilometres away, a small outcrop where the land rose above the level of the canopy of the jungle and where it would be possible for choppers to land. Although the mission had been a global failure, control had no wish to lose such a valuable asset as this team. Also, as was the organisation of the SAS all controllers had to have previous real-time on the ground experience. All of them had been there on the sharp end of the line, they understood that the team need to be out, ASAP.

"Immediate evac granted."

"Right, let's move," said JJ. "We have four clicks to cover and then we are out."

"They will come fast," said Will.

"Then we better move faster," said JJ.

Stealth was now abandoned, speed was required so they changed formation and ran in single file. Will was at the front once again, using his knowledge of the terrain to increase their pace. They moved fast but remained organised, spaced approximately ten metres apart, still a professional unit. They were now in real danger and they knew it. All the previous advantages that they had, greater firepower, far superior comms gear and anonymity were now all turned against them. They were in a race against a massively superior force who were unhampered by heavy weaponry, who knew the jungle better than they did, with one exception, and were built to run. Not a single member of the guerrilla force now pursuing them, nor anyone else who lived in this conflict zone, had any excess body fat. The SAS team ran fast. They knew their survival depended on them reaching the extraction point first, once there they would be relatively safe. It was a scenario that they had practised in training many times before, *hostile extraction* it was called in the training manual. On arrival they would be able to establish a defensive perimeter and call in a set pattern of pre-programmed airstrikes to preserve their position and make it virtually impossible for any land-based force to seriously threaten them. The coordinates of the extraction point were already being loaded into the fire-control computers of the destroyer lying two miles offshore, the same ship that had dropped them into harm's way just ninety-six hours previously. Once they had arrived at the pre-planned extraction site they would remain in the so-called fifty-by fifty-metre square safe box while they could call in a rain of destruction that would fall precisely around them, launched from the destroyer and vaporising anything or anyone in a 200 metre circular perimeter of their safe box. This lethal airborne arsenal of destruction could be coordinated locally from the ground and also through satellite imagery under the authority of their central control in the event that communication was lost with the ground team. It was only four kilometres and they were highly motivated.

As it was they reached the extraction point unchallenged, covering the distance in just under thirty minutes. The reason for their calm passage was a combination of indecision and inferior technology. The leader of the local guerrilla force had only recently taken over command from his now recently deceased predecessor and he was nervous. Although he would never publicaly show his nervousness, in reality he was not prepared to commit his newly gained force against an unknown, but clearly highly armed and efficient enemy, without clearance from his superiors. Even a disorganised guerrilla force had a chain of command and he was well aware of the personal consequence of failure. It took some time to establish a line of communication back to the capital and this gave the soldiers all the window of time they required. They arrived at the extraction point, set their perimeter and called in the transport. The overhead satellite imagery confirmed that it was safe for the helicopters to land and their control coordinated the rest. In contrast to the intensity of the previous hour, their departure was relatively calm.

CHAPTER FOUR

As Will and the other seven members of his unit loaded into the helicopter he could feel the savage intensity of the last ninety-six hours begin to ebb away. The XC90 was the pony they were now riding. It was a medium-range helicopter, normally used as a workhorse transport vehicle or occasionally, as in this case, capable of being transformed into an attack ship of devastating capability; mounted under the fuselage bilaterally there were two AC70 rotating-barrel machine cannons. However bland and snub-nosed, these protuberances could deliver over one thousand rounds per minute of 1.59 calibre projectiles into a highly accurately controlled area, nothing could withstand this onslaught. Once in the protective armoured cocoon of the centre of the helicopter the men began to unwind. As they lifted off and left the hostile environment in which had just been seriously unwelcomed tourists, the rhythmic beating of the rotors began to work their mesmerising effect. Will had experienced this before, the regular metronomic beating of the rotors combined with the physical and mental exhaustion of the last few days was hard to resist. He could see in the weary faces of his friends that all of them had been deeply affected by the man-made cruelty they had passed through. All of their souls had been tainted by the carnage they had seen, it was not possible to remain whole when touched by such evil. Will saw this mirrored in the drawn faces of his friends. He felt it in himself.

As they cleared hostile airspace and started to head out over the crystal-clear African ocean towards the Type-45 class destroyer which they had left four days previously Will found himself wondering. He found himself lingering on the inescapable fact of why was such human cruelty possible, why it seemed to endlessly occur and would it ever stop? If history could teach us anything, he thought, it was unlikely any time in the near future. Why it was that one group thought it was reasonable to exterminate another if they did not agree with their rules or abide by their creed? Why did the human race have the seemingly inbuilt visceral need to remove others that did not comply with their view of the world and why was this normally dressed up as either a form of religion or belief? This was not a new phenomenon as he moved back through recent history. Currently Syria was ripping itself apart, gripped by a bitter civil war based on religious culture. The IS movement appeared to be at war with the entire rest of the world who did not hold to their ultra-idealistic philosophy. This inward-looking behaviour was not limited to so-labelled terrorist groups or Third World countries. Germany, the effective leader of the European Union, had arguably carried out the worst genocide ever performed just eighty years ago, less than two generations in the past. In the concentration camps of the Second World War millions of Jews had been systematically murdered, simply because they were Jewish, not because they were a danger or capable of any threat, just because of their religion! More recently the US had gone into Iraq on the basis of weapons of mass destruction, so-called WMDs that were never found probably because they never existed. They had rained down death and destruction from on high through bombers and naval artillery possibly only to guarantee oil rights to the region, seemingly unconcerned by the innocent human cost. This macabre theatre seemed to be repeated generation on generation, going back through the centuries the Christian nations, galvanised by the nobles of Britain had plundered Arab lands in the name of crusade and the Christian religion. No single group or nation was any better or worse than the other. And here, today, they had witnessed first-hand, up close and personal, the real human cost. When would human nature change? Would it ever change? What was it within our nature that drove us to such cruelty? Why did the collective mindless action of a group strip away the basic morality of an individual?

Will found his mind wondering over such wide-ranging and broad thoughts and then he rapidly jolted himself back to reality, to the here and now. He dismissed his musings as the foolish whims of a child. Human nature was what it was, the good and the bad and it had not changed over thousands and thousands of years and likely never would. Acceptance of this was the reality, resisting it would lead to insanity. He was a professional soldier, a marine commando of the Royal Navy, attached to a unit of the SAS. He had a job to do and completing it, without question or hesitation, was the only way forward. He had already made his choice many years previously. He had joined the British armed forces and he had enjoyed all the benefits that accompanied this, it was time to pay his dues, that was the deal, and he was fine with it. After all it was a far, far better situation than his former life.

Not many individuals had lived two distinct lives by the age of twenty-seven. Will had. He had tried so hard to bury his former existence, to forget. Officially he had succeeded, there were no records of his existence before the age of fifteen. However deep within he knew he would never truly be able to leave that previous life behind. As they whipped over the white crests of the ocean waves below the rhythmic beating of the rotors continued to work their soporific charm. Will succumbed to sleep, yet in his last few conscious moments he knew where his exhausted slumber would take him, it often did. It would take him back. Back to the beginning.

CHAPTER FIVE

BEGINNING

He was born at eleven o'clock at night on Christmas Day, almost exactly a year after his mother had arrived at the sanctuary. She died on Boxing Day, Will was one day old; she almost made her nineteenth birthday.

Thankfully maternal mortality was a vanishing rarity in the Western world, perinatal or otherwise. However, in underdeveloped West Africa a quarter of a century ago it was not unusual. She had a condition called *placenta praevia*. It was bad luck really, that is all, no one's fault, just bad luck. The placenta had grown in the incorrect part of the womb and had blocked the exit of the baby. As Will was born his passage into this world had torn through the soft friable placental tissue. It was not his fault, he had no knowledge of the fact that his arrival into this world would herald his mother's departure. As he was born the ripped placental tissues bled, causing a massive peripartum haemorrhage. In the Western world this was relatively easily dealt with and the risks of any serious adverse outcomes are low. However, in rural Africa, with no access to medical support, the die was cast. She quietly surrendered six hours after Will was born, slipping peacefully away with her defenceless newborn infant cradled on her chest.

She had arrived at the Sanctuary of St Xavier one year previously. Her father had endured and eventually died from AIDS. With his passing she was left alone in her village without any means of obtaining food or protection. Her choices were limited, either marry rapidly or turn to a life of prostitution, the only realistic options available to a lone female in this part of Africa. She chose a third option, she fled. She ran to the Mission of St Xavier. St Xavier's was a Catholic run mission established several years previously for the shelter and protection of displaced women. There had been a financial grant from an American-based institution to establish a centre for vulnerable women and children. It was a trendy cause, popular with the affluent and idle sections of high society. As well as a highly sociable evening spent with the great and the good of American celebrity society, those attending felt that they were doing a good deed by donating and returned home to their security-gated mansions with a smug inner glow of self-satisfaction. No matter their origin, the funds raised had been substantial and had allowed not only the building but also the permanent staffing of St Xavier's, organised and run through the Catholic church.

Will's father was one of the several Catholic priests that ran and staffed St Xavier's and he took his father's name. Father Wilhelm had been born and raised in the foothills of the German Alps and physically he was a giant of a man, standing at six foot nine inches tall. He had all the true Germanic characteristics of his origin with striking, almost white blond hair and piercingly clear blue eyes. Like most of the other priests he had been sent to St Xavier's in Africa due to his previous misconduct. Deep down in his soul he was truly a good man. He had two unshakable beliefs; firstly was that the only reason for his presence on this earth was to help others and secondly was his total commitment to his religion and all the good that it could deliver. The problem was that he was normal, he was a normal man with the normal desires for human contact and company and he had struggled to suppress these normal desires as was demanded by his religion. Wilhelm was attracted to the opposite sex. Will's mother was not the first time he had strayed from the path of abstinence demanded by the Catholic church, unfortunately for him in the past he had been caught. He had been in an "inappropriate relationship with a female in his diocese", which was the official description of his previous relationship. He had been given a choice, either leave the Church or leave Germany and travel to a new mission being established in West Africa. There had been little option for Wilhelm, so he had simply packed and left the following day.

Will's mother had understood the situation almost immediately after arriving at St Xavier's. She understood the needs and desires of the priest for female companionship and there was no coercion required, she was a willing participant in a deal from which she gained friendship, stability and shelter. One year after she arrived Will was born. The infant was named Will, after his father. He had no surname, he was just one of many orphaned infants in Africa, yet he had the good fortune to have been born within the confines of the Mission of St Xavier's and so he survived when, by all the laws of natural selection he had no right to do so, an infant alone in Africa. He was cared for by the many other young women who had sought shelter from the conflict inside the walls of the mission. He was one of several children who had been born in the mission as a result of the union between the women who fled there for shelter and the priests who lived and worked there. As he grew from infant to boy it became more obvious who his father was, Will had inherited many of the physical traits of Father Wilhelm. To start with he was tall, very tall and stood head and shoulders above the other children of his own age. His hair was not white but neither was it the dark jet-black of his mother, it was fair, and his skin was paler than the other children so that he could easily pass for European rather than African at first glance. His height was combined with the powerful muscular bulk of his African heritage which gave him strength and stamina. Even as a boy it was obvious that he had been gifted a phenomenal physical build which would only grow in size and strength as he grew in years. However the most striking physical attribute was Will's eyes. He had inherited the piercing stony blue eyes of his father's Germanic race.

As well as the standard chores required of all the youth in the mission Will's early years were remarkably traditional. He was living in a Catholic mission after all and as such he was required to attend school. For six hours a day, six days a week he was in lessons, mainly based around religious teaching, and by the age of eight he could recite the entire Bible verbatim. Where he demonstrated competence in his basic education he had an uncanny ability and an unusual thirst for knowledge for different languages. His father spoke to him in German and English, the other children and women in the mission used mainly French and the few men from outside allowed into the mission used the many native dialects of Africa. By the age of eleven he was fluent in them all and his natural ability delighted the priests who then in turn invested more effort in his education. And so it continued until one day shortly after his twelfth birthday. Up to that point Will's memories were blurred into one of his early childhood, with no real specific points of reference. However that changed. It was the day he was always dragged back to in his fitful dreams.

The helicopter plunged fifty metres downwards as they passed over the top and through a thermal current. The rapid descent snapped his head backwards from off his chest and woke him momentarily. He stared around the cargo hold of the XC-90. All but the pilot and co-pilot were asleep, safe in their own private worlds. The pilot rotated the throttle and regained altitude, the rotors continued in their unbroken mesmerising rhythm and Will returned to unconsciousness, once again.

CHAPTER SIX

It was a Tuesday afternoon, like any other, nothing out of the ordinary. Will was finishing his afternoon lessons in the mission school with the other children as usual. Then they came, without warning and brought death and destruction in their wake. St Xavier's was about to become the victim of its own success. Over the last few years it had attracted more and more women and children to the relative safety of its shelter. This success had dramatically increased the fund-raising potential of the Mission; a viable humanitarian project in a poverty-stricken, conflict-torn country had become a more and more intoxicating proposition to the affluent First World societies who donated their funds. As financial support poured in the number of both staff and refugees increased exponentially. When St Xavier's had been a small and inconsequential development the dominant guerrilla force of south-west Cameroon, the LPT organisation, had no interest in its affairs, it had been nothing but an irritation to be ignored, a fly, unimportant in the grander scheme. However now the fly had grown. The existence of such a rapidly growing safe harbour, independent of the brutal rule of the LPT was becoming a serious issue. The people were beginning to talk, beginning to question the possibility of another way, an alternative to the vicious rule that was imposed upon them. The Mission of St Xavier's had simply become too successful, too big, too obvious. It was time for what had once been an irritating fly to be swatted, it was time for a very public demonstration that there was no other way, no alternative to submission and obedience.

So in the late afternoon they came from the west, stealing out of the thick jungle silhouetted by the setting sun and flooding into the Mission like a plague. There was no resistance as there were none at St Xavier's who were capable of mounting any. The women who had taken refuge there over the last few years tried to flee as they knew what was to come. A lucky few who were out of the centre managed to escape, for the majority their fate was sealed. The priests initially were relatively calm, they did not share the abject terror and panic of the women, they had no previous experience of what was about to pass and as such were slow to realise the mortal peril they were in. As they were herded like cattle into the central square of the Mission the women cowered, paralysed by fear. The children, Will included, infected by their fear fell silent, hiding behind their mothers as best they could. Initially the priests, Will's father included, did not understand. They tried to reason calmly with their now captors in a way they would have expected from their previous lives in different parts of the world. There was to be no reasoning, no discussion. As all the men over the age of approximately fifteen were roughly separated from the group of terrified humanity corralled in the square, they began to understand. Then it began. There were no last requests, no last thoughts, there was no honour in death. All the men were simply grouped together and then executed. Now they all understood that these were to be the last few precious seconds of their lives. Some stood still, paralysed by the events unfolding in front of them, some began to sob, some began to pray. It made no difference. The guerrillas' orders had been highly specific, an example was to be made for all others to fear, no other option was to be tolerated. It took less than thirty minutes, under half an hour and then there were no adult males left. The once peaceful central square of St Xavier's Catholic Mission, refuge for displaced women and children, was now defiled with a pile of bodies. The previously rock hard, dusty sun-baked ground had been turned into a crimson-tinged sticky mud. The ear-shattering noises of the last few death-filled minutes were now replaced by a relative silence which fell over the remaining few left alive in the Mission square, the killing ground. As the fighters poured petrol over the bodies piled unceremoniously on top of each other, they lit the pyre. The unforgettable mixture of the thick acrid fumes of burning flesh mingled with the bitter cordite from the expelled shells and the sickly-sweet odour of the blood spilled around him, filled Will's nostrils. It was a scent like no other and it choked him, sticking in the back of his throat, infecting his lungs, seeping into every pore of his body. As the guerrillas now turned their attention to the remaining few the scent overpowered him, drowning out all of his other senses. It was the scent of total human devastation. It was his first concrete memory and was to be the start of his new life. That unique scent would never leave him.

Will woke with a jolt as the helicopter touched down on the landing pad on the deck of the A-class destroyer. Wearily, he dismounted, along with the other members of his team, and then dragging their gear with them they were escorted to the decontamination area under armed guard. All returning missions were treated in this manner, initially checked for any unauthorised explosive devices or extra personnel that were not expected. It was just part of the routine that they were accustomed to and thus they remained under armed guard until they were officially cleared. Decontamination took ninety minutes and once declared clean to proceed they were allowed into the lower decks of the destroyer, back to their quarters. The official debrief would not start until tomorrow and it would last some considerable time. It was pointless to expect men both physically and mentally exhausted by lack of sleep, strenuous exercise and deflated after the intense emotions of combat to provide any meaningful data immediately. Tomorrow, after sleep, washed and fuelled they would be fully debriefed, each and every aspect of the last few days dissected and digested. While they had obtained some valuable information on balance the mission overall had been an abject failure. They were supposed to perform reconnaissance and information gathering but most importantly remain undetected. Lethal contact was not anyone's definition of covert or undetected. Will knew however that those debriefing him and his team were professionals themselves, having been there themselves, in similar situations in the past. Not only was it to share the information they had gathered this well-established process was not for recrimination, it was for reflection and improvement for the future and was part of the constant evaluation and self-development engendered by the British forces.

Will could still recall every aspect of the semi-conscious wanderings of his mind, it was not the first time he had revisited that particular place, his first real memory. He had buried it deep within himself but knew that he would never be able to leave it behind for ever, never to return. While he would be, as always, totally transparent in all of his actions to the debrief team those private thoughts would remain just that, private for him only. Once complete, all questions answered there was only one place he wanted to be — asleep — and, as he slowly slipped into unconsciousness, safe in his bunk in the depths of an immensely powerful A-class destroyer of the Royal Navy he began to reflect on the years that had led him to be where he was, what he was. How had he journeyed from that terrified, shocked just-turned-twelve-year-old-boy, overpowered by the scent, standing facing death all around him in the killing ground, to become the soldier he was now?

CHAPTER SEVEN

Once the raging crimson flames had died down to burning white embers and the guerrillas had taken all they wished, had destroyed anything left standing, they turned their attention to the remaining few. The elderly women and infants were simply ignored, they were not a threat and certainly of no value. To their now captors they were a total irrelevance, not worth wasting any effort or more importantly not worth wasting the precious resource of a bullet. They were allowed to go free, they were not given a second thought and simply allowed to fend for themselves, whether they lived or more probably succumbed to the harsh environment of Africa bothered the guerillas not. The younger women and girls were all taken. In contrast they were of significant value; the younger, more attractive girls, and in particular any virginal girls, would be sold as future wives for not insignificant amounts. If not purchased they would be employed in the prostitution trade monopolised by the LPT organisation. All the remaining women who fell between these two groups were also taken to be used as either domestic slaves or as wives for some of the guerrilla fighters. It was not an enviable choice but there was no other option and, with the practicality born of generations of persecution and continued survival, they accepted their fate with calm resignation.

That left only one small group remaining, the boys. Those boys, old enough to care for themselves yet not old enough to be considered a threat, not yet old enough to have significant memories or any unbreakable allegiances. There were five of them remaining and they ranged from twelve to fifteen years in age. Will was the youngest but due to his size did not appear so. Of the 412 souls previously inhabiting the Mission of St Xavier now there were only five. They stood or sat in silence awaiting their fate, it was pointless trying to hide or to contemplate escape as there was nowhere to go. As it was, unbeknown to them, they were in fact the most valuable individuals to the guerrillas in the entire Mission. They were of an age where they could be taken, trained, for ever changed and then could become guerrilla fighters themselves. They quite clearly now had no attachments, there was no one else left to be attached to, and they were now totally alone in the world. They were old enough to run and move with the guerrilla force without being a significant burden yet they were young enough to have their morality and loyalty reset to a new, more vicious campaign. Also in reality there were not that many young males left in the region who would be suitable so, when the opportunity came to replenish the stock, it was not to be wasted. And so Will was taken.

He now entered a new school with very different rules where only strength, endurance and ruthlessness counted and he was currently at the bottom of the pecking order. While a reluctant recruit he was now bizarrely dependant on this organisation for his continued survival. Will and his four child companions were fed and sheltered to a degree by their new leaders and without them they would die. Thus when the team moved, they moved. They learnt to move fast and silently, unobserved through the jungle or open ground. The first hard-learned lesson was that survival relied on keeping up, much like a pack of wild wolves. One of them, the smallest and weakest of the five began to fall behind. He had been injured as an infant and the shattered bones of his left leg had healed in an unnatural position. Although overlooked initially it meant that he was slow, he failed to keep the pace set by the guerrilla fighters on the move and he grew progressively weaker until one day he was simply left. There was no ceremony, there was no remorse, none stopped to help as they could not. He was simply left to perish.

Combined with the extreme physical demands that were placed upon them, the constant lack of basic humanity that now surrounded them began to work its influence. Slowly, gradually, bit by bit they began to lose any remnants of compassion, their moral compass was being reset. They learnt to become ruthless, emotion was now a weakness to be hidden. After a year Will and his remaining companions were becoming accepted into the group. They were no longer the smallest, weakest or slowest and their relative standing in their reluctantly adopted society was growing. Most of the fighters of the LPT had been taken in this way, ripped from their families at a similar age and now Will was no longer the most recently added to the ranks, such was the way of life for many of the young men in Cameroon in the nineties. At the age of thirteen Will took up his first gun. It had previously belonged to one of the more senior members of the LPT who had been killed in a skirmish a week previously. As with everything in this harsh conflict nothing was wasted and the so AK-47 was recycled. It came to Will as it was his turn, he was next in line. At the time he recalled that he had been pleased, even proud, a recognition of his rapidly rising status in the harsh world that he now inhabited. It was his weapon now and it gave him a place in the fighting force, it gave him status and it became part of him. He slept with it, ran with it, could assemble and disassemble it in total darkness in seconds, it became an integral part of him and over time he became deadly proficient in its use. By the age of fifteen he had become a fully-fledged guerrilla fighter, scarily efficient with either blade or gun. He had been hardened to unfeeling steel at the school of the LPT, he was able to kill without compassion, without remorse and without hesitation. He had excelled and had graduated with honours.

Now on the outside, reflecting back, it seemed strange, almost impossible to conceive what he had become then, at the tender age of fifteen. But in truth he had revelled in the physical challenges that were ever present each and every day. He actually sought out the mental highs of conflict as a drug addict searches for their drug of addiction. And all compassion, any emotions of kindness, empathy, mercy had been stripped from him. It was not by his own design that this transformation from innocent child to lethal, emotionless adolescent had occurred, it was simply the environment that he had inhabited for the formative years of his young life. It was the deal that he had been dealt and had created the individual he had become.

By the age of fifteen and three quarters Will had become a section leader within his local contingent of the LPT force, he was now a fully-fledged and even respected member of this consciousless killing machine. His previous childhood was rapidly fading into a distant memory. Physically however he was growing into the man he was born to be. He had inherited his father's stature and Germanic frame and now stood tall at six feet, seven inches or in modern terms 2.3 metres. In addition to sheer size he had retained the muscle bulk and stamina of the African nation from his mother and the combination had become a weapon that he was now not afraid to use without hesitation whenever required. His eyes however still remained incongruous, piercing, pale and faultlessly blue.

He had been involved in many skirmishes, mainly small and medium size in scale as the conflict between the LPT and the new free, democratic government of Cameroon intensified. Unfortunately for the LPT currently its influence had now outgrown this uncared for region of Africa and, mainly due to their actions, in particular their harsh treatment and random abduction of women and children, had now become known to the wider international community. Now as the LPT and its actions became more widely publicised in Western societies they had officially become an unwelcome organisation and as such unacceptable, not to be tolerated. It was no longer possible for the Western world, who had been aware of them for some time, to continue to publically ignore them. The consequence of this was the huge support now pouring in, from America, to the new pro-American government of this region. The government's forces were now swollen with US Marines, in so-called advisory only roles, plus sophisticated weaponry and the knowledge to use it. More vitally however was a now total dominance of the skies with complete air support from the F14 Tornado fighter bombers launched from *Invincible*, the second largest aircraft carrier in the world, now stationed 160 nautical miles off the coast of West Africa. With this US-led support and vitally total dominance of the skies it was now only a matter of time until this vicious conflict, that had ripped this previously lush country apart, was over.

Will and his fellow fighters knew nothing of the wider picture, to them the fight simply continued. He now had personally been responsible for the death of many, too many to count or remember even if he had been interested. More striking than his physical development and evolution into the highly skilled soldier that he had been forced to become was the change in his mental state. His basic morality and basic human values had been totally reset. He could take life in an instant, without compassion or self-reflection. He now knew only one way of existence and this was through the demonstration and ruthless use of strength and power. For Will there was only one way to resolve a situation and this involved unfettered aggression combined with mind-blurring speed, a formidable combination, speed and aggression, without warning. He had learnt how to survive in the environment he had been forced to live in and he had excelled. He was surrounded by those with the emotionless expressions of men who had seen and done terrible things and he recognised this in himself. He now had the statue-like, drained face with empty, stone-cold eyes, devoid of any emotion be it anger or pity that belong to ruthless, unrepentant killers. He had come a long way from the happy innocent boy, conversing in four different languages with the priests of the Mission of St Xavier's. He was losing his basic humanity and it was almost gone for ever. Almost.

CHAPTER EIGHT

Redemption for Will came by pure coincidence, pure chance. It was only blind luck that led his path to cross with that of Christopher James, for them to both meet on that day, at that precise moment in time.

The conflict ruining his country was reaching its final bloody conclusion. Christopher James, like Will's own father, had come to Cameroon to help. He was part of a United Nations-sponsored food convoy that had been delivering bottled water and freeze-dried food packages to the starving people displaced by the conflict. They had been en route to the main refugee camp just across the border when his convoy had been ambushed. All the food and supplies had been taken, but the Westerners delivering the supplies had been simply left to fend for themselves. Killing foreign nationals was currently very poor public relations and only led to significant air strikes in recrimination. Chris was thus left with the drivers of the convoy, all of whom had been born in Cameroon and understood the situation; they were alone, some 160 kilometres away from any form of civilisation or safety, in an active war zone. They did not linger but fled as fast as they could, they did not need to be asked. Chris, although reasonably physically fit at forty-three years of age, did not have the stamina, knowledge or skills of the African drivers and was soon left behind, alone. Although untrained he figured that to remain in open view on a main supply route was a bad idea and so he wandered into the farmlands of the lower plains of Ekop, heading back the way he had come. He continued doggedly, alone for two days without any contact, persistently heading back towards civilisation. He had been lucky, he had remained undetected for two days, it was unlikely that he would survive a further two, his luck was due to run out.

Will and his group were moving fast, they were in trouble and they knew it. The pressure on them had built relentlessly over the last few weeks, spearheaded by unbelievably accurate and persistent air strikes that had stripped them of any of the safe havens of the past. The reinvigorated government troops, bolstered and actually led by tough and well-equipped highly trained Western soldiers were squeezing them into an ever-decreasing area. Their influence and power was shrinking and, to make matters worse, they were now being forced out of their traditional higher mountainous regions. In the higher passes of their country they were relatively safe, there were abundant caves and steep valleys to hide in and, even if detected, the terrain was not passable by any mechanised infantry so pursuit had to be by land-based troops. "Boots on the ground" was the common term for such conflict and it was a highly costly and extremely politically unpopular solution. Recently however they were being corralled down into the more exposed, cultivated flat lands of the central plains. Here they were vulnerable. The balance of power had swung, when once they were dominant, the hunters, now they had become the hunted.

Will was the fastest, strongest and most skilled of his group at the front. Leading, but also searching for any food or potential assets they could take. They had been moving through the cultivated arable lands of the flat plains now for two days. It was unfamiliar territory for them and they were uncomfortable. As dusk fell on the second day Will had drawn ahead of the main body of his tiring force and was now a clear kilometre ahead of them. As darkness enveloped the land he would retrace his route and re-join the main force. Just as he turned, preparing to return, he heard it — the sound of a man, moving towards him. Immediately all of his senses rose to full alert, as if a wave of energy had flooded over him, in an instant he was suddenly the feral animal that he had become, ready to instantly neutralise any threat. He froze, not making a sound, slowing his breathing, in total control. As he waited he could hear the other man blundering noisily towards him, he was close enough now for him to smell his unwashed odour. It puzzled him. It was not the noise of an enemy, trying to move in silence and remain unheard and unobserved, rather it was more a cacophony of a stranger to the forest with no intention of masking his presence. It was the sound of an exhausted man, unfamiliar with this unforgiving environment and deprived of food and water. As the stranger, the threat, moved closer Will silently drew his knife from the scabbard flush against his back. It was a crude but highly efficient weapon; the blade was sixteen inches of razor-sharp tempered steel embedded in a rough wooden handle that had moulded to the shape of Will's hand with years of use. It lay snugly within the smooth leather scabbard that rested in the small of Will's back, in the natural curve created as his lumbar vertebrae joined his pelvis. The knife had been his constant companion for the last five years, to him it was like a security blanket, he had never been without it and had used it on many occasions in the past, often at close quarters; when silence was required there was no superior weapon and Will was scarily proficient. As the exhausted man stumbled to his left, Will silently shuffled to the right, positioning himself in precisely the correct position to strike, he knew from experience, from instinct, that as this man fell out of the tall maize fields into the clearing at the edge of the forest he would be there, almost invisible and ready.

His breathing slowed, his heart rate dropped and Will coiled himself to strike. Chris, blissfully unaware, emerged into the remaining half-light of fading dusk, simply pleased to at last be free of the tall, strength-sapping stems of the maize field. Will was about to launch himself at the unsuspecting victim in a lethal assault with speed and aggression, as he had come accustomed to and then suddenly, unexpectedly he hesitated. There was an instant that caused Will to hesitate — a wholly unfamiliar action to him, hesitation. As the man had stumbled out of the maize field the dying rays of the setting sun had reflected off something dangling from his neck. It was a silver crucifix, strikingly similar to the one his father had worn, a distant memory from what seemed a lifetime ago. Due to this simple trinket Will had hesitated and, as he did, the exhausted man looked up into those cold, expressionless blue eyes and saw nothing but rage and impending doom. He did not attempt to escape, did not attempt to fight back, he simply stood still — all Will saw was acceptance, an emotion he had long forgotten. They stood, just centimetres away from each other in silence for what seemed like an eternity but in reality it was no more than a few seconds. As the silence stretched out the sun disappeared, falling rapidly behind the horizon plunging them into darkness.

"Thank you," uttered the exhausted man, in English.

"You are welcome," replied Will, automatically in English.

His reply stunned them both. The fact that this armed fighter, who seconds before was preparing to kill him, had replied politely in fluent English was startling enough to Chris James. More startling was Will's reaction to himself. The single word of thanks had elicited an automatic reply that five years previously would have seemed normal, now it seemed so foreign, so utterly out of place it stunned him into inactivity. With this three-word phrase automatically given as a reply long-forgotten memories of his previous life came flooding back to him; memories of his schooling and his delight in his linguistic ability, long-forgotten memories of kindness and affection that he had been shown at St Xavier's, memories of his father.

They continued to stare silently at each other, Chris on the brink of collapse, Will confused. Both felt amazed by the polite and brief exchange that had just occurred in a foreign language under surreal circumstances, yet neither knew what to do. Chris, mainly due to exhaustion, sat down in front of Will, an act of necessity and also submission, not one of fear or threat. Will thought for a moment, he did not know what to do, so he sat too. They sat facing each other in the darkness. After several minutes of silence had passed the exhausted man appeared to regain some of his strength and was able to speak. He looked directly at the young man-boy in front of him, calmly holding his slightly unnerving gaze, and then did what came naturally. He introduced himself, "My name is Christopher James."

Will looked directly at this spent man, appraising the situation but also slightly uncomfortable, so unused to formal introductions. Yet due to his past education, engrained into him by the priests and by his own father in St Xavier's he replied formally also.

"My name is Will."

Will knew that if he did not soon return to his main force, now camped just one kilometre behind them, there would be no immediate concern. However if he did not return by daylight they would assume that he had encountered government forces and had been killed. They would expect to find some evidence of combat, at least a body and the animals of the forest would lead them to his corpse. He also knew that if they found no such evidence they would soon become suspicious. Desertion from the cause was perhaps the ultimate crime that was never forgiven, to do so would allow many others who wished to leave the ability to do so. Will had seen first hand, how those foolish enough to try had been mercilessly hunted down and then very publicaly and painfully punished. He also knew that he now had to choose what to do with this other human being he had encountered. If he simply left him he would soon be discovered by the other members of the LPT and most likely killed. Worse however would be the questions of why Will had allowed him to live. He would have shown weakness in their eyes and they would not understand that, somehow, this desperate man had stirred a degree of long-forgotten compassion buried deep within Will's soul. At best this lost individual might remain lost, undetected, however unlikely, but then he would surely perish alone in the wild. Will knew his choice was binary, kill him either actively now or by inactivity in the future, or help him. These thoughts flashed through Will's highly intelligent brain as the minutes ticked past and they both remained stationary, sitting, facing each other in silence in the darkness. What was it about this totally vulnerable man that had awoken long-hidden emotions within him? Was it his helplessness, was it the complete acceptance of his fate openly displayed on his face and in his eyes? Or was it simply the crucifix that lay around his pale neck that reminded Will of his father and his former happier years in the Mission of St Xavier? Whatever the reason, Will knew that he could now not simply dispatch him as he had so many others in the past. He knew he could not simply pull the trigger or use his deadly blade that was still drawn and ready to strike. He knew clearly that he did not want to kill this man and so therefore there was only one other option available, he would have to help him. As so often a simple choice, with significant consequences.

CHAPTER NINE

Decision made. Will was going to help this man, Christopher James, a man he had been planning to kill just minutes previously, and with this decision he felt immediate relief, indecision was one of the few things that caused him anxiety. They sat facing one another hidden by the lush growth of the tall maize fields in the total darkness that only occurs a long way away from the artificial lights of civilisation, where there was no other ambient light.

"I will help you," Will said in English, before giving the man some water from his flask and some of his food that he carried. This was not a totally altruistic act for if he was going to run with this man, if he was going to try to restore him to civilisation and evade the soon to be chasing LPT, he needed him to rapidly regain some significant strength. Chris looked at Will, completely perplexed. Minutes before this enormous man had appeared out of nowhere and was about to kill him; just minutes before he had looked into his unnaturally pale blue eyes and seen his impending death. Now this man was going to help him! With the simple acts of offering food and water and the exchange of a few words in his native language a glimmer of hope of self-preservation began to spark within Chris.

For the first hour they sat and rested, allowing Chris to regain his strength and they began to talk. In truth Chris did almost all of the talking, Will was unaccustomed to conversation, and so Chris explained how he had come to be alone in this harsh land, a long way from home which was London, England, and how he had been part of a relief convoy heading for the refugee camps at the border when they had been attacked. Will hardly spoke, there seemed little to say and, when Chris asked how he had learnt such perfect English, he simply replied that he had been taught it at school. Once an hour had passed and Chris had rallied physically it was time to move. Whether it was the urgency in his voice or the complete confidence that his command would be obeyed, Chris appeared to understand the necessity to be distant from where they currently were. Will led, Chris did his best to follow. He was forty-three years old and by normal standards he was extremely fit. Triathlons had long been his sporting pursuit and recently in the UK, mainly due to notable success in recent Olympics, triathlon had now become the fastest growing sport in the UK, in fact it was positively trendy. At forty-three he was officially classed as veteran, a label that niggled him, however he had been good. He was a single man of considerable financial means and so had been able to dedicate significant chunks of time to his training. By Western standards he was supremely fit for a man of his age. Despite his best efforts however he was not able to keep the brutal, unforgiving pace that was set. Will was almost twenty years his junior and he had been born and bred in this environment. Soon Chris began to tire and, as each hour passed, Will was forced to gradually slow their pace and rest more often. While they had travelled a significant distance by normal standards during the night they had not travelled nearly far enough to keep them safe from the now awakening force of the LPT. They pushed onwards through the following morning until the combination of the rising heat of the day and Chris's complete exhaustion forced them to stop. Will knew that now in daylight, with the absence of any evidence of his death, the LPT would have discovered his desertion. He knew now that they would be chasing him with unbridled rage that could not be easily satiated. He calculated that they had approximately a single day's lead but this would not last long, for while he was forced to proceed relatively slowly and rest often due to Chris's growing fatigue, the honed fighters of the LPT would not cease in their relentless pursuit.

As they sat, propped up against the bank of a man-made irrigation stream, they shared the last of the food and water and Will quietly, succinctly spelt out their current precarious situation to Chris. During the last twelve to sixteen hours they had been together Chris had begun to realise that the individual he had taken to be a full-grown man was in fact a boy, much younger than he had at first thought. Although physically enormous, intimidating even, he was in chronological years just a teenager. He found this contradiction difficult to assimilate, such strength, confidence and power in one so young who sat calmly, eloquently, explaining his likely fate. Chris was old enough to be this man-boy's father yet here he was totally and completely dependent on him. Will had recognised that for the last few hours they had entered cultivated arable land which required water and a plentiful supply to flourish. If they could reach the river supplying this delta they had a small chance of escape, if they could float away towards civilisation, just maybe they could survive.

As the heat of the day evaporated and the still calm of darkness came it was time to move once again. They had rested for over four hours and Will knew that they had to find the river before the end of the night for there was no chance that they would be able to evade the chasing pack for another day. So they pushed on, travelling gently downwards with each mile, the cultivated vegetation became lusher with each passing hour. Eventually, after what seemed an eternity, in the small hours of the morning they stumbled upon their goal. As they fell out of the organised and groomed maize fields they came to the river. It was vast and slow flowing and they could not see the opposite bank. Chris waded in with gay abandon but Will was more cautious. The truth was that Will was actually a poor swimmer, while supremely confident in his physical ability on land in the water he was less able. While his genetic inheritance had endowed him with enormous size, strength and stamina his significant muscle bulk and increased density associated with his African roots meant that simply if left alone in the water he would sink. It was not his fault, it was simply his physical makeup and it was not unique; as in high level sport while most sprinters and runners originate from hotter climates there are no successful black swimmers, each genetic trait having its own advantages to be celebrated. Chris on the other hand now felt invigorated. Part of his triathlon training had been regularly swimming long distances, often in open water, and now for the first time, here in the water, he began to feel slightly more confident.

Will started to search the river bank. While he had no hope or anticipation of finding any craft in this isolated stretch of the river, he needed something that would both keep them afloat for the coming hours and also mask their presence from the casual observer. They stumbled downriver in the muddy shallows for a further mile in the half-light of the impending dawn until they eventually found a small tree washed up and caught by its branches in the river bank. It was not perfect but they were desperate and time was running out. The first rays of the morning sun began to reflect of the ripples of the constantly moving river. Together they heaved it out from the mud where it had lodged and pushed it out into the deeper water of the slow-flowing river. As their feet lost contact with the silted bottom they felt the current strengthen and they kicked together using the last vestiges of Chris's energy, propelling their makeshift craft into the faster flowing central part of the river. They clung to the dead tree, obscured by its remaining foliage and began to float faster downstream, moving away from the pursuing LPT who, with a bit of luck, would now be unable to follow.

Several hours passed as they drifted further and further downstream, pushed by the ever-strengthening current, further away from danger. Yet as the sun reached its zenith at midday Will began to tire — this time, today, it was not Chris but Will who was weakening and there were two very distinct reasons for this. Firstly Will was the weaker swimmer and the effort required to just stay above water was not insignificant for him. However secondly, and the principle reason that Will was struggling, was that he still had all of his weapons, now weighing him down in the water. They had been a part of him for so long, his lifeline, an almost integral part of his body and he had not yet been prepared to relinquish them. As the afternoon lengthened it became obvious that he would either have to let go of his weapons or let go of the tree keeping them afloat. While there was no choice still he could not easily discard something that had been so vital to his survival for so long. Eventually, through abject necessity, plus some encouragement from Chris, he shook of his weapon and let it sink away into the murky waters of the river. As he watched the matt black metal of the AK disappear below the opaque surface of the turbid water it was almost as though he was leaving that part of his life behind him, almost as though he was allowing the river to wash it away. Not fully however was he able to relinquish all means of protection for, strapped to his back, flush against his sodden skin remained his knife, snug within its scabbard slung across his back. Not only was it the practical necessity of the blade it was also the physical link to his current existence and he was not prepared to discard it yet.

They had travelled many miles propelled by the strong flow of the river and as dusk arrived they reached a natural curve where the current weakened. They kicked together, slowly moving towards the muddy river bank and, exhausted, both physically and mentally, hauled themselves and their new craft up the steep banks and took shelter under the cover of the rich undergrowth that grew at the junction of the forest with the river. They were coated in thick black river mud and hidden under the roots of the trees feeding off the river; they were totally hidden, incorporated into the natural landscape and both fell into a fitful sleep, totally spent.

CHAPTER TEN

They continued downriver for three more days, sleeping during the days, half swimming, and half floating during the nights to avoid detection by any hostile parties. As the time passed they began to talk. While Chris was far more open about all aspects of his life based in London, Will was initially tentative. However, slowly small snippets of his brutal life and his journey to this point began to emerge. As dawn broke on the morning of the fourth day they began to taste salt in the water, a gradual transition from the freshwater of the river to the increasing salinity that marked an estuary. They realised they were close so they continued in the growing daylight, and then they arrived. As the river spat them out into the harbour of Kribi at the head of the Kineke River like all the other flotsam and detritus washed down from the higher regions, they knew they had reached civilisation of sorts, they knew they were temporarily safe. In the strengthening light of the late morning sun they hauled themselves out of the water and for the first time in days lay on solid ground on the harbour wall. As they lay there shoulder to shoulder, gradually drying themselves and their sodden clothes, the next problem came to them both simultaneously, what next?

While they had been entirely focused on evading capture and making it to some form of civilisation, neither had any idea of the next step in the journey for each of them. Chris knew that as a British national on a sanctioned UN humanitarian mission he needed only to find his way to either the British Embassy or to any of the many United Nations stations in the port. This was the main import and export route for the entire region and all of the vast quantities of foreign aid flowed through it. Chris knew that once his identity had been confirmed he would shortly be on his way home. Will on the other hand had no idea where this day, or any of the next would take him. He had lived his entire life either in the Mission of St Xavier's or practically living wild as part of the LPT moveable force. He had never seen such things as the metal cargo ships towering high above him or the huge concrete structures that surrounded him in this massive port. The normal hubbub of a busy port waking up, starting its routine daily business, seemed deafening to him compared to the silence of the forest or the still air of the mountains which had been his home. This environment was as foreign to him as the wild had been to Chris and he felt totally and completely alone.

They stood and looked at each other, almost as though the time to part had now come and Chris, in contrast to the last few days, now saw uncertainty, even fear in those piercingly pale blue eyes. Suddenly he saw a young boy in front of him, rather than the terrifying man he had initially encountered just four days ago and in that moment he knew what he had to do. He realised like a jolt of electricity now the reason he had come to Cameroon, even perhaps why he had been placed in harm's way when his convoy had been attacked. He realised that it was his turn to return the favour to this boy and save Will, just as Will had surely just saved him. A surge of almost paternalistic protection swept over him, taking him by surprise. Chris looked at Will and said.

"I will help you."

CHAPTER ELEVEN

They were just two more bedraggled, displaced individuals among many. Due to the years of turmoil thousands upon thousands of displaced refugees had passed through the port of Kribi seeking asylum, fleeing from the violence that had ripped their country apart, looking for a way to leave, searching for a better life. They were not unusual, nothing out of the ordinary and no one paid them any special attention. Slowly they made their way through the endless queues of desperate refugees, all hoping for a way out. Eventually they came to the outer parts of the UN-sponsored aid camp that had been the original staging point for Chris's aid convoy. With a wry smile he reflected that the last time that he had been here he had been the one delivering the aid, he had even looked at the snaking lines of desperate people with a degree of pity. How easily had it been for him, himself, to now be in the same desperate situation? His previous position of relative safety and wealth had been so rapidly reversed and now he was just the same as all the others, desperate for help. There was no possible way to jump the queue of refugees and so they took their turn and waited. After almost four days of waiting, relying on handouts of food and water to survive they eventually made it to the UN staging post for processing. Once Chris's credentials had been verified he became an almost overnight celebrity within the community of aid workers. They had received news of the ambush of his convoy and in the absence of any news had assumed the worst. The story of his journey back to civilisation, pursued by the LPT yet at the same time bizarrely rescued by a member of that same violent group, brought hope to the others.

Chris had decided to take Will back with him to England. He had tentatively floated this option to Will on the third night of their wait in the refugee camp. Will had very few options available to him, he certainly could not return to the LPT, that would be met with the harshest punishment possible and a certain painful death. To remain a refugee in Kribri, homeless and penniless in the port was not an attractive second choice. So with the practicality bred from necessity he accepted. Chris had anticipated that there would be many bureaucratic hoops to jump through, however in the end it proved remarkably straightforward. The combination of the fact that Will, at sixteen and three quarters, was still a child under UK law and the liberal application of large quantities of cash, which Chris had in abundance, meant that the wheels of bureaucracy turned relatively rapidly. This fortunate combination meant that it was relatively simple for Chris to be granted temporary guardianship of a one Master William James, officially classified as a minor with no attachments or living relatives. Up until that moment he had not considered the need for a last name, he had never required one and had just always been William after his father. When asked the question at registration he had shrugged, confused by the request. The logic was that it made the transaction easier if he shared Chris's surname and so there and then he had become a one Master William James. Within a week both had temporary passports and exit visas. Their transport was to be one of the supply ships, chartered by the UN that had just delivered further humanitarian supplies pouring in from the West. Will had never been to sea, in fact he had never even seen the ocean until the week previously when they arrived at the port and as they boarded the ship he felt severely confined, caged, with no immediate exit route. To him the physical limitations of the perimeter of this vessel seemed to close in on him much like the wall of a prison cell. Having been accustomed to always having the option to flee, to run and escape when required, this new confinement was unnerving. To his surprise however as the voyage continued the passage across the ocean had exactly the opposite effect. The gentle movement of the tanker on the never-ceasing pulsation of the waves soothed him. The taste of salt on the crisp, fresh sea air was a total contrast to the oppressive heat and dust of the forest he had previously known. However, more calming was the endless serenity of the blue ocean topped with the white crests of the breaking waves that appeared to continue uninterrupted, almost without end, to the horizon and beyond. As hours followed hours and turned into days, the magic of the ocean began to work its mesmerizing effect.

The tanker was huge, it was ungainly, even ugly in appearance, it was designed to carry massive loads efficiently across the ocean and it was certainly not built for speed or comfort. The net result of this was that their voyage took a little over two weeks. During this time they slowly, tentatively began to talk and, as time passed, Will began to do something he had not been able to do since he was so abruptly ripped from the Mission of St Xavier's. He began to trust. As they talked more and more over the coming days that trust grew and Will found himself drawn to the older man as he had been to his father in the mission and eventually he felt able to tell Chris the story of his young life. How he had been so violently ripped from the sanctuary of the Mission, how he had entered a school of human conflict where there were no second chances and how he had been forced through necessity to become such a proficient agent of violence. Chris was many things some good, others not so good, that Will would discover later, but he was a good listener and he allowed this physically and mentally scarred half-man half-boy to pour out his soul to him. As he listened, absorbing and assimilating the events that had shaped Will's young life, he also slowly accepted his trust. While he had gone to Africa ostensibly to deliver aid he knew that part of the reason was also to provide himself with a degree of personal satisfaction. Much as a devout believer draws strength from their religion, he knew that he was gaining some inner satisfaction from being able to help, his journey had not been completely altruistic. This was the truth for almost all of the aid workers if they were true to themselves. Never in his wildest dreams however had he expected this to happen, he would not have gone in the first place if he had been able to anticipate the dangers he had faced. He would never have left the safety of the streets of London for the perils of the forest and the terrifying float down the disease-ridden river. Most shocking of all however was that he could not have anticipated that now he was responsible for a young man, so clearly damaged by a traumatic early life, who appeared to be placing his trust in him. The harsh reality was that just as Will had saved Chris, delivering him out of the forest and back to civilisation, Chris was now in the business of saving Will. Just before he slipped for ever into his previous world of brutality pure luck had led to his redemption. While he had survived five years in that harsh violent environment it was unlikely that he would make another five — there were very, very few who did. However what was for certain was that if he had remained in the LPT any vestiges of the better human emotions such as pity, kindness or remorse would have been gone for ever. The trust that was growing between them was beginning to restore Will's humanity, the morality that had been almost completely stripped from him.

CHAPTER TWELVE

Overnight their tanker had serenely glided through the still waters of the English Channel and had docked in the main commercial harbour at Plymouth. They were cleared through customs and as they set foot on English soil the next chapter of their journey was beginning. After a short bus ride to the main station, Will and Chris boarded the early train on the main line and hurtled at just over a hundred kilometres an hour towards London, Chris's home. The journey along this part of the South Western rail network was nothing short of spectacular. As they barrelled past the South Devon coast, just metres from the initially red gritty sand and then pebbled beaches falling into the clear sea, then along the lush green wooded estuaries of Lympstone and Exeter, the natural beauty of the scenery flashed by at speed. The completely foreign images, to Will, distracted him from the new experience of yet another mode of modern transport, it was overwhelming; to Chris it was the familiar route home. With each mile closer to London the scenery became more populated, more urban and then the dull established monotonous grey of London took over from the green of the countryside as they drew into Paddington Station.

Chris lived in the top floor penthouse apartment of a block of flats in Belsize Park, in fact he actually owned the entire building in this highly trendy and desirable area of affluent North London. He was rich, actually very rich. He had made his considerable fortune in IT design. He had started as essentially an IT techno geek but, by a combination of intelligence, hard work and good luck all in equal measure, he had designed a computer system that was now used by the majority of the financial offices in London and, in turn, across the world in their financial option trading departments. His key selling point was that he had made his system simple, so simple that even these traders became familiar with it within minutes and hence its popularity. Not only did he now receive a considerable regular income from the continued use of his system whenever there was a problem, a glitch in the smooth operating of the system they called him, or his company. London traders were not the most patient of individuals at the best of times and, when their computers crashed, so did they. More importantly with every second of downtime they lost money and consequently Chris and his team could charge extortionate amounts for fixing it. Now his role was more supervising and overseeing the smooth running of his company and ensuring the standard of their service delivery remained outstanding. This lack of direct contact, the lack of a new challenge had subconsciously irked him and was the real underlying reason why he had become involved with the UN and had agreed to go on the aid convoy in the first place.

As the weeks passed the complete culture shock of this totally polar opposite environment of one of the largest, busiest metropolises in the world, compared to the forests and mountains of Africa, receded and Will rapidly and remarkably acclimatised to his new surroundings, adapting in a way that only the young can do so well. As the summer drew to a close Will did what all other seventeen-year-olds did. He went to school. He had been enrolled in one of the better-known fee-paying public schools in England, he was to be a resident boarder at North Field School on the outskirts of North London. The considerable expense was not an issue for Chris, rather he had purposely chosen North Field as it accepted a wide range of pupils from diverse cultures and different backgrounds. Academic ability was not a prerequisite for any of these pupils, far from it, rather it was the correct financial backing that was the determining factor to admission. Consequently the school was full of highly affluent children, mainly from overseas, whose families had sent them to London, England to gain the benefits and social status of an English boarding school education. Will found that, surprisingly, he fitted right in.

He was now a boarder in the lower sixth of a multicultural school where academic excellence was frowned on by the pupils, instead either the financial position of one's parents or more importantly sporting prowess was seen as the most important quality, and in this Will excelled. His sheer size and physical ability guaranteed his success in a wide range of sports but particularly in rugby he found a gift. In this sport it seemed that physical domination and controlled aggression were actually encouraged, both of which he had in abundance. In languages also he demonstrated considerable talent, stemming from his childhood time in the Mission. In reality he was fluent in English, French, German and several African dialects but he was wise enough to hide, to a degree, his considerable talents in this area to avoid any awkward explanations about the origin of his unusually wide and diverse range of languages. The first term came and went without incident and all appeared to be going smoothly. He had made the transition from forest to school with consummate ease and had adapted as only the young can. However it was not destined to last, perhaps it was just too much to ask.

It happened towards the latter part of the second term. Three of the senior and most popular boys from the upper sixth, the final year and the year above Will came at him. They were irritated by his instant popularity and it was time, in their opinion, to re-establish the natural pecking order. As the three of them, all physically large and fit cornered him, their intention was obvious and Will reacted to impending conflict in the only way he knew how. He reacted through instinct, not logic, and reacted with unbridled speed and aggression. Before any of the three had any chance to even initiate an attack Will struck first and with complete conviction. With blurring speed he launched his entire body forward, slamming his leading rigid forearm into the soft exposed part of the throat of the nearest and largest of the three would-be assailants. Driven by his entire weight moving ferociously forward at high speed, the cartilaginous structures of the boy's cricoid and thyroid rings, the structures that form the moveable skeleton of the throat shattered into multiple segments and he collapsed instantly, fighting for breath through the shattered remnants of his airway. Without checking his impetus, without the slightest hesitation or thought of restraint Will continued forward, continued to attack, and drove his other fist in a vicious upward arching movement into the epigastrium of the second boy, striking the central area just below the ribcage and doubling him in two as the air was driven from his lungs by the force of the impact. As he buckled Will lashed out with his right leg, striking the inner aspect of the left knee of the winded boy at such an angle that it forced the knee sideways and outwards in such an extreme position that he could hear the instant popping of the cruciate and medial ligaments of the knee joint. Unable to bear his weight, gasping for breath, the second boy fell and, as he did so, Will scythed his other arm down at speed, increasingly dramatically the velocity of the boy's descent and crushing his head into the floor. He hit with the sickening unmistakable sound of skull bones breaking on a solid surface, once heard and never forgotten a dull crump with a slight echo. Fortunately for all concerned, the room was carpeted and it was only this that saved him from a mortal head injury, instead he instantly lapsed into unconsciousness. Will rounded on the now not so confident, now alone third boy. He had just seen his two friends wiped out in seconds in such a brutal and ferocious manner he could never have imagined. Fights at school he had previously witnessed had been far more gentler and a lot longer, he had grown up in the closeted sheltered society of affluent Britain and in the finest education system that money could buy. Will on the other hand had an entirely different upbringing and this type of instant and brutal conflict had been his not so long ago reality and he had just snapped right back into it by instinct. Faced with this naked wild rage so obvious and uncontrolled now just inches from him he was scared, truly sacred and so he turned and ran. What should have happened is that it should have been the end of it. Will should have let him go, but he was now back in the jungle, he was the instinctive lethal combatant he had been forced to become in order to survive. Instinctively, without conscious thought, he reached behind him to the small of his back, fully expecting his open palm to grasp the rough wooden handle of the long lethal blade that months before had always been there, an extension of his body, welded to him, part of his core. If it had been there he would have slipped it from its sheath and in an instant he would have impaled the boy, thrusting the blade past the two-winged scapula of his shoulders and out through his sternum, straight through his chest from behind without a second's hesitation or a single thought of mercy. It was fortunate for both that of course the blade was no longer there. Will however was still instinctively in the killing rage and so he threw himself forward without hesitation after the fleeing boy and caught him with his full weight, barrelling him out of the room and down to the floor. Again Will should have stopped, his victory was complete. However, to leave a living, functioning opponent was akin to committing suicide in the world he had previously occupied, for if they could, if there was any opportunity, any chance at all they would turn and strike back with the desperation and ferocity of a wounded animal. Everything he had learnt in the past, all his basic survival instincts that had been nailed into him by the harshest of lessons compelled him to further violence. He struck the remaining fallen boy once more, a vicious powerful blow to the temple and the third would-be assailant lay still.

The entire encounter had lasted only a few seconds, certainly less than a minute. None of the three now unconscious bullies had even come close to harming Will. In fairness to them they had no knowledge of his particular skill set and certainly would not have ever entertained such a foolish action if they had been aware of a fraction of his abilities. He had simply neutralised them before they had been able to harm him, he had reacted through instinct engrained into him by his previous existence, learnt in order to survive. He had reacted with lightning speed and unbridled aggression that was part of him, the combination of speed and aggression had kept him alive in the past. While he had superficially adapted to his new environment of civilised society, he had not left his previous, far less civilised one behind. It was part of him whether he liked it or not and always would be. Despite the veneer he put over them, the animal instincts that he had needed in order to survive were hard wired into him. The trauma he had lived through could never be fully erased, the fire within him would always burn. That was the legacy of his youth.

CHAPTER THIRTEEN

Scuffles and occasional all-out fights between boys were not uncommon, in fact they were the norm. When just over 300 testosterone-fuelled sixteen to eighteen-year-olds were in close proximity, conflict was inevitable. Normally such an encounter would result in a single week's suspension for all concerned and then would be forgotten. Normally however three boys did not end up in hospital, with one in intensive care with a tracheostomy tube now replacing his shattered windpipe. Initially Will was suspended for two weeks. Unfortunately for Will one boy's father happened to be chairman of the school governors, the committee that oversaw the financial running of the school. Where there were standard rules for most circumstances there were also situations that did not change across different cultures. It was suggested in the strongest possible terms that Will's continued presence at North Field was unacceptable and so he found himself in conversation with the headmaster with Chris by his side. In the incredibly, almost too polite manner, only possible by the upper classes of British society, it was explained to them both that his time at North Field had now come to an end. And just as the door was closed on his very brief academic career in the way that again only the British can do, another door was opened to him. Will could clearly remember as if it were yesterday how it had been politely suggested to him and Chris that his talents may be better appreciated elsewhere, how his particular skill set may be better suited to a career in the armed forces. And once again in that ever so British way the school had already arranged for him to meet with the recruitment officer for the forces who just happened to be visiting in the very near future. As North Field had firmly closed the door on his short time with them they had opened another, to the start of the next chapter of his life.

The following week, again with the ever-present and supportive Chris by his side, he found himself in front of Lieutenant Colonel R. Saunders. He was the chief recruiting officer for cadets and officer training in the UK and Will stood in front of him, towering over him in reality, while he read a glowing letter of support from the headmaster of North Field. Only the British were able to see what a poor situation was and create something positive out of it, one of their better qualities. The combination of Will's obvious physical size and the report of the outcome of his recent exploits ensured that his acceptance into basic training was never in doubt, in fact for Lieutenant Colonel Saunders it was the easiest decision he had to make all day. There were very few individuals of such marked physical ability who could fluently speak three mainstream languages and several other African dialects who also had a proven track record of decisive and effective violence. It was a no-brainer and so he simply asked Will which service he preferred, Army or Navy? Commandos or Marines? Will remained silent, inwardly contemplating the step he was about to take. Although only seventeen he had already lived what for most would have been a full life's worth of experiences and he was not naive. He knew that if he accepted this generous offer he would be returning, to a degree, to that world of conflict that he knew so well. Would it be different as part of a First World-organised army, or would it be just the same disguised by a different name? These thoughts flashed through his highly intelligent brain and the lieutenant colonel repeated his question, a touch of irritation creeping into his voice, unused to having to ask anything twice. Again Will paused, not sure if he should commit, hesitant on the threshold. In the past he had never been given the luxury of choice, he had simply adapted to survive. Now he was acutely aware that to proceed would be at his own personal volition to go back to that dark world that he was unfortunately so comfortable within. The lieutenant colonel started to draw breath to possibly ask a third time, more likely to dismiss him, and before he was able to utter a syllable Will answered: "Marines."

The reason he willingly stepped over this threshold, answering "Marines" was twofold. Firstly it was due to the slow voyage back from Kribi on the tanker across the rolling ocean. The new experience of being afloat on the sea had for a brief and completely unexpected period of time instilled in him an inner calm that he had never known before and so when given the option he had chosen the Marines over the land-based Army. However, the main reason for his acceptance was based in stark reality. The harsh naked truth was that he had little other option, what else was he going to do? He had nothing else to give.

CHAPTER FOURTEEN

Basic training for Will was simply a walk in the park. Once complete and now at the age of seventeen and three quarters he was moved to the Royal Marines' training base at Lympstone Common in Devon. This was the home of the elite special forces of the Royal Navy, the Marines, where any weakness was filtered out and only the strongest were allowed to continue. The initial training programme was a nine-month, gruelling for most exercise where the aim was to break you down, both physically and mentally and then, just before you folded completely, to remould you as a fighting special forces Marine. Will excelled in every facet of the training, for him it was child's play. The more straightforward physical training involved what was commonly termed being "beasted" around the endless muddy hills of Woodbury Common. This entire area, rising high above the River Exe was filled with thick sharp gorse covering steep hills and criss-crossed by tight, dark and slime-filled tunnels designed precisely for this purpose. Will's natural strength, speed and stamina made light work of everything they threw at him. He outpaced all of the other recruits with ease, most of them had never experienced such hardship, for Will it was a far, far gentler life than he had previously been forced to adapt to. When it came to weapons training however, he had an obvious advantage. While the current weapon of choice of the Royal Marine Corps, was the L119A Canadian-made light carbine rifle, recently replacing the M16, a weapon of supreme accuracy and firepower for its compact and portable size, it was not so different in its basics to the AK-47 that had been part of Will's life for so long. He could break down and then reassemble all of the weapons they gave him in seconds with an unnatural familiarity. On the range, against targets, he used them with such skill and rapidity, with both rifle and side arms, the ballistics officers began to question how one so young acquired such skills that had to be learnt by constant practice. It was not so much as his obvious ability, it was the unnerving way in which he would incorporate each weapon they gave him into his own movements, such that each became a lethal and seemingly natural extension of his own body that he could deploy with mind-blurring rapidity and consummate skill.

While there had been quiet mutterings among the training team they really began to question Will's origins when it came to hand-to-hand combat. At the end of his first session the instructor had been carried out with a broken nose and dislocated patella. He had told Will to hit him, as he did with all of the novices. All in the past had tried and failed, ending up flat on their backs and in pain, an exercise designed to stamp his authority on the future sessions. What he had never encountered before was the unbridled speed and aggression with which Will reacted. When instructed Will reacted, instantly, decisively striking the instructor directly on the bridge of his nose with his rigid flattened palm, instantly shattering the cartilaginous membrane supporting the centre of his nose. In startled anger he had lashed back — big mistake. Will had anticipated the recoil and had easily moved away from the older, much slower man's flailing arm. Using the unbalanced forward momentum of the instructor, he had kicked out with his leg striking the instructor's knee directly, tearing the patella, the mobile bone on the front of the knee out of its socket. The injured instructor would not walk without pain for the following six months, the next instructor was more cautious.

As the time at Lympstone rapidly passed with continued success the instructors, all experienced in real-time conflict zones around the world, began to further question Will's obvious abilities. How had this unknown eighteen-year-old developed such advanced skills? While his physical ability could in part be explained by his immense size, how could he have such skills with any weapon, gun or blade that they gave him? How could one so young have developed such a rare and refined skill set? As these unanswered questions and his ability filtered through to the higher echelons of the Marine command structure any further questioning or rumours abruptly stopped. While they knew that there had to be more to this young man's background, they were wise enough to question no further. They were fully aware of his potential, of what they had now inherited, they did not care where he came from or what he had done in the past. What they knew was that they now possessed a highly skilled individual with an exceptional skill set, strong, fast and lethal. They had no intention of alienating him with pointless prying into his past, for them it was enough that he was with them and they welcomed him into their family of sorts. Will loved it; he rose to the physical challenge and revelled in his success and marvelled at his instant acceptance, irrespective of his past, into this group and for this he was supremely grateful. He now felt he belonged.

CHAPTER FIFTEEN

Chris attended Will's passing-out parade as he accepted his green beret and became a fully-fledged marine commando. It had been two years and three months since they had crawled together out of the stinking river, starving and exhausted with nothing, yet now he stood tall in his number-one uniform on the parade ground of 23 Commando. How life could change so rapidly and radically; once an innocent, a child in the Mission of St Xavier, then taken, forced into a brutal life of self-preservation and conflict, then by pure providence taken back into civilisation, of sorts. These thoughts flashed through his highly tuned brain as his commanding officer, walking with a slight limp, shook his hand and passed him his beret. Chris watched with no small degree of pride. While his business had been financially successful, beyond his expectations, there had been a void in his life that Will had unexpectedly filled. By a strange twist in fate he had become responsible for this boy, now rapidly growing into a fully developed man, and as he watched him accept his beret he felt a genuine swell of what could only be described as paternalistic pride.

So Will stepped forward, accepted his beret and accepted the start of the next chapter of his life. He graduated with both the sword of honour as the top cadet in his year and also the gold medal as the top commando, the first and still the last individual to achieve both accolades. The Navy knew that they now had an extraordinary asset and had no wish to probe the how or why he had developed such skills, skills that did not just grow overnight out of the ether. They were well aware that he must have a past they could guess at but they were simply happy to have inherited such a potential weapon. They were not afraid to use it, to use him!

Shortly after graduation he was deployed, along with the rest of his unit, to Afghanistan where he spent two six-month tours on the ground, based at Camp Bastion. His innate survival skills, hard and quickly learnt as a child saw him through this conflict, while he learnt with every new experience. Then there was a further period of training with the US Marines based in San Diego and then once again deployed into harm's way, fighting the pirates of Somalia off the North African coast. While the high-tech surveillance capabilities of the many satellites orbiting 3,000 miles above earth could detect any unauthorised activity in the region they were powerless to do anything about it. That basic task, the task of neutralising the threat was left to the Marines and in this arena Will excelled further. Their role in essence was the pursuit and then destruction of the pirates and traders in human misery. With his language skills and his ability to deal out swift retribution, engrained from his youth, he rapidly became the number one squad leader. And so it went for several years in different combat zones around the world. Will had learnt his basic craft as an adolescent in the forests and mountains of West Africa in order to survive, now they had been honed to a razor-sharp point by the various professional armed special forces of the modern world. He was the complete package, fluent in many languages and most proficient of all in the language of death. He had found his role, his place in a modern world.

CHAPTER SIXTEEN

PRESENT DAY

Will awoke from his fitful reverie as the engine note of the huge ship dropped. They were drawing into Plymouth Sound and the deep throaty roar of the powerful diesel engines fell away, to be replaced with the almost silent hum of the more easily controlled electric motors. In reality it had only been four and a half days since their disastrous so-called peacekeeping mission in Cameroon where the peace had been shattered so violently and decisively. They had been thoroughly debriefed, both as a team and as individuals, during the four days that it had taken to cruise back from North Africa to the UK. One of the many advantages of ultra-fast satellite communications was that this laborious process could occur pretty much anywhere in the world and be done by their normal control team, based in the UK. So on docking Will was free to go, free to go home.

All combat missions have a minimal period of one to two weeks' downtime after any enemy contact, it is termed uncoupling and Will and his team had just about completed the minimum acceptable time aboard the destroyer. Bitter past experience had taught the armed forces of not just the UK but of all developed nations that in general it was not a sensible idea to simply release combat-ready troops back into civilian life. When ratcheted up to such a high level of alertness, trained and ready to react to any threat, potential or real, with extreme rapidity and force, it required a decontamination period to essentially unwind these men and women, back towards normality. This was absolutely necessary to avoid unfortunate incidents on their introduction back into the normal reality of civilian life. So, as the engines of the destroyer began to gradually cool, Will slipped away from the ship. He strolled along the featureless grey concrete quays of Plymouth naval docks and, along with the many other returning service men and women of all ranks, joined the orderly queue for the busses to take him to the main railway station. There was no welcoming committee for Will as there was for many other returning heroes, rather he simply waited in line for the next train. Forty-five minutes later, quick by British Rail standards, he was slowly chugging along the local line to Totnes station. From there he caught a taxi to the stunning estuary of Salcombe. He was almost home.

Over the last nine years during Will's formal training and active service career he had little, if anything to spend any of his hard-earned wages on and so shortly after his commission in the Navy, he had bought her. She was a thirty-six-foot sailing yacht and to him she was beautiful.

To the hypercritical she was ever so slightly swollen in the centre to provide both increased stability and an extra cabin, normally reserved for Chris, however to Will her lines were perfect. She had a single main mast supported by four high tensile coiled halyards that slapped in the wind against the aluminium of the mast in the most characteristic manner, creating the rhythmic high-pitched sound that he loved so much, the sound of a sailing boat at rest. The decks were teak lined and weathered in the way that only a regularly used vessel can be, the combination of smoothly varnished and polished hardwood caressed by the gentle touch of the sun and saltwater created a finish like no other. But most importantly, the heart and the soul of his beloved boat were the sails that drove her forwards, lifted her on her way. She was currently rigged with a single undersized mainsail that could be used in all conditions, even when rough and a functional roller-jib, easily deployed by a single pilot from the cockpit and a genoa, a larger forward sail that, when opened and filled by the fresh wind, sprang to life with a crisp smacking sound as the tethered material, once canvas and now high tensile Dacron polyester, filled with the power of the wind and lifted the bows of the boat out of the water, driving it forwards with silent power and grace. Will's only possession in the world was this thirty-six-foot boat. Being on her, sailing her in the open sea gave him peace and balance, it was the only place on earth he felt completely at ease. To him this was home. Her name was *Amnesia*.

The water taxi skipped over the small ripples of the still waters of the estuary, rapidly leaving the small but main passenger pontoon at the centre of the tiny village in the distance as they turned left and headed up Batson Creek towards the swing mooring where *Amnesia* lay. As Will drew closer to home, as it always did on his safe return from being once again in harm's way, his excitement grew and as he tasted his first breath of salt-tinged air from the spray of the speedboat he as always marvelled at the serene beauty of this place. Similar to the very first time that he had visited Salcombe, with Chris, repeated with each time that he returned from various conflict-ravaged zones of the world he always found his mind stilled and his soul rejuvenated by the simple fact that such a naturally stunning location could remain unblemished by man's cruelty. For those who had never been it was without doubt one of the most naturally striking and simply beautiful locations on God's earth. The estuary itself teemed with boats, particularly in summer, of all shapes and sizes and it was walled on each side by steeply rising deep green wooded hills that plunged directly into the ever-changing colours of the crystal clear water, dependant on the weather conditions. The junction between the lush unspoilt forest and the ocean was boarded by the yellow-white sand, washed clean twice daily by the tidal surge that ebbed and flowed. The combination of the serenity and unmatched beauty of this small and relatively unknown area of the South Hams with the comfort of his home, *Amnesia*, always restored a degree of reality and calm to Will's life. A life that was based in, and had only really known, violence and strife.

CHAPTER SEVENTEEN

The following day Chris arrived to join Will on *Amnesia* as they usually did after any significant period where Will had been away for some time, especially if that time had involved a combat mission. They met, as always with understated pleasure, as Chris boarded *Amnesia* and then on the rising tide, while Chris held the tiller steady Will hoisted the undersized, but easy to control, mainsail. As they cleared the underwater bar that limited free sailing within the estuary, and indeed could only be passed on the higher parts of the tide by a vessel of their size, Will unfurled the roller-jib fixed to the forward halyard and they both felt the intoxicating sensation as the silent energy of the harnessed wind surged through the boat, pushing them outwards into the gently rolling waves of the open sea. For the next four hours they sailed easterly at a modest pace, dictated by the weak but steady force two wind until they reached a little-known harbour popular in the summer season. However now, in September, it was almost deserted. As they turned towards the shelter of the coast and entered the lee of the headland called Bolt Tail they felt the incessant movement of *Amnesia* settle as the drew into calmer waters. As they approached further they passed a man-made break-water that protected the small cove and dropped anchor between two remaining leisure craft and one obstinate professional fishing boat. She was scruffy and called *Girl Jean II*. Unknown to them she belonged to an elderly local fisherman called Jarvis, still living in the old ways, still pulling up lobster and crab each morning, still resisting the irresistible change to modern fishing practices, a dying breed unlikely to be seen again.

As was their routine, unofficially established over the last few years, once the boat was secure and the anchor fast only then did they begin to talk. Chris would start with the more mundane details of the exponential success of his tech company. Always the more reticent of the two, Will would release small snippets of his recent deployment, never furnished with any specific detail that could potentially embarrass him or put Chris in potential danger, just the overall outline. This was the way it had gone over the last few years between them, a bond that was originally born of necessity, on both sides, had grown stronger and stronger with time. Now both trusted the other implicitly. Neither had any family members, neither had anything like a regular girlfriend, nor had any other significant friends. They depended on each other and the trust that each had in this relationship was absolute and unshakable.

As dusk fell the stillness that normally arrives on the South Coast in the summer descended like a blanket of serenity on the cove. As the day's thermal breeze, driven by the heat rising from the land over the sea dissipated, the sea became as glass and all was almost silent. They rowed ashore on their small tender and dragged it up the sandy beach, leaving it safe above the high tide mark, their toes digging into the now cooling sand. They dined in a small but friendly local pub, aptly named the Hope and Anchor, the sort of unique establishment that can only be found in English country seaside villages, warm, welcoming, unpretentious with quite simply stunning food and ale. Later they returned to *Amnesia* in the moonlight that seems to have a special life when reflected off the rippling sea of the harbour at night. They continued to share their lives together and it was on rare occasions, such as this, that Will felt completely and totally at ease. For once safe! He was in the one environment that he loved and called home, with the one person in the world whom he trusted and called family, he felt at peace.

It was not to last.

CHAPTER EIGHTEEN

Over the following ten days the two drifted from harbour to harbour in splendid isolation, their pace dictated by nothing more than the vagaries of the strength and direction of the wind. They left their sheltered cove and, riding a strengthening westerly breeze, cruised past Start Point and then Prawle Point, ancient land markings for fisherman of the past, and from there onto and into Dartmouth. Here they moored once again and spent the evening enjoying the high quality dining and fine wine experience that was offered in this exceptionally affluent harbour, catering to the massed floating wealth that frequented the area. Financial constraints had ceased to be an issue in their lives, noticeably over the recent couple of years, as Chris's affluence had grown exponentially and also inexplicably. Will had questioned him several times over the past one to two years over this seemingly bottomless financial ability and unending disposable funds, yet Chris, on this one subject was evasive. This was the one single subject where they were not completely open with each other, almost as though Chris was trying to shelter Will, the hardened soldier from the harsh realities of the financial markets. Chris would generally answer that the IT business was going well and expanding, or that the global markets were on the up, but never with any specifics. Will always wondered where such extreme funds came from, in his experience nothing was free in this life and it always left him slightly uneasy if he pondered too long.

The wind disappeared for two days while they were moored in Dartmouth so, to avoid idleness and boredom, they took what they needed and in the small tender half rowed, half floated with the tide, up the Dart estuary. They passed the ancient steam train that ran along the east bank of the estuary, once an essential travel link, now a tourist attraction, and then pushed further inland. At Stoke Gabriel they forked left along one of the larger secondary tributaries of the estuary and eventually arrived at a totally isolated stretch of the river where they landed and set up their camp for the night. They were in splendid isolation on a dairy farm that occupied 300 acres of some of the most expensive real estate land in the country. It was simply called Tom's Field. Later that night, as the sausages were almost ready on their campfire Tom, as was his custom, appeared to share the evening's feast. He wore the same clothes as when they had last visited a year previously, the same tweed cap with a hole in the worn peak and his trousers were held up by bailing twine used for making hay bales, he was unchanged and unaffected by the modern world. Tom had never left his farm for long and had certainly never strayed out of Devon, everything about him testified to that. He led a simple life on his farm and was happy for his friends to come and go as they pleased as long as they left no trace of their passing. The contradiction in his life was, that if he had been of a mind to sell his land, he would have been a multimillionaire many times over. What he personally would do with the funds no one would ever know as, for him, this was his home and he liked it as it was.

Sadly this wonderful downtime, just the two of them doing exactly as they pleased came to an end. Will by routine would have a two-week period of leave after each active deployment and would always take *Amnesia* and disappear from the world, with Chris if possible. As the wind found her strength once more it was time to return to reality, Will back to the Marine Corps and Chris to the world of IT and finance. Will returned to the commando base at Lympstone where, bizarrely, the railway station for this elite fighting force was little more than a single concrete platform with no other amenities. It was so small in fact that the trains would not stop unless specifically requested to do so and so Will found himself requesting that the conductor stop so he could disembark. On arrival on base as always he was immediately engulfed in further training, it was the Navy's way of re-establishing routine, to ensure such an asset remained fit and ready to be deployed at a moment's notice, always good to go. The days drew into weeks and they were filled with a combination of physical training, often ploughing through the thick energy-sapping mud of the estuary, and further refinement of his considerable skills, either on the firing range or in the affectionately nicknamed "kill zone", the bunkers they used to simulate close contact urban conflict. The routine and familiarity of it was relaxing to Will, it was the regular life that he was comfortable with and had led for the last nine years. To most it would be a mind-blowing combination of excitement and exhaustion, to him it was reassuringly boring.

Then everything changed. Mid-morning, on a routine Tuesday, he was unexpectedly called off the grinder. This was the name the Marines had affectionately given the assault course at Lympstone, so called due to the effect it had on the men and women forced to endlessly go over, around and through its soul-crushing obstacles. This course had ground all but the fittest, the strongest and most importantly the irritatingly obstinate into submission and hence its name. He was politely but firmly requested to proceed directly to the office of the base's commanding officer as the Metropolitan Police wished to speak to him. This was all the information that was currently available and in itself was not that unusual. When the police wished to speak to a Marine it was normally due to bad behaviour, often alcohol fuelled, normally involving excessive celebration and then a fight of some sort. This was the natural assumption of the young and inexperienced CO who had only been on base for three weeks and did not know Will. Will held the digital handheld phone, equipped with safe line technology if a more private conversation was required, totally bewildered as to the reason. The next few words caused his world to crash down around him, to implode about him.

"Are you the next of kin of a Mr Christopher James?"

The officer repeated the question in the neutral level tone that he had been trained to use. Will knew what this simple single line request meant. Chris had no other family, no other significant friends, there was only one reason that someone would ask such a question. Chris was dead!

In a monotonous tone the police officer explained that there appeared to have been a burglary last night at Mr James' apartment that had gone disastrously wrong. It appeared that Mr James had returned while the criminals were still on site, there had been a knife, there was panic and Mr James had been killed. There were very few details and nothing more that they currently knew or some such trite phrase that the policeman used to curtail any of Will's initial questions. With this two-minute phone call Will knew that once again everything would change. He had been alone for most of his life and had become hardened, ice-like in attitude. However in Chris he had trusted, he had opened his soul to him and he was the only thing resembling family he had ever known since being ripped away from Father Wilhelm and the mission at St Xavier's. Now it would seem that once again this had been taken from him. He could sense the isolation creeping back over him, the cold descending over his inner core, even as the line abruptly went dead.

His grim expression and the tone of the brief conversation told the others in the room all they needed to know. To his CO the situation was classified as a standard family bereavement and he simply needed time to "attend to matters" as it was termed. As he was not currently on active service or in any specific good-to-go status it was a relatively straightforward process for him to be released.So he was granted two-weeks of compassionate leave, the standard length of time for any serving naval personnel, two weeks and no longer. Will now found himself once again on that visually breathtaking train journey up to London, ten years previously as he had just arrived in the UK when he had marvelled at every second as the scenery flashed by. This time he was oblivious to it all, cocooned in his own zone of personal grief. Outwardly to any observer he appeared as calm as always, however on the inside he was in turmoil. The external visage of the guerrilla fighter was always there, it never left him, the stony blue eyes now set in a paler face than before never changing, expressionless, almost as though devoid of life, the featureless expression carried by so many who had seen too much human misery and death. However he knew that he had been robbed of the only person in his adult life that he had cared for. Since being forced from St Xavier's as a child he had hardened every aspect of his being, both physical and emotional, outwardly hard as rock, inwardly cold as ice. Chris however had taken him back to a degree of humanity, even allowed a degree of human frailty to creep in. Now it was once again banished. There was not a single shred of self-pity at the unfairness of the situation, pity was not part of his persona. However there was a growing anger, a deep rising fire the embers having been lit deep within him. Anger, which without any doubt, was part of his makeup.

CHAPTER NINETEEN

Late that night, close to midnight, Will let himself into Chris's apartment in Belsize Park, North London feeling almost like an intruder in familiar circumstances. Although he had spent many days and nights with Chris in this apartment over the last ten years it had never really been his home, *Amnesia* was his home. As he moved around the luxurious and totally integrated high-tech apartment, with each second, he more acutely felt Chris's absence. Everything in this place reminded him of Chris, everything had belonged to Chris and, in keeping with his position as a CEO of a major IT company there was every IT gadget that one could conceive and several more that Will had never heard of, all hard wired into the infrastructure of the building. In each room there was a massive wide screen curved monitor that had touch screen technology that not only controlled all of the gadgets in the apartment but was also permanently linked into the mainframe of Chris's business computers. It was nothing less than one would expect from an individual in Chris's position, someone whose technology not only served but also to a degree controlled some of the higher financing option traders of the UK capital and so of the financial world. Although Will's skill set was very much in a different area he was not without a basic knowledge of this other cyber-world that Chris had been a master of. On their many nights together, normally floating around the South Coast of the UK on *Amnesia*, occasionally more formally in town, he had not wasted the time and had schooled Will on the basic nuts and bolts of his IT empire. More importantly he had forced Will to imprint in his memory all of the passwords necessary to give him unrestricted back-door access to Chris's entire IT network, the ability to bypass all of the firewalls that had been put in place to protect his system. So naturally, as he had been taught, he found himself installed at one of the work-stations in the apartment accessing the system, Chris's system, now his system, by inheritance, as he saw it. His main reason for opening up the network was to try and piece together the last few hours and days of Chris's life, to somehow see what he had been doing before this bungled unprofessional burglary had robbed him of his future. *Access Denied*, was all he achieved!

Access denied. For the first time ever since Chris had shown him the network, made him commit the passwords to memory, Will appeared to be blocked out. He tried again with the same result. Will could not comprehend why now, now of all times, just after Chris's death, he should be blocked out, why his normal passwords were ineffectual. It just did not make sense. If Chris was gone who could have blocked his access? Will spent the next two hours attempting to bypass the numerous firewalls that Chris had built to protect his IT system from cyber-attack and as the minutes passed he became more and more uneasy, more and more uncomfortable. It was not that the system was blocking him out that really unnerved him, it was the fact that the entire network had been shut down, almost as though it had never existed, simply erased. He did not understand it, where had Chris's system gone?

Will eventually succumbed to exhaustion and fell into a fitful sleep. Death was not a new event for him, neither was accepting its consequence nor rapidly moving on. It had been part of his youth, his upbringing that had remained buried for the last eight to ten years albeit not lost or forgotten. It was not the loss of Chris that woke him, rather it was the fact that Chris's IT network had been so permanently deactivated. In order to terminate such a large system it required not only considerable skill but also considerable assets. To achieve this in under twenty-four hours was an extraordinary feat. The resources and willpower required to achieve this were not inconsiderable and this bothered him like a splinter in the back of his mind. Who would possibly want Chris's system shut down so rapidly and so permanently and why? These questions churned around his mind, despite his best efforts to ignore them and kept him from his slumber. Something was just not right, all of his instincts told him so, and every fibre of his being knew that something was out of place. He had long ago learnt to trust those instincts.

CHAPTER TWENTY

He woke early from a fitful sleep with two fixed appointments already confirmed. The first was mid-morning at number 5 Queen's Stable, the outrageously expensive upper set law firm that had been tasked with the serving of Chris's estate, the second, later in the day, was at the mortuary.

He took the Tube, to Embankment station, surfacing from the hot, stuffy, confined depths of the underground network into the freshening autumn light of a London morning. He turned left and leisurely strolled along the South Bank of the Thames. Big Ben chimed as he passed the |London Eye on his way to Tower Bridge. Now the perfectly smoothed paved walkway was more often used by joggers and commuters, rushing past without the slightest recognition of any of the great monuments to past conflicts and the sacrifices of the many that were regularly placed along this stretch of the river. He left the great river behind him and moved northwards through the Inns of Court towards the Royal Courts of Justice. This was barrister land and indeed a very special place, unique in any busy capital city. It was hard to describe the polar opposite that was created in this unique part of London; as you step through a gated doorway you passed into a world of tranquillity, leaving the rush and bustle behind by just passing through an arch, almost as though stepping into a different world as in a children's novel. The Inns of Court are a semi-private cloistered area that in all essence is identical to a Cambridge college, transplanted into the centre of one of the busiest capitals of the world. It was quiet and tranquil. It is populated by the sharpest minds of the legal world and oozes wealth from every pore. It is a small island hidden in plain sight in the centre of the capital and home to those who exist in this pampered zone, very much separated from the people and consequences of the real world.

He exited the protected quadrangles of the Inns of Court as abruptly as he had entered and was directly in front of the Royal Courts of Justice, once again thrust into the noise, hustle and bustle of a major London street. He turned immediately left and came to the front offices of 5 Queen's Stable. Will's unease was growing with each second, with each pace he took into this polished unfamiliar world. He was aware that these chambers were more used to dealing with multimillion-pound international fraud cases. Why therefore was he here, for a simple transfer of a family estate? These thoughts had been barrelling around his mind throughout his journey across London and they did nothing to settle his growing unease.

He was instantly greeted by Stephen, the senior clerk of the chambers, yet a man who was on Will's wavelength.

Steve was forty-nine years old and had been born only three quarters of a mile away. He had no formal qualifications at all, unlike all of the barristers who he oversaw, and had spent his entire life in apprenticeship. He possessed not a single degree nor any embossed letters of higher qualifications after his name, but he was streetwise. He was savvy and he was the extremely well-paid head clerk of a multimillion-pound chamber of lawyers. When a case arrived at his chambers it was he alone who chose which barrister would take it, he had control over their work and hence their income and he deployed each of them as a stable owner would use his stock of prize stallions. His confident but unassuming manner immediately put Will at ease and this was his particular gift, the skill he had acquired over the years of apprenticeship.

Will was alone so Steve sat with him through the reading of Chris's last will and testament, which was a good thing as the information, delivered in a monotone, was simply staggering. Chris had no other beneficiaries, his parents were dead, and he had no siblings and had neither married nor had children. What he did have was a mind-blowing fortune in disposable cash and that now all passed in its entirety to Will. The fact that Will had inherited all of Chris's estate was no surprise, however what was a mind-blurring fact was the magnitude of the sum. One hundred million pounds sterling, and change! How had Chris ever amassed such a fortune? Yes, Will knew that his business was successful but one hundred million? Over the last eighteen months to two years Chris had become excessively focused on his financial affairs but still, so much for just one individual and now it was all Will's. It was both disconcerting and exhilarating at the same time. As the incessant words poured out from the emotionless lawyer as he read the final details of the document of transfer the reality began to dawn on him. He was rich, unbelievably so. He would never want for any material object in the future, he would never have to work again, never have to go once again into harm's way, never have to fight again. However, at the back of Will's mind there was a nagging doubt like a splinter in his mind, where had all this money come from? It just did not seem real. Will knew in his core that above all else that there was never, ever anything completely free in life, he did not really expect this fortune to be so either. There was simply no such thing as a free meal and money unfortunately just did not grow on trees. It must have come from somewhere or someone.

As he left the refined environment of 5 Queen's Stable and emerged once again into the real world of London his head was spinning. With Chris's death he, the penniless boy from Africa had just inherited a fortune that was truly difficult to comprehend in its magnitude. As he emerged he looked up and saw the statue of Queen Victoria towering above him at the apex of the Royal Courts of Justice. She held forward a set of old-fashioned scales representing the balance of justice, action against consequence, reward against responsibility. He wondered whether the balance would come for him, the deposit had just been made, out of his control, would payment be required and, if so, where and when?

CHAPTER TWENTY-ONE

Will was now already late for his second appointment of the day but he figured they would wait. One of the attendees of the meeting certainly was not going anywhere. He hailed one of the many black cabs rushing down the road and soon found himself winding through the backstreets of London, avoiding the main traffic that clogs the capital's main routes, as only the professional cabbies know how, and in no time at all was soon approaching the Whittington Hospital. All victims of crime in North London, whether alive or dead, are taken to the casualty department of this hospital and as such it is a busy place, highly favoured by junior surgeons and emergency doctors for the training and exposure they receive to major trauma. It is normally as a result of drug-fuelled gangland violence or occasionally, perhaps once or twice a week a more high-profile client from the maximum-security Holloway prison would be resident. The vast majority arrived still breathing and almost always left in the same situation, the unlucky few, Chris among them do not make it and so they eventually found their way to the mortuary, located in the basement of the hospital and called, almost macabrely, Rose Cottage. Will found himself escorted into the grey, sterile building that smelled of formalin and disinfectant, by a silver-haired man, probably in his sixties but ageing badly. He was as polite and formal as all British officials seem to be and referred to Will simply as the next of kin, rather than by his name, almost as if this would depersonalise the situation. Will was here to identify the body, it was a legal requirement and he was complying.

He passed through the reception and descended the plain concrete steps to a lower level. He was now below ground, without ventilation or natural light, such a contrast to the luxurious offices of the law firm where he had spent the morning. Chris was lying on a steel bench covered in a starched white sheet. The bench was angled with a drain plug at one end, presumably to catch any secretions or body fluids and enable efficient and easy cleansing of the sterile steel surface. Will noted these odd details as he formally identified the body as Christopher James, previously of Belsize Park, London, his friend, his only friend. This proximity to death, to a corpse was nothing new for Will — however there was something about Chris's body that bothered him. He could not place it but he knew that there was something not quite right, an inconsistency, a minor detail. As he left the mortuary having completed the necessary documentation and of course paid all the required fees, he was left with a nagging doubt that there was something just not as it should be. Chris had simply been a victim of a robbery gone wrong.

He was rich and lived in an extremely affluent apartment and had been the innocent victim of a knife crime. He had been unlucky. That was the conclusion of the Metropolitan Police and Will had no reason to doubt them. Why then was there a relentless splinter at the back of his mind, gnawing away at his subconscious? There was something wrong, he knew it but could not identify it.

He dismissed these thoughts as paranoia born from his past and left the mortuary on foot, slowly heading back towards Chris's apartment, now his apartment. Whether it was the recent revelation of his new-found wealth or more likely his recent personal isolation he allowed himself to push these dark thoughts away and he strolled away from the Whittington and through the grandeur of Regent's Park and up Primrose Hill. As dusk fell he paused for a moment and looked back, taking in the stunning vista sprawled out below him to the south. The backdrop was one of the greatest cities on earth as darkness fell and the lights began to pick out the skyscrapers and monuments of the capital. It was quite a spectacle and emanated power and financial resource, to him however it was nothing compared to the sight of the moon rising over a calm sea from the stern of his beloved *Amnesia*, currently anchored peacefully in Salcombe estuary. As darkness took hold of the city he found himself in the lift slowly ascending towards his newly acquired penthouse apartment, moving upwards through the building that he now owned. As the heavy doors of the polished lift silently opened a sudden chill entered Will's body. The door to Chris's apartment, now his apartment, was not as it should be. It was not open, nor was it locked, rather there was a tiny crack of light visible originating from the inside. The door had been pushed shut, after it had been forcibly opened and left as such to hide the evidence of forced entry. In an instant Will was ready to react, it was part of his training, both as an adult and as a child. There was no panic, there never was. Panic only ever lead to disaster. There was an issue and he was ready to deal with it, simple as. Instinctively he reached for a weapon, as he had done for many years he felt for a gun, yet there was none. His second instinct was to run his right hand to the small of his back where his blade had always been, an integral part of his body in his previous life, it came back empty. In Britain the carrying of such weapons is strictly forbidden with very severe penalties, probably why so few fatal crimes occur, Will however felt naked. Despite this he moved cautiously forward through the shattered door, ready to deal with any potential threat. Instead he found an empty apartment, empty that is but completely ransacked.

To the casual observer the place was in chaos but to Will it was obvious that the apartment had been thoroughly searched. He had done this before in the past and he recognized the signs of professionals. There was no possible hiding place left unexposed, no cavity or floorboard spared. To Will, a professional himself, it was clear that a dedicated search team had spent several hours here methodically searching for something. This was not the work of burglars. The question that immediately presented itself to him was had they found what they were looking for and why would such a professional team have been here in Chris's apartment? Suddenly he knew what had been bothering him ever since the mortuary earlier in the day. His anxiety had started as he had formally identified the body and he now realised what was wrong. It was the pattern of the wounds on Chris's body. They were not random! They were not the result of a panicked burglar who had been disturbed, they were precise. There were three entry wounds, two on the left and one centrally. The first was high on the left chest, almost in the armpit and would have immediately caused a condition known medically as a tension pneumothorax. It occurs when the lung cavity is pierced, as it would have been by this blow, and with every breath the pressure on the lungs increases as air is sucked into the ribcage, compressing the lung itself. With every breath the victim becomes more and more breathless, squeezing the life out of them, until eventually the pressure becomes so great that the lungs can no longer function. Alone this would have been a fatal wound within minutes, however it is easily treated using just a simple needle or even a hollow pen if you know how. The second wound was slightly lower in the left chest, in fact precisely three rib spaces lower. An attack at this site would generally damage the heart itself and if long enough the blade would sever the ascending aorta, the great vessel rising out of the heart carrying the lifeblood, and would prove fatal within a few brief moments. The third wound was centrally placed in the upper abdomen. A blade placed there in the epigastrium angled slightly upwards, sliding in under the ribcage, would find the pericardium, the sac that contained the heart and several other major structures. Will knew from previous experience that a wound here was always fatal, although not as rapidly so as the previous two. This was what had inadvertently captured his attention in the mortuary earlier in the day, this was what had caused him such subconscious mental disquiet throughout the day. In an unskilled knife attack the blows originate from above and are angry random slashes that inflict wounds on the outer aspects of the forearms as the victim tries to protect himself, or the shoulders and superficially on the chest, although often disfiguring, rarely do these result in major injury. The wounds to Chris were precise, targeted and highly effective, they were in the same pattern that Will had been taught in the past and they were with without doubt the marks of a right-handed professional who had very efficiently carried out his, or her work. Suddenly he realised the ugly truth. Chris had been professionally murdered! While it had been made to look like a bungled robbery there was nothing random, nothing left to chance. Chris had been struck by three precisely aimed blows, each of them fatal on their own, delivered by a professional, someone with significant training. A professional with similar training to himself.

As the cold reality of these unescapable facts dawned on him the question of why leapt to the forefront of his mind. Was it because of the money? No one could amass one hundred million by chance. Nothing was clear. What was crystal clear however was that the one person in whom he had trusted, the only friend, the only family he had remaining had been violently ripped from him. Chris had been murdered, the why and by whom was yet to be determined. Through the confusion his training kicked in and he knew that he could no longer stay in the apartment, it was not safe, for whatever reason it had been compromised. He left rapidly, touching nothing, taking nothing and headed back outside to the nearest open space. He found himself back in Primrose Hill Park, the slightly raised extremely elegant green area overlooking Regent's Park and then down to London's central financial district. Will found himself hunkered down with his back firmly pressed against the solid trunk of one of the larger Poplar trees that flourished here, hidden from sight by the low-hanging foliage, he had returned to what he knew and here he knew he was safe. He was not alone however, there were several others sheltering in the darkness of the park, now he was just one amongst the many other unlucky souls who were homeless in this city, desperately searching for a safe dry place to stay. After several hours passed he allowed his body to slowly relax, yet his mind was on full alert trying to put together the unfolding situation. Chris had been professionally assassinated. Why and by who?

As he mentally worked through the situation he was not sure if he wanted to know. He was alone now with not a single personal attachment and he was apparently exceedingly rich, as of yesterday morning. If he wished he could simply leave and chart a new independent course for his life, an incredible opportunity, he could go where ever he wished, do whatever he wanted. This was not an opportunity that would present itself again. But Chris was gone, professionally terminated. Clearly whatever his assassins had wanted they did not get from him or there would have been no reason to search the apartment. What could they have been looking for? What had Chris been involved in? All of these questions and options spiralled around his brain like disorganised fireworks on bonfire night as he half lay, half slept in the shelter of the tree. A multimillionaire, he was now a vagrant in one of London's most beautiful parks, the almost comical contradiction of his new-found wealth and his current circumstances did not escape him. He was rich, he was sad, but most of all he was once again truly and completely alone.

CHAPTER TWENTY-TWO

As the sun's first rays began to warm his body Will woke, immediately alert as always, and left the park. Rather than returning to the apartment he walked to the nearest gym, of which there were many that served the young professional population that lived and worked in this part of North London. A young, slightly scruffy, a little worse for wear, man arriving at six a.m. requiring a change of clothes was not unusual, in fact it was the normal routine, and so he was able to freshen up and then once again found himself in the grey featureless reception area of the Whittington Mortuary. Chris's body was officially released to him, the tedious paperwork having been completed. To the expressionless mortuary technicians it was just another body, another unfortunate victim of yet another senseless violent crime in North London. To Will however he had been the one and only person he had trusted, his only friend, the only thing he had approaching a family.

The funeral arrangements were made surprisingly easily and rapidly. He was just another in the system to be processed, although Will's new-found serious wealth certainly oiled the wheels of bureaucracy and sped up the process, an ability that Will would be happy to get used to. Holland and Holland were a three-generation run family undertakers and were the standard go-to company attached to the Whittington's mortuary. They were normally accustomed to dealing with the less savoury end of society so a well-spoken naval officer was a refreshing change for them. However they were above all else discreet, and never, ever asked any prying questions. With their standard clientele they knew that inquisitiveness was unwise. All arrangements were complete, payment had been electronically transferred between accounts and the funeral was scheduled for nine o'Clock the following morning.

Later in the day Will had been contacted by the police to officially notify him that the case was closed. In their language they had informed him that they were satisfied that this had been a simple burglary gone wrong and, in their view, there were no other active lines of enquiry. As there were no other victims involved they were not pursuing the investigation further. The officer droned on about recent cuts in police funding as an excuse for their lack of interest, but nothing he said was of any consequence. Will knew the truth that this had been a professional assassination although he had no hard evidence to support this. He rationalised that to open this particular can of worms with the police force would be pointless and so he remained silent and simply politely thanked the officer for the phone call.

The following morning Will trudged alone up Highgate Hill towards the designated cemetery. In contrast to Archway, the location of the Whittington Hospital, just a few hundred metres up a steep hill lay the highly affluent and far more desirable suburb of Highgate-on-the-Hill, North London. Like most large cities there are areas of extreme affluence living adjacent to areas of extreme poverty and it normally took a few minutes at a leisurely walking pace to move from one to the other, a fact that can often lead to jealousy or fear, dependant on one's point of view and often leads to conflict. And so Will walked into the beautifully kept cemetery of Highgate-on-the-Hill where Chris was due to be buried. There was no funeral service, there was no need, and it was pointless as there was no one else there to listen. Will simply stood silently in the tranquil gardens of the cemetery as Chris was lowered into the ground. He was alone, a fact that struck him as bizarre. How could a man worth one hundred million pounds and change not have a single other friend to attend his passing? It just did not make sense. Will knew that Chris's parents had died when he was young and he had no other family, but not one single other person? He had long understood that Chris's passion in life had been his computer, a world in which he had buried himself. He had also known for some time that Chris had been on the brink of a personality disorder, autistic almost in his personality. While he was the master of his high-tech IT world, whilst he could navigate the complex world of the computer system that he had built the straightforward acts of basic human interaction were difficult for him, almost impossible. Will had also understood that for Chris, in bringing him back to the UK, adopting him and rescuing him from certain eventual violent death Chris had found a degree of human interaction that was enough for him, one he could emotionally manage without causing personal distress. Apart from this Will knew remarkably little else about Chris's life, he had just accepted him at face value. What he did know however was that most people would normally have someone to attend their funeral, certainly those worth one hundred million. Why was there no one else?

As the heavy damp clods of earth thudded down onto the polished mahogany coffin these thoughts blurred with the bitter emotions of sadness and loneliness circulating through Will's mind and soul. It was a grey damp morning in North London and for once he was now not sure what to do. Uncertainty was not a status he was accustomed to, in fact, it was so far detached from his normal status quo it unsettled him. In the past, in his youth it had been simple, move fast, stay strong, survive and when called for kill or be killed. The Royal Marines were not so different and as his skills had been fine-tuned in the British special forces uncertainty had not played a major role, it was not part of a soldier's armamentarium. Above all he was now alone. However he was also now very rich! So like most people when uncertain, when out of familiar circumstances he resorted to the place he felt most comfortable, home. So, he hailed a cab and, not bothering to return to the ransacked apartment, he travelled directly to Paddington station. He caught the next fast train to Plymouth and within a few hours was once again tasting the familiar salt spray in his face. The water taxi skipped across the glass-like surface of the waters of Salcombe harbour as the low setting sun, reflecting on the smooth surface, turned the water into liquid fire. He boarded *Amnesia*, lying peacefully at her swing mooring out in the middle of the estuary and immediately felt relaxed, at home. As the last rays of the late autumn sun left the estuary Will sat with his back braced against the base of the mast, feet outstretched, gently rocked by the motion of his yacht. Dusk was the time of day when he was able to gather his thoughts and here was his favourite place. As darkness enveloped him he began to consider his options.

The Navy had allocated him the standard two weeks of compassionate leave and their rules were not made for breaking. In a few days he would be expected back on base in Lympstone, ready for service, able to be deployed if required. Being on a twenty-four, or forty-eight hour or occasionally the luxury of a one-week good-to-go level of alertness had been his life for the last few years and he had not regretted it. The Navy and more specifically the Marines had been good to him, they had given him a purpose and a place in life and he was grateful. In addition they had trained him, extensively, building on his considerable innate skills and had moulded him into a serious weapon, confident moving in multiple arenas, both rural and urban, different countries with his various languages, different terrains, he was more than competent in them all, he was the complete package. But now everything had changed, with Chris's passing the unavoidable fact was that he was now exceedingly rich. He was in a financial position that could only be dreamed of, the origins of which were still unclear. However while mentally questioning where the money had come from he was hardly going to turn it down. He was now in a position where he could do practically whatever he wanted and as this reality crept over him he realised that for the first time ever in his life he was completely free, unchained from any restrictions. If he wished he could simply leave, he could just set sail on his beautiful *Amnesia* on the rising tide tomorrow morning and go wherever he wished, totally independent, beholden to none. After all the years he had been forced to fight in the jungle or forest, avoiding death from either starvation or violence, for all the time that he had served in harm's way with the Marines, now he was free to leave.

As the darkness became complete, enveloping the yacht in a blanket of silence he went below having made his decision. Tomorrow he would contact the CO at Lympstone and officially resign. Then he would leave. He did not know exactly where he would go but it did not matter, from now on he would be able to determine his own direction.

CHAPTER TWENTY-THREE

The sound! It woke him as though an electric current had been passed through his body. There was a sound that was out of place, foreign. Yachts are never silent, there is always perpetual movement and as a consequence perpetual background noise; whether it is the caressing flow of water gently slapping and flowing around the smoothed fibreglass hull, the intermittent high-pitched squeak of helical ropes pulled tight and then relaxed as the swell oscillates the yacht against its moorings, or the ever-present unmistakeable screeching of the halyards vibrating against the hollow aluminium mast and rails. To most it was simply noise but, for those who have a deep affection for boats and the sea, it was the sound of tranquillity. Despite this constant cacophony there are other sounds that have no right to belong, they should simply not be there and it was such a sound that had jolted Will from his slumber. It was the soft dull thud of another smaller craft bumping into *Amnesia's* hull. Will heard it for a second time and now he was certain, there was another small boat, probably a tender of some sort brushing against the sides of *Amnesia*. This meant only one thing, someone was planning on coming aboard and, as far as Will could recall, he was not expecting visitors.

Immediately alert he silently rose and padded noiselessly on bare feet towards the opening of the cabin, where the tender had tied on. As he looked upwards, completely invisible in the dark interior of the cabin he could see two uninvited guests vault over *Amnesia's* rail and drop down into the cockpit at the stern of the yacht. Silhouetted by the moonlight he could see then clearly while remaining undetected in the blackness of the cabin. As they moved he could immediately tell that they were both men, both agile and both powerfully built. They landed perfectly balanced on the polished teak hardwood of the cockpit, rapidly assessed their surroundings and slowly moved forwards. There was no communication, no discussion between them and glinting in the moonlight he could see that each man was armed. The reflection of moonlight from the dark matt metal was unmistakeable, each man held a Heckler and Koch HK-7 semi-automatic pistol fitted with an extended barrel and snugly fitting ugly silencer. These were not casual visitors!

Every one of Will's highly tuned survival instincts was screaming with alertness. These two had not come for a social call. By the way they moved, the weapons they carried and the lack of any need for dialogue they were without doubt professionals. He knew immediately, he recognised them, he was one. The question was, why had they come? Was it to simply search *Amnesia* as Chris's apartment had been. Or more importantly right now had they come looking not for something but for someone, for Will himself? Either way the question was academic, now was not the time for polite conversation. As the two professionals started methodically, to search the cockpit Will was not shy in taking advantage of their temporary distraction. He remained in the blackness of the cabin, confident that he could not be seen and quickly moved forwards to the bow of the boat. Silently he slipped the forward hatch open, reached up and, as the two would be assailants entered the cabin, he raised himself upwards, through the small hatch and into the fresh chill of the night air. Slowly and silently he shut the hatch, fastening the bolts securely. Now the only way in or out of the cabin was through the main entry at the stern. The two uninvited guests were now contained, trapped and completely unaware that Will was alert to their presence. Underestimating a quarry was very often a fatal error.

This time, unlike forty-eight hours previously in London, Will was not naked, he was armed, he had a weapon. As he had ghosted through the gloom of the cabin he had instinctively reached for his blade. The old well-worn long-tempered blade that he had carried for many years through the forests and jungle, like his past he had never quite been able to let it go. In truth he did not want to fully relinquish his past, it was part of him and he had kept it. As his fingers automatically grasped the rough wooden handle of the long, razor-sharp instrument the familiarity of it was instant, almost comforting in a macabre manner. As he firmly grasped his old friend the ruthless, merciless soldier returned. Now there was no place for the well-spoken, well-mannered marine who had politely thanked various individuals over the last two days for their help. Now he was the weapon he had been bred to be, initiated in the jungles and then refined and trained by arguably the best in the world. The only person he could call family had been executed and now, when he was ready to leave and disappear for ever, two professionals had come to his home, looking for something or worse someone. He was cold, emotionless, and ready. First priority as always was survival, to survive the current situation, it appeared that this meant that two others would have to go down, and so be it, he felt no remorse it was the way of his world. Second priority was information. It was time to find some answers.

Down below the two men had turned on the cabin lights and were methodically searching the boat. They knew that torches flashing on and off, intermittently illuminating a boat may arouse suspicion but a vessel with its cabin lights on at night was just normal, an owner up for the evening. From the outside, now brightly lit, Will could see them both clearly. Both were armed not only with the HK-7 semi-automatic handgun but also a second even more lethal automatic machine pistol slung almost casually over each shoulder. They had come prepared and it was obvious that neither would simply leave if politely asked to do so. Will remained motionless now in the relative darkness of the cockpit, observing, waiting. Will was the cold, ruthless weapon he had been built to be and he instinctively knew what now had to happen. Although stationary his entire muscular body was coiled with patent energy, tense and ready to be instantly released. As the two men moved through the cabin, focused on their search, his moment came, for just a fleeting instant both were turned away from the entrance to the cabin, the now only entrance or exit, and as they were momentarily unsighted Will unleashed his attack with unbridled speed and aggression. Speed and aggression, a combination that had never failed him in the past. He lunged forwards and downwards into the cabin, his entire six feet, seven inches of hardened muscle now straight as a human javelin and moving twice as fast, the leading point of which was not his blade as would be expected, but instead it was his left fist and rigid arm, the blade would come later. With unstoppable force generated by the ferocity of his lightning-fast movement he slammed into the back of the nearest uninvited guest. As the completely unexpected force of the impact struck him the assailant was catapulted forwards and downwards at a sickening pace and crashed into the solid wood floor of the cabin. As he hit the deck his skull struck the solid teak wood with the unmistakeable resonating dull thud of bone striking a solid and inflexible object, and, as in all such circumstances, when the human skull is stuck so violently it does not simply bounce back as in so many unrealistic films. Instead he was of course immediately rendered unconscious and was not going to be going anywhere for some time.

As the impact of Will's initial silent attack laid one of the unwanted visitors incapacitated he rolled forwards, instinctively leading with his non-dominant left arm and shoulder, protecting his right side, leaving his dominant right arm free, the one clutching his blade. He had calculated that while there was no doubt that the first opponent would fall without warning, without any opportunity to counterattack or without any opportunity to discharge their weapon, the second would be a different matter. With the sudden noise of decisive action the second man whirled around to see his colleague collapse unconscious under a fast-moving giant. This must be the man that they had been briefed about, warned about, that they may encounter. Treat with extreme prejudice and respect had been the term used to describe him. As he took in his new situation he began to take the briefing information more seriously. Will on the other hand did not hesitate for one single moment and continued his forward momentum from his initial lunge, rolling forwards and upwards now directly facing the second and only remaining assailant. As Will stood tall, now immediately in front of his would-be attacker in the cramped confines of the yacht's cabin he could see the dawning realisation in the other man's eyes that the situation had been reversed, the hunter had become the hunted and now he was in mortal danger. In that precise moment the second unwanted house guest began to do what he had been trained to do, instinctively he began to raise his right arm, the one holding the HK-7 moving in an arc that would in a fraction of a second come to rest pointing directly at Will's torso. Will sensed the movement, he had been expecting it, he reacted first, he was faster. There was no conscious thought, just a pre-programmed reaction to an action, when only decisive and absolute action would allow one to survive and the other to perish. As the unknown man's arm approached him Will moved even further forwards, continuing his initial momentum and as he drew within striking range he used his left arm and shoulder to deflect the lethal pistol headed for his torso upwards. As they collided he used his free left arm to grip the outer aspect of the assassin's wrist that held the HK-7 in a vice-like grip and violently jerked his wrist downwards and outwards. In this position the tendons of the extensor compartment of the forearm were so violently and painfully pulled that it was not possible to effectively hold onto any object. Will felt the silenced gun jerk twice in the dismayed grip of the attacker as it ineffectively discharged two rounds, now harmlessly flying over his head and ploughing into the deep, soft velvet that covered the ceiling of the cabin. In this position, locked together as they were, the assailant's entire abdomen and chest were now exposed, vulnerable and he could do nothing to protect them. Without a second's hesitation, without the need for conscious thought Will used his free right hand, that he had, up until this time, protected, drove the full nine inches, twenty-seven centimetres of his old blade upwards and forwards into the helpless man. The blade passed through his epigastrium, through the diaphragm and pierced firstly the pericardium and then the cardiac muscle itself. It was a lethal wound, both knew it. The almost silent fluid movement that had just occurred lasted less than four seconds and was now over. Will found himself face to face with the second man, entwined together almost as lovers in an embrace. He held him there, pressed against his body for a few slow heartbeats longer until he was sure that there was no further threat. He felt the warm flow of his lifeblood pulsing out through his wound, flowing over his hand and arm and down onto the floor of the cabin. He saw the light in this man's eyes slowly begin to fade, his pupils constrict, his eyeballs begin to roll. It was over, his life-force had left him. There was something imperceptible that leaves a person in the moment they die and it could only be appreciated if you were there at the exact moment when it happens. Some call it their soul, others their being, whatever it was there was a moment when something undefinable, untouchable suddenly goes, never to return. Some believe it is passed onto the next generation, most however who have witnessed this event just realise that life is precious and life is finite and you only get one shot at it.

Once again Will's instincts had saved him. Awakened from the moment by the groaning of the still-incapacitated first assailant he was jolted back to the present and turned to the prostrate form on the floor. The man was beginning to regain consciousness so before he was any further awake Will took action; he flipped his long blade in his hand and using the rough solid wooden handle he delivered a blow just behind his ear. Twelve minutes had passed since he had been suddenly awoken, just twelve minutes and now there was one dead man and one unconscious one on the floor of his cabin. There had been no significant noise, nothing to alert anyone on the outside to the lethal drama that had just unfolded. There was no panic, there never was. Panic only ever lead to disaster. Will was stonily calm, just earlier that evening he had decided to leave, to disappear for the foreseeable future, yet the events of the last few minutes were now going to threaten that, push him in a different direction. Why had these men come? Had they come for something or had they come for him? Either way the question was slightly academic. They had been professionals, that was obvious and now their mission, whatever it had been, was a failure. Professionals and the organisations or individuals who controlled them did not simply accept failure and just move on. If this first team had been unsuccessful a second larger, more powerful, better armed and better prepared team would come until the task was complete. They would continue until the mission, whatever that was, was complete, until they had got what they wanted or who they wanted. This was how professionals worked, Will understood this; after all he was one. Now however he needed to know why they had come, who had sent them.

Once again practicality took over and, using one of the many spare ropes on board, Will securely bound the unconscious man, there was no need to bind the other. Once he was satisfied he was secure he briefly checked the tide tables to see when there would be sufficient water to clear the bar, the sand bar that provided underwater shelter to the estuary, neutralising the swell of the channel, but also preventing a large yacht such as *Amnesia* from leaving unless two hours either side of high tide. He knew he had to move and the top of the tide was at six o'clock in the morning so, at just after four a.m. he silently crept out of the harbour, with two uninvited passengers. For once he had turned off his running lights, he did not now want to be observed as he left port. At four in the morning there was no wind to propel his sleek vessel so he slowly cruised out, pushing through the growing swell using the power of the throaty diesel engine. He hugged the coast eastwards for a couple of hours and as the tide reached its zenith, he pushed *Amnesia* through the surf of Bigbury Bay and around Burgh Island, once the location of famous detective novels and now a luxury spar hotel, and into the calm waters of the Avon estuary. On the flooding tide he moved further up the unknown and deserted estuary towards the tiny hamlet of Averton-Gifford and on rounding one further meandering bend in the river, he eventually dropped anchor and moored in a deep-water pool that left enough water for her to remain afloat once the tide had ebbed away and left the rest of the estuary bare and mud covered. It was a spot Will had discovered by chance several years previously and there was now not a single soul within ten miles of him and absolutely no possibility of anyone reaching him until the following high tide in twelve hours' time. He was alone, isolated and for the near future safe. It was time to find out some answers.

CHAPTER TWENTY-FOUR

As the summer sun rose over the calm waters of the isolated estuary, bathing *Amnesia* in its growing warmth the one remaining assailant awoke. He found himself bound securely with his four limbs splayed out in front of him in a sitting position. As he slowly regained consciousness he found himself faced with a huge, powerfully built man of unrecognizable nationality who had apparently incapacitated him and dispatched his colleague. As he began to shake off the last vestiges of unconsciousness the throbbing pain in his head began to increase and the seriousness and uncertainty of his current situation began to dawn upon him. Will started with kindness; he gave his would-be assailant food and water and then left him, alone but securely bound, below deck to contemplate his imminent future. Will stood barefoot on the smooth teak deck and took in the serene natural beauty that now surrounded him, silently evaluating his current options in his current situation. The Avon estuary is a special, undiscovered place where the lush greenery of the English countryside rolls down directly into the deep blue, green waters of the ever-moving estuary, purged twice daily by the flow and ebb of the tidal surge. The contrast struck Will as almost comical. Here he was, in one of the most beautiful places on God's earth and yet he was on the brink of crossing a line that would plunge him right back into the ugly mire of human conflict. Yesterday he had resolved to leave, to relinquish his violent past and simply float away aiming to lead a life of tranquillity, of boredom even. Yet now by the actions of two unwelcome visitors, dictated by someone as yet to be determined, he had been thrown right back into that life of base human conflict.

He knew that he had a simple choice; leave or stay. His lifelong training of analysing a situation and breaking it down to two or perhaps three simple options had not left him, it never would. For some reason, as yet completely unclear, these men had come for something that may or may not be on his yacht, or perhaps even for someone, for him. Whichever option it was they, or more importantly their supervisors and directors were not likely to simply give up and leave. With initial failure they would redouble or triple their efforts, exponentially increasing the resources allocated to the mission until their goal was achieved, until the mission was complete. Will was sure of this, he knew it in his core, and these individuals who had come to his boat were professionals, like himself. They did not operate in any other way and would not just conveniently go away. Failure was not an acceptable option and they would just continue until the goal had been achieved. As he worked through this unescapable logic it meant that he now had a straightforward black and white choice, a decision to be made. He could either run or stay. If he chose to run, to flee right now and remain hidden for the future he knew that he would be successful. His training over the last ten years had involved evasion in many circumstances in many different countries. He was highly skilled at it and fluent in so many languages with a face that could pass for almost any nationality required. He knew he could run if he wished and in fact this would be the sensible choice, the smart option to take, but there was a problem, a big problem. If he ran now he would always be running. He would have to live with the constant threat of pursuit or worse, the constant looking over his shoulder, could the next turn in the next street be his last, would the person serving him his morning coffee turn and shoot him dead, the constant, never-ending pressure of being hunted. If he stayed on the other hand he would be embarking on a journey back into the depths of depravity of his old world, his previous life where ruthlessness, pre-emptive violent attack without warning and ultimately death were an integral part of his survival. If he stayed he had to find answers, he had to know why these men had come and what, or who, had they been sent for. He would have to go further, he would have to determine who had sent them and then he would have to neutralize that threat. If he was to live a future without fear, without having to constantly look over his shoulder there was really only one option and he knew it. Despite his faultless logic it was not an option he wanted to take. He had striven to leave that brutal part of his previous life behind, with Chris's help. He had excelled in the Royal Marines and had carved a new and almost respectable life for himself and he did not want to leave it behind. Unfortunately, life, as it often appeared to do so for him, had not been kind, had given him no realistic choice. To live in constant fear of reprisal was to live a life half lived and Will knew deep in his soul that he could not do that. He did not like the situation but there was only one realistic path that he could take. He did not like where he suspected it was going to take him, but he figured that he had been given no other option.

The cruel irony of his current situation did not escape him as he stood alone, silently surveying the stunning natural scenery that surrounded him and his uninvited guests. As with most choices in his past the current choice was simple. Run and live in perpetual fear or stay and find a solution, wherever that may take him? He chose the only one he could. Pretty much all of the few choices in his life that he had any control over had been straightforward, black or white, binary. He had always reacted in order to survive, kill or be killed, so again, he did not hesitate. However this time he realised that he was about to cross over a line from which there was no coming back from. Since leaving Africa he had regained the few intact remnants of his humanity, with Chris he had known friendship, compassion and kindness. Will was all too well aware that this future journey on which he had been launched, by none of his own actions, had no place for such civilities. He realised that he would never again be able to return to the Marines as a serving officer. He realised that he was plunging head first back to the cold, ruthless and unfeeling human weapon of his past. He did not want to go back there but it seemed that he had been given no realistic other option. He knew what he had to do, in the tranquil dawn light he had decided. If he could not run he would have to neutralise the threat before it neutralised him. Again a simple binary choice. It was the only possible way for him to have a future. With these concrete facts solidified in his mind he turned away from the warmth and light of the sun and with ice in his heart and steel in his soul and went below to join his one remaining breathing uninvited guest. He knew there was no turning back. He was once again the unfeeling guerrilla warrior of old, buried but not forgotten. It was time for answers.

CHAPTER TWENTY-FIVE

He approached the prostrate bound man in silence. His ex-colleague lay motionless on the floor of the cabin nearby, cold and stiff, Will's conviction was not in doubt. The assailant from the night before, now captive had been in solitude for the first part of the morning to contemplate his situation and, as Will stepped down next to him, his face only centimetres apart, their eyes locked. Neither spoke, it was painfully clear that a polite request for the information required was not going to suffice. Throughout his years with the LPT Will had observed several different techniques for extracting information, some more effective than others, some more brutal than others. As with all efficient techniques it was never about the degree of harm inflicted, rather it was the degree of implied future suffering that was to come that was the key. If an individual was totally incapacitated it became futile. However if that individual remained well but truly understood the potential harm that may be rained down upon them in the very near future there were very, very few sane men or women who would not divulge any information in exchange for safety. And so Will, hardened by his earlier decision, quietly and slowly, explained the situation to his one remaining living captive.

He needed the answer to three simple questions. Why had they come? What had they come for? And who had sent them? Why, what and who, simple as ever. As expected the initial enquiry was met with silence. Will expanded on the imminent future. There is a very old and exquisitely simple procedure developed in the late thirteenth century in the ice lands of the Russian tundra, favoured by the Russian security services of the time and revived in the Second World War by parts of the NKVD, the Russian secret service. It is called only *pain*. It's not high-tech and requires nothing save a strong arm, a degree of accuracy and a hammer. One starts with the toes, then methodically moves upwards, through the metatarsals, the small bones of the foot, then the ankles, then the tibia and fibula, the long bones of the lower leg and slowly and methodically upwards, the knees, hips, spine, not forgetting the testicles of course and then onwards and upwards pausing briefly at every joint, although no one has ever been recorded as reaching the ribs. With each fall of the hammer another bone breaks, with each strike the pain increases, with each strike the level of permanent disability increases until there is nothing much left. There is no doubt that the poor victim will succumb, they always have in the past, it is just a question of how much damage they wish to endure first, how much future disability they wish to live with for the price of information. Will, without any emotion or excitement in his voice, very specifically spelled it out for his unwelcome guest and then placed the winch handle down in front of him, resting it between them. While he did not have a hammer the winch handle if anything was heavier, normally used to crank the circular chrome deck winches to raise or tighten the sails. With this inevitability laid bare in front of him combined with the touch of the now chilling corpse of his former colleague lying next to him, there was no need for any further action. He took the wise choice and simply disgorged any and all information that he possessed.

Both men were ex-army and now worked for the security department of a large multinational company called Monaghan and Clark. Both reported directly and solely to the head of this security department a one Mr Timothy Jarrett. They had been given this assignment specifically by Jarrett himself, which in itself was unusual. Two weeks previously they had been instructed that a single individual, Christopher James, head of the IT system used by the banking branch of M&C, had developed a system that was syphoning large amounts of cash illegally from the corporation. Their instructions had been simple, the system had been temporarily blocked through its cloud access but the hard discs with the program on were still in existence and needed to be destroyed. They were to regain them and destroy them. Will had not expected them to know even as much as this small amount of intelligence. Will had been on many missions in the past where the pre-action mission brief had been even less forthcoming. What had happened was that Chris through stupid stubbornness had refused to surrender the discs, worse he had attempted to flee and then when that had failed had made a bad situation worse and had even more stupidly attempted to fight. A struggle would imply a degree of two-way conflict where in reality there was none. When the discs had been demanded Chris had refused, he then ran and being blocked foolishly started to fight back, bad decision, in fact a terminally bad decision. A forty-five-year-old computer techie versus two highly trained professionals. It was not even a conflict, however brief, the outcome was inevitable and when faced with a threat the two professionals reacted instinctively. They simply neutralised the threat, rapidly, silently, efficiently.

With Chris removed from the equation they had searched his apartment but in vain and had failed to acquire the discs. Then after the funeral a second option had presented itself, Will. He was Chris's only next of kin and the only other person who may have the discs and may have some knowledge of the illegal IT system that Chris had designed and this was why the two men had stolen in the dead of night onto *Amnesia*. Their instructions once again had been specific but again short on factual information. They were to identify and retrieve the discs and then to neutralize him. Since both individuals with any potential knowledge of this system were gone, the system would be deactivated permanently, if either remained there was a possibility, however remote, it could be rebooted. This was a possibility that was unacceptable to the corporation of M&C. He knew no more, Will had not expected him to have more information. He was a foot soldier, given the information he required to complete his assigned task, no more and no less. However breaking it down into bite-sized chunks these two had assassinated Chris. They had then come looking for some discs that had the potential to reactivate a system, whatever that system was, and more importantly they had come looking for him, with strict instructions to take him down. They had been sent by a man named Timothy Jarrett, head of security at a company called Monaghan and Clark. This gun for hire knew no more, further questions were futile.

He had taken an initial step forward on a path he did not want to follow but now had no choice. He had a name, Timothy Jarrett, this man had sent a unit to kill him, driven by the need to acquire some computer discs, that he had never seen, that could potentially reactivate a system that he had never heard of. Unfortunately, it had clearly been Chris's system and now by vicarious liability Jarrett mistakenly had assumed that he had some intimate knowledge of it. His underlying basic course of action was now clear, he needed to find one Mr T Jarrett and either radically change his opinion of the situation or, if not possible, neutralise that particular threat before it neutralised him. Once again a seemingly simple black or white choice, run and live in fear or stay and remove the threat before it removed him. Neither was a great option, neither was of his own making, but the choice was clear.

Returning to the immediate situation there was one remaining problem that needed to be resolved right now, what to do with the man below? He knew the answer but was not prepared to accept it. He could not simply release him, he would fight back or run directly back to Jarrett and the security department of Monaghan and Clark, removing any slight advantage of surprise and uncertainty that Will now had. Alternatively he could not just leave him bound where he was to slowly die from dehydration. This was the man who cold-heartedly had killed Chris, he had little sympathy for him, and so he turned, and headed back down into the poorly lit interior of the cabin, now once again the cold, ruthless, emotionless guerrilla warrior of the past. The silenced pistol, once belonging to this man, now belonged to Will, coughed twice, no other sound was audible and it was done. With this cold act that had taken no longer than a couple of seconds Will had launched himself backwards, back to where he had started, as an unfeeling teenager all those years before. It was a massive retrospective step but there was no other realistic option and there was certainly no going back now. Events beyond his control had now forced him to embark on a path he had not wanted to take, it had started in lethal violence and he was sure that there would be more to come before it was over. He had no choice now but to follow it to its conclusion.

CHAPTER TWENTY-SIX

As the sun reached its dazzling zenith at midday, Will prepared to leave. His decision had been taken, the events of the last twelve hours could not be undone; now he was fully committed. In reality such binary black and white decisions were easy for him. Stay or run, hide or attack, kill or be killed. These were the snapshot decisions that he had been taking all of his life, the way he had been trained to be and he was at ease with this. Indecision, uncertainty created anxiety for him, neither was present now, his new path was clear and it had definitely started. So as the afternoon sun lit up the otherwise deserted and silently peaceful Avon estuary, Will left his beloved *Amnesia*. He was confident that his early morning exit from Salcombe harbour had not aroused suspicion, Even if his departure had been observed and logged by the harbour commissioners it would not have raised any alarms, a single sleek pleasure yacht among so many leaving this stunning harbour on the rising tide was not unusual. He was confident that his early morning entry in darkness through Bantham, silently stealing into the Avon estuary had been witnessed by not a single soul and he knew from past experience that there were very, very few who ever came along this particularly isolated stretch of water. The occasional canoeist or even more infrequently a group of swimmers, half swimming, and half floating along with the current out to sea would pass this way, but all they would see was a rather elegant large yacht moored in one of the deepwater pools of the estuary. This was not unusual in the summer and would raise no suspicion, rather envy at the location and the beauty of the vessel. He was confident that he was leaving *Amnesia* safe and unobserved and that there was a relatively good chance that she would still be there on her swing mooring if he returned. That is if he lived through the events that were about to unfold over the coming few days and months.

As the flow of the tide reversed and slowly swung *Amnesia* around, Will left. He simply drifted on his canoe, pushed upstream by the incoming tide flooding the estuary, leaving his home behind. Securely strapped to his canoe were two waterproof barrels that fitted snugly in their bindings. Within them were the three essential items that he would require for the immediate future: cash, weapons and information — the essential tools of his trade. Will had never had any trust in the banking systems of the modern world, much to Chris's disgust. He had never fully been able to shake off his past and the thought of entrusting any of his significant belongings in the care of a corporation he did not know was too foreign to him. Chris had been the only person he had trusted and so he had squirrelled away a not insignificant amount of liquid cash on *Amnesia*. Over the last eight years as an officer in the Marines he had almost no opportunity to spend any of his not inconsiderable wages. Frivolity, holidays or expensive cars were not his style and so he had gradually accumulated a large amount of disposable cash that he had stored in the underfloor lockers of *Amnesia*. Now this money was carefully wrapped in multiple waterproof bundles, each worth ten thousand pounds sterling, and sealed in a closed, vacuum-tight barrel, now strapped securely to the top of his canoe, sitting in plain sight just in front of him as he slowly paddled up the estuary, back towards civilisation. The second vacuum-sealed barrel, slightly larger, slightly heavier was secured behind him, its weight lifting the bow of the canoe slightly out of the water and balancing it perfectly. This barrel contained the second of the three requisites, weapons. While Will, as a professional soldier in the special forces, had his own personal set of highly advanced weaponry issued by the Royal Marines, all of it was very safely and very securely locked away in the gun racks on base in Lympstone. This was Britain. Unlike several other so-called advanced countries running around with one's own personal set of defensive or offensive weapons was just not acceptable, it was just not how it was done. Despite the fact that he was a highly trained professional it made no difference, there were no exceptions, and as such all weapons remained the property of the Royal Marines and as such never left the base unless to be released in an active conflict zone. So this barrel contained the weapons that he had liberated from his two uninvited guests from the night before, who had no further use for them. For a team of only two they had been remarkably well equipped. He now possessed two HK-7 sidearms or handguns, each with an effective silencer for covert work and enough full magazines for the foreseeable future. In addition there was a machine pistol, capable of delivering three thousand rounds per minute which, although inaccurate at any distance, when deployed in a crowded environment could be simply devastating. It was not one of Will's favoured tools but he knew from past experience that it was extremely effective. As well as these conventional weapons each had possessed a new 5-G mobile phone, each with the same single pre-programmed number on its main screen and no other numbers in the contacts or memory. One of these phones was now shattered into multiple fragments that were slowly sinking through the thick dark estuary mud, the other was securely wrapped in a waterproof bag safe in the barrel. Next to it was its battery and SIM card, both having been removed and wrapped individually. Will could reactivate this 5-G phone whenever he wished to and indeed planned to do so in the not too distant future, however devoid of energy and without a SIM card the mobile could not be tracked and his location could not be revealed. The final weapon was his blade, kept from his previous life, snug like an old friend in the small of his back. It had not been there for some time but now, in the current situation, it did not seem out of place, it was a different environment but the basic situation was the same. Will was under no illusion, by no choice of his own he was now in direct conflict with a large and powerful corporation that had already demonstrated it had the means and motivation to use lethal force to achieve its goal. The gravity of the situation had not escaped him but the rough caress of the haft of his blade between his shoulder blades, the unconventional comfort blanket he had clung to for so long in the past, gave him a degree of unwarranted and bizarre reassurance.

The third and most unfamiliar object was not packed carefully within the two barrels, instead it hung from his neck, safely in a waterproof pouch hidden from sight nestling against his muscular chest under the neoprene of his wetsuit. It was a disc. He did not yet know what it contained, however he did know that whatever information was on this disc was, for a certain Mr Timothy Jarrett, worth killing for. He had found it almost immediately. He had guessed that if not in Chris's apartment the only other logical place would be on *Amnesia*. As it happened it was not hidden at all. He had found it in plain sight on top of the chart table with a plain yellow stick-it note attached to it. It read "For Will, from Chris, Sorry". That was all, five words and it reflected Chris's almost autistic character, there was no emotion, no explanation, just five simple words. Perhaps that was why Chris had been so successful in the world of financial computing and IT support. Whatever this disc contained it was clear that to M&C and Mr Timothy Jarrett it was of significant value, enough to send a team of professionals not only to retrieve and destroy it but also to destroy anyone, namely him who may have been exposed to any of its contents. Will now had this information, this disc and he knew that this was his bargaining tool, his leverage against Jarrett and the corporation of M&C. It was his only real significant resource, with this disc he had something of value that he could use and it was now vital to his survival.

Two hours later his loaded canoe ground gently into the gravel base of the slipway of the Totnes rowing club. He had arrived at the head of the river at a landing and launching area that was used constantly by various small craft entering and exiting the estuary. The slipway belonged to the Totnes rowing club and he simply blended in with the other members launching and recovering their boats. He hauled the canoe out and stacked it in the visitors' racks. He slung both barrels over a shoulder using the straps that had held them fast on the canoe and ambled up the slipway without raising the slightest interest, just another sportsman using the river, and melted into the cosmopolitan throng of humanity of Totnes town. He knew that today time was not his friend, the longer it went the more obvious it would be to Jarrett that something untoward had befallen their team. They would have been required to provide regular sit-reps back to M&C and, as they inevitably missed each deadline, the anxiety would grow. Then a second, larger and better prepared team would be dispatched to find out exactly what had occurred. Will knew he had to act soon to take the initiative away from Jarrett and his team, to readdress the balance of his current situation. However to embark on this course of action without any prior knowledge of his adversary, without any solid intel, went against all of his instincts and training. All he had learnt over the last few years in numerous counter-insurgency operations with the Marines told him to stop, to gather information about the individual and corporation he was now pitted against. So he decided, on balance, to wait one day, twenty-four hours. There was no real possibility that Jarrett could be aware yet of the events of the last twelve hours or of Will's current location. For the next day, he should be safe.

CHAPTER TWENTY-SEVEN

Totnes is an unusual town. Anywhere else in the Western world a sixfoot seven inch man walking barefoot along the main street of any town with two large barrels strapped over his back would arouse suspicion, or at least look unusual. However here it was almost normal. Totnes is a town filled with individuals seeking an alternative life to the mainstream existence and is famous for this fact. The open attitude of the place and total unquestioning acceptance of difference acts like a magnet to travellers, old or new age hippies or anyone seeking a different life, most commonly those who have lived and often prospered in the hectic bright lights of the city and who are seeking an alternative, calmer rhythm to their lives. Here the sickly sweet scent of marijuana is normal and there are more street vendors pedalling magic crystals than newspapers. In fact the town is officially twinned with the mythical city of Narnia by deed poll of the town council and, for those who dwell in this unique town in South Devon, this does not seem out of the ordinary. The open-minded approach to life of this town draws in those seeking an alternative existence like bees drawn to the irresistible scent of nectar. So Will, calmly and peacefully strolling alone, dressed as he was, down the main street was not unusual. What he needed now more than anything else was information. He needed protected access to the Internet and some protected time and so he found himself installed in a café with free Wi-Fi. He was in a restaurant cum coffee bar of sorts called the Vegan Cat which primarily catered for ladies and their feline friends. Will found himself installed in an isolated corner of the coffee bar, surrounded mainly by kaftan-wearing middle-aged women displaying multiple body piercings almost as a badge of allegiance. It did not matter as the Vegan Cat also recognized the fact that free unlimited Internet access also drew in the customers as well as the specific alternative ethos of the place. So several hours later and after several cups of virtually taste-free herbal tea Will was able to extract some of the basic intelligence information he required.

The World Wide Web is an extremely powerful tool, often underestimated by the generation who have simply grown up with it as an integral part of their lives. Will was not a computer buff as Chis had been, but neither was he incompetent nor computer illiterate, and after a few well-spent hours, he had built a basic profile of a one Mr Timothy Jarrett and his security company, the security department of Monaghan & Clark. When Will sat back to make a judgement on the information available, Timothy Jarrett seemed the perfect individual to be in charge of a security firm for a large multinational corporation. He was fifty-four years of age, married with two school-age children and lived in a large detached house in North London. He had been a career officer in the British Army for the requisite nineteen years and then, after serving mainly in Northern Ireland during the troubled times of the IRA and then in several other combat arenas, had retired. Then for just over a decade there was no information at all, not a trace of his existence, nor a single snippet of any activity, a complete information void until at the age of fifty. Ten years later he emerged as the newly appointed head of security at M&C. For such an individual to have not a single mention for ten years meant only one thing. He would have been part of the clandestine shadowy world of intelligence gathering, special forces operations and government officially deniable espionage. As Will began to build an initial picture of this individual the basic information that he could glean gave no hint to the underlying nature of the man. However, from past experience Will knew that such individuals were just simply not warm and welcoming, it was not the nature of the beast. They were mentally hard, cold, mercilessly calculating and also prepared to order others into harm's way without the slightest hesitation or self-recrimination. Mr T Jarrett and his team were not to be underestimated. In addition to the basic factual information he had obtained he was able to download an image. It was of Jarrett from his retirement dinner on leaving the Army and, although over ten years out of date, it was something that Will could work with. The man was well built and still physically fit with grey streaks beginning to edge into his ash-coloured hair. His face however was blank, emotionless and unreadable, as would be expected from such an individual.

While the information on Jarrett was sparse and difficult to find the opposite was true regarding the giant corporation of Monaghan & Clark. There were pages and pages and it was immediately obvious that M&C was an extremely large and diverse multinational corporation that operated via a well-integrated global network. There were divisions and then subdivisions each with slightly differing financial expertise, insurance, international trade, offshore banking. There were investments in construction, mining, mineral wealth, transport infrastructure and many, many more industries spread around several continents, and the list continued. While it was impossible to gain any specific answers it was immediately obvious that this was a global company with enormous resources operating on a level way above plain simple national interest. The other essential task that he accomplished while ensconced in the Vegan Cat was to copy the disc. He did not have the time yet to examine its contents but he knew it was of significant value to Jarrett and M&C, significant enough to be worth killing for, and so he made several hard copies that he could keep as insurance. When he had more time, he would scrutinise the discs carefully, but for now he had lingered in the same place for too long. As he logged out and quietly thanked the owners for their hospitality he left and moved out into the half-darkness of dusk. He had spent the majority of the day gathering intel on his new adversary and, although he had nothing concrete, he did know some solid information about the company and the individual who had dispatched a team to kill Chris and to take him. None of the intel gave him any comfort, yet he now had a face, an image of the man responsible. He also had a phone number, the only number preprogramed into the 5-G phones he had liberated the day before. It was a start. An identity, a method for contact. It was a start.

Calmly he strolled along the single street of the town towards the railway station, mixing with the other restless souls who passed through, desperately searching for a different life often without really knowing what it was that they were searching for. In the station he used cash to buy a single on the slow sleeper to London and again cash for a pay-as-you-go mobile phone with a new SIM card, both the phone and any cash transaction was untraceable, as his previous flight and evasion training with the special forces ingrained into him. Without any means of mobile communications he felt vulnerable and this small purchase helped to settle his nerves. He boarded the night sleeper that intentionally chugged slowly cross-country to arrive in Paddington, London in the early morning. The train stopped at many small provincial stations on the way up to the metropolis to intentionally slow its progress and also to open up business from different parts of the country, arriving always precisely, if sedately, on time at 0600 at Paddington station. In the lonely darkness of the cramped cabin, jostled by the incessant rhythmic motion of the train juddering over the imperfect tracks, Will began to formulate a plan of action, a possible way to move forwards, a possible way to regain his life, a possible way to be allowed to simply go free, to be able to live without the constant threat of lethal recrimination. He did not want to take anything. He did not ask for much, he just wanted to be left alone.

CHAPTER TWENTY-EIGHT

As the elegant train drew inexorably into a wakening London Will knew that time now was not on his side. It was approaching twenty-four hours since he had left *Amnesia* lying silently on her swing mooring and by now Jarrett and his team would surely realise that something untoward had occurred. With no contact from their first two-man team they would be desperately trying to locate them, not out of concern for their safety but out of pure selfish self-protective anxiety to know what had occurred and whether these as yet unknown events could leave them exposed, corporately vulnerable. His security team would by now have built an initial profile on a one Mr W. James and would now know that he was a currently serving naval officer in the marines and had been so for the last ten years with an outstanding service record. They would know that he had served across different continents in multiple different environments including both rural and urban conflicts. While specific details were classified a shrewd team would be able to plaster over the gaps in the easily available information. They could not be sure but would correctly surmise that he had significant skills and knowledge of street craft, counter-intelligence, evasion and assault based on his past experiences of hostage rescue and urban conflict. What they would have no knowledge or even the least premonition of was his former life, a more brutal existence, as with Chris gone there was not a single living person who did. They would have zero appreciation of his unique and specific physical and mental skill set, his almost animal ability to survive combined with his multilingual skills and razor-sharp intelligence, hopefully they would have not the least suspicion of this formidable individual armamentarium. However in the brief time that had now elapsed Jarrett and his team could not really be sure of anything and because of this, because he still remained an unknown quantity, an uncertainty, a small but important advantage that he could use, he had decided to accelerate the process.

As the train finally juddered to a halt at the terminal, adjacent to the platform Will was woken from his thoughts. He gathered his possessions, disembarked and moved forwards along the long thin grey concrete platform towards the exit, engulfed in the throng of commuters pushing forwards almost as one. Paddington is always a scene of constant motion, twenty-four hours a day seven days a week. It is one of the two main railway stations that serves London with a population of over ten million people, most of whom enter and exit on a daily basis. On average three and half million souls pass across the central concourse of this fine old station each day and this morning was the same as all others. It was six fifteen in the morning, the start of the crazy rush hour and there were literally thousands upon thousands of commuters passing through every few minutes as newly arriving trains disgorged their human cargo. They pushed and shoved their way forwards, scurrying across the concrete platforms smoothed by the passage of endless feet, all trying to get that tiny advantage, any edge on the rest of the competition for the day. Will simply flowed along with them, with this unstoppable flow of humanity, like a huge herd of mindless beasts moving as one without a single individual thought. Having purchased a grey featureless suit from one of the charity shops the day before he now simply just blended into the massive crowd, just another faceless commuter.

Paddington station is unusual in its structure in that it is a covered building in the heart of central London but it is open to the environment on two sides. This creates a very distinct air flow in that there is always a constant breeze that flows from one end to the other, always in the same direction, driven by the thermal difference between the main entrances through which the trains move and the much hotter and narrower exit that all the thousands of people funnel through. As Will moved slowly forwards hidden in the crowd he breathed in deeply, it was a familiar scent as unique as it was distinctive. The heady mixture of diesel fumes mixed with the odour of thousands of people tainted by the tinge of air pollution from the city diluted by the ever-present breeze through the station. It was the scent that he had been greeted with on his arrival in England a little over ten years previously. He had been struck then at how different it was from anything he had known in his turbulent adolescence. Now it was almost comforting, it was always the same, unchanging in a recently highly uncertain personal world.

As the never-ending flow of individuals rushing to get to their desks or offices headed for the entrance to the Tube. Will stepped sideways out of the mainstream, just like clambering out of a river. He moved into the quieter commercial concourse of the station and sat down at the first available seat which was the sushi bar right in the centre of the concourse. In order to not look out of place he reached for one of the plates that passed in front of him on the revolving miniature conveyor belt that ran around the surface of the rectangular bar carrying different plates of meticulously prepared raw fish. After the first mouthful of the amazingly nutritious food he suddenly realised that actually he was ravenous, he had not eaten for hours. After several more plates to fill a hole he moved further into the financial areas of the station and strolled into the atrium of the Hilton, the hotel directly linked to the station by a glass-clad walkway. This highly comfortable and successful hotel was packed with either tourists passing through or city dwellers engaged in business meetings, huddled over their laptops and ever technologically advancing handheld devices. He squeezed his large frame into a booth in one of the more secluded parts of the bustling atrium and placed two mobile devices on the smooth polished surface of the table. It was time for him to take the initiative, enough time had elapsed. He had decided to stay, rather than run, and therefore neutralise this current threat to his continued existence. A simple binary decision. The decision was easy, as always achieving it was the difficult part. It was time to start the process.

He made two calls. For the first he used the pay-as-you-go phone he had picked up the evening before. He phoned the office, he dialled in to the secure line at four-two commando base at Lympstone and asked for the officer of the day. He was swiftly put through to a voice he immediately recognised as belonging to a one Lieutenant Simon Tapp. Will knew him from the past having worked with him previously. Lieutenant Tapp was perfectly suited for his specific role in the Marines, in fact this was one of the strengths of the armed forces in that they were able to identify each individual's potential skills and could in general find a role that was ideally suited to them. Everyone had a certain skill set and if placed in the correct environment it can be productive, placed in the incorrect environment these personal traits led to individual stress, inefficiency and mission failure. Tapp was an administrator and a really, really good one. His communication skills were non-existent, his physical skills poor but his obsessive nature and almost pathological attention to detail, which to some could be seen as at best irritating and to others as a personality flaw, in this role made him exceptional. He ensured that the correct personnel were at the correct point at precisely the correct time with exactly the correct equipment required. All organisations require such individuals in order to operate efficiently and Tapp, in this role, was extremely efficient. However he was not someone who could consider in any way bending the rules, in fact he loved rules, he loved regulations, and they gave him a fixed structure to hang his professional and personal life around.

"Simon, it's Will," was all he had to say.

"Jesus bloody hell where the hell have you been?" was the startled reply. It was to be expected. The Royal Marine's function very effectively based around a tight set of rules, as do all the armed forces. Will had now been absent without official leave for over three weeks, this was way over the ten days of compassionate leave that he had been granted. The rules did not allow for any more extra time and he had now been officially classified as absent without official leave, AWOL. This was a disciplinary offence and taken very seriously by the Marines, they had their rules, he knew them, and he had lived by them for almost ten years and he had now well and truly broken them. These rules were not for breaking, not even bending. Will succinctly explained that he was not currently in a position to be able to return and that he was not currently able to provide a valid reason. Simon, to whom adhering rigidly to the rules was second nature almost had an epileptic fit. Will was currently scheduled to be available for active duty on a twenty-four-hour good-to-go notice to any location to be determined based on urgent need, being AWOL was just not acceptable. This was the special forces branch of the Royal Navy and such behaviour was simply not tolerated. The conversation was brief. Will understood that that continued absence without a really goddam good reason would almost certainly end his naval career, but right now he had no choice. He had to get his life back, whatever that life would turn out to be in the uncertain future. He had no excuses so he simply wished Simon well and told him that with luck he would see him sometime soon and with that ended the call. He knew that the call would be officially logged and recorded and he would now official be classified as AWOL. If detained and caught by any of the national services, either armed forces or domestic, he would be taken as a common criminal, imprisoned and detained pending questioning. He had cut off his previous safety line but this was currently the least of his worries. He had made the call out of loyalty, the Navy had been good to him, a surrogate family of sorts. He had paid back that debt many times over the past decade by his actions but he still felt that he owed them honesty, if nothing else.

The second call was more pertinent to the situation at hand. For this he reactivated the phone he had liberated from his two uninvited house guests from the night before, replacing the battery and SIM card that he had removed previously. He seriously doubted that an essentially financially based corporation such as M&C would have tracking capabilities, but old habits die hard and cautiousness had kept him alive in many previous situations, he saw no reason to change this hard-learned pattern of behaviour now. The phone had only one single number pre-programmed into it and he pressed *dial* on the touch screen. It was seven thirty in the morning and he only had to wait for three rotations of the bland call tone for an answer. A crisp, business-like voice answered with a single word.

"Jarrett." Then there was silence, waiting for a response, expecting an answer. Will waited a full five seconds, which was almost an eternity in a phone conversation and there was nothing, silence.

"You came for me with force, it was a mistake."

Will said no more and simply waited. He did not have to wait long as the reply came without hesitation in a calm, level tone and without any hint of anxiety.

"Major James, I apologise."

The coldness of the reply almost, almost took Will by surprise. Yet it also supplied information, any exchange always did, no matter how impersonal there was always some information to be gleaned. Jarrett was clearly an individual who not only had significant intelligence-gathering resources he was also prepared to lose two of his employees without the slightest regret. In the short time available he now knew who Will was, that was to be expected, but more importantly was the lack of any element of panic, just cold emotionless control. It reminded Will of the many missions he had served on in the past where distant controllers, sitting in the safety far from danger, linked by satellite communication and imagery had sent him and his previous comrades into harm's way. This robotic response, lacking any surprise, devoid of emotion told Will that Jarrett was a serious adversary, whoever he really was and whatever organisation he represented. Will was not fazed, just warned, he had faced far worse situations in the past and survived.

"I have something you want," was the brief reply. He did not want to get into a conversation. Not only did he wish to remain an enigma, he was conscious of the fact that he was using the mobile taken from his would-be assailants. He was dealing with a private security firm of a multinational corporation, clearly extremely well-funded and obviously by its actions of the last few hours ruthless, but a private firm all the same. Will had made an educated guess that they would not have access to significant satellite tracking technology and they would certainly not have access to the vast network of security cameras that linked almost every place of interest across London. He had used them before in previous operations when his unit had often supported the clandestine services but this was not MI5 he was up against, that would have been a much more daunting prospect. Jarrett might however be able to track his own company's phone and that was one of the reasons he had removed the SIM and battery up till now and was one of the reasons he wanted the conversation to be brief.

"What do you want?"

There was no room for subtle negotiation, he was brutally direct, precisely to the point. It was clear that Jarrett was a professional, dealing efficiently with the situation in hand.

"I want two things," Will replied. "One million pounds sterling in cash and I want to walk away, for ever."

The money was not really the main issue for Will, money never had been. However he knew that for individuals such as Jarrett and certainly for M&C money was always the only issue and as such they would expect him to want some, they would be suspicious if he did not demand some. He was now pretty confident that all his previously recently inherited wealth would be gone. A huge financial corporation such as M&C would already have reached its sticky tentacles into his bank account and taken the one hundred million left to him by Chris. After all it was their money really since Chris had stolen it in the first place and, as he recalled, it was sitting in an account in one of their subsidiary banks. Anyway, simply transferring funds was a routine part of their daily practice. He was sure that the money was gone. There was a silent pause over the phone for almost ten seconds. This is such a short period of time but Will could feel each second slowly ticking by and then the silence was broken.

"I accept your terms."

It was all Will needed, he knew now that all the money had gone, he had expected it but the confirmation was strangely final. Oh well, it had never been his money to start with and while he had been a multimillionaire for a day he was now back to normal. He quickly snapped back to the present and delivered specific instructions.

"You will bring one million pounds sterling in high denomination notes in a single black wheeled travel case." It would fit easily, Will knew this from a previous hostage rescue mission he had been involved in as armed support.

"You will deliver this and then I will leave. Once safe I will give you the location of the discs. There are no copies. I will disappear and you will never see or hear from me again, nor I from you."

"Accepted," was the monosyllabic reply followed by the expected enquiry. "Location?"

"Paddington station, wait under the main central screens at six p.m. tonight. You will deliver the case in person. This is non-negotiable."

"Accepted," was again the reply. Will then immediately terminated the call. There was nothing further to discuss.

The rapidity of the conversation, particularly its conclusion, bothered Will. It was almost as though the final part was of no consequence, almost as though Jarrett had already decided on a course of action, independent of Will. He pushed these nagging doubts to the back of his mind, principally as he had no other realistic choice. He wanted his life back, Jarrett wanted the discs; it was a simple exchange. He knew that there was something out of place but he had no other option but to proceed, if he ran he would be running for ever and that was unacceptable. He had already made his decision, neutralise the threat. Simple decisions, easily made, achieving them was the difficult part. It was just before eight o'clock in the morning, he had ten hours to prepare.

CHAPTER TWENTY-NINE

Will decided that the first thing he needed to do was to eat. No army marched or fought on an empty stomach and neither did he, he was no exception to that age-old adage. The station has over four million passengers passing through it each day and it was well equipped to cater for them, so Will took the escalator in the main concourse up to the twenty-four-hour restaurant that overlooked the entire central area of the station and ordered a full English breakfast with extra toast and coffee. As he munched through a large plate of sausages, eggs, bacon, mushrooms and toast he began to collect his thoughts and formulate a basic plan. He had been involved in similar exchanges in the past while serving in the Marines, normally in a support role for either financial or occasional hostage exchanges. However in the past he had always been part of a fully organised and highly trained team, normally with a full pre-action brief and significant prior intelligence. Never previously had he been a lone individual and now he was completely and truly alone, isolated. Looking on the positive side however he was facing a private security firm, albeit employing ex-military personnel, but not the British professional armed forces or secret service. To be in direct conflict with such organisations would have been an entirely different prospect and may have altered his decision to stay.

As he finished his third cup of semi-decent black coffee he began to crystallise his thoughts for the upcoming few hours. He was under no illusion that Jarrett would come alone, rather he would certainly come with a team for protection at the least. He may also come with a team for more than just protection, the purpose of the team may be offensive, they may be tasked with taking him, rather than exchange, this was a very real possibility based on the evidence of the last twenty-four hours and he needed to be prepared. Paddington however was a good location for such a meeting, he had not chosen it at random, not only was he already there and as such at an immediate advantage the station itself had many favourable features. The foremost of which was that there were literally thousands of people at any one time in the station, particularly at six p.m. in the evening, the height of rush hour. No one but a complete madman would want to start a firefight in such a human-rich environment and Jarrett did not strike Will as being insane, if anything he was the exact opposite, complete cold logical control. While he had temporarily paused over breakfast to collect his thoughts and create a rational plan the time for thinking was over, it was time to move. First stop was the left luggage lockers located on the far left of the station, down a single flight of polished marble stairs and then back on oneself to essentially end up underneath platform one. He paid in cash for three lockers, each separate from each other among the many rows of dull metallic identical boxes. He first placed the discs that had caused so much trouble into one of the small code-operated lockers. If all went to plan, once he was clear, he would simply text Jarrett the locker number and the four-digit code that he now programmed into the digital keypad to close the door and secure it shut, then he would be free to just move on. In the two remaining larger lockers he placed some, but not all of his equipment that he carried. While he still had the two semi-automatic pistols, the two high-powered handguns and his cash securely bundled he could not keep it all with him and remain easily mobile and able to move swiftly if required. After brief consideration he decided to keep one of the handguns with three magazines and a moderate amount of cash, everything else he placed in the two larger lockers. He figured that if it got anywhere close to a situation needing the more impressive firepower he was leaving behind, he would already have lost and he knew he would never ever realistically be able to use such destructive force in such an crowded environment packed with thousands of innocent civilians. Almost everything else was left behind, almost everything but as always, he still had nestled in the small of his back his knife, snugly sheathed in its smooth leather scabbard. To leave this behind in the current situation would be like walking naked. Its familiar presence against his bare skin gave him a form of comfort and almost as a talisman returned him back to the state he now needed to be in. The rough simple blade took him back to his roots, back to the ruthless guerrilla fighter he had been forced to become in the past, able to react in a heartbeat to any situation of personal threat with decisive action, with lightning speed and unbridled aggression, without a second's thought or hesitation. He needed once again to exist in this state, it was once again time for him to become that creature of conflict created by his brutal past.

With his extra equipment squared away and the discs safe but accessible the next step was to create a situation where he could observe the exchange arena yet remain unobserved himself. He flashed back to his training in the Marines, this skill of observing the enemy and remaining hidden had been drilled in to him time and time again. He had used it many times on many reconnaissance missions in many different environments, both rural and urban, over the last decade and the optimal situation was to be as far away as possible from the zone of conflict, ideally observing through the cross hairs of a high-powered telescopic lens some significant distance away. Hidden yet with significant influence, minimal personal risk with maximum impact. Unfortunately today that was not going to be possible, the paradox today was that he not only needed to control the exchange zone he unfortunately needed to be directly in the exchange zone. In the past he had usually been in a support role, never right in the middle and never alone. He was dragged back to his training and could still hear the dogma incessantly shouted out from his instructors that he had been made to repeat over and over again. Where possible observe from a distance, minimise your exposure. If not possible become insignificant, the insignificant remains unnoticed and poses no threat. He had repeated these lessons in the past, how now to become insignificant yet remain on site? The rules reverberated through Will's mind, the principles were sound, yet how was he going to put the principles into practice?

He still had several hours before six p.m. but time was beginning to run short, so he began to walk the station familiarising himself with every possible entry or exit point. Although he had travelled through Paddington many times in the past it had always been as a normal passenger, arriving by train and leaving through one of the main exits or vice versa. Now he needed to know each and every point that a potential enemy — for that is what they were now — could come from and, all possible exit routes, particularly if he needed one in a hurry. This took longer than he had anticipated simply due to the fact that there were so many. The station was virtually open on two sides and there are a plethora of possible entry and exit points. This was both disconcerting in that there were multiple points of potential attack, but also a comfort in that there were numerous options to evade and escape if required. Too many for any team to cover effectively, no matter how large that team was without locking the station down completely.

Next he returned to the main concourse that overlooked the entire central area of the station. If he were running such an exchange, he would have at least two members of his team located in this high ground, able to observe, give instructions with the benefit of the overview of the situation and, if it came to it, able to provide effective fire support from above to anyone below. Once again, his isolation as a lone individual struck him and highlighted the disadvantage he was at, it could not be helped. He was committed now. Fleetingly he considered just getting onto one of the many departing trains and running, fast. As fast as the thought came to him he dismissed it faster. A life lived in perpetual fear would be a life less than half lived and he knew this in his heart, soul and mind and so he pushed those thoughts away. There were two obvious areas in the higher levels of the concourse that he would have used. The first was in the top-terrace bar that overlooked the entire station. It was another floor up connected by an elegant escalator and an individual seated at one of the tables here, normally reserved for the high-paying executives of London's financial elite, would have a grandstand view of the entire station. Although they also would be in full view of the public so while they could observe, relay information and give commands they would not be an immediate threat. Far more worrying was the second area which was a scaffolding tower in the left corner of the concourse. There appeared to some maintenance work being conducted and it would be simple for a trained professional to remain out of site with a sniper rifle, able to spit instant death while remaining totally unobserved. This was the principal threat to the exchange zone, the distance was a little less than two hundred metres and even the most unskilled marksman could deliver a lethal projectile with no warning at all with deadly accuracy at that short range. Will considered climbing up the scaffolding or destabilising it somehow but decided that any such action would draw far too much attention to himself and, in his current situation, he needed to remain completely anonymous. So he did the best he could in the situation he was in, he stood at the base of the scaffold tower and estimated with a trained eye the arc of fire that any sniper would have from the tower. The right-hand side of the station was completely exposed but there did appear to be a small window of opportunity, there was a small area, just behind and to the left of the central information screens that was blocked from view. Right in the centre of the station there stood several massive screens mounted on cylindrical steel posts that provided all the information required on arriving and departing trains. These screens blocked out an area, created a shadow in the arc of fire-controlled form the scaffold tower and it was this shadow area that Will would have to remain within.

Time was ticking on and Will was satisfied that he had done all he practically could in the brief time available to familiarise himself with the area and to isolate a relatively safe zone for the exchange. In the past on similar operations he and his full team would have spent many days preparing for such an event, studying maps, learning the entire geography of the area, even rehearsing over and over again for all possible eventualities on real scale mock-up models of buildings and entire areas. Today he was alone, but in the last few hours he had prepared as well as he possibly could. Now it was time to become insignificant.

CHAPTER THIRTY

London is one of, if not the most racially diverse cities in the world, perhaps challenged only by New York. In every five-second period every possible skin colour, shade, race and varied sexuality crosses over the central platforms of Paddington. Will initially thought that he could simply blend into the throng of thousands upon thousands of commuters rushing through the station. But then a commuter who stops, who lingers in a single location for too long is no longer a commuter on a hurried journey, they are suddenly stationary, no longer part of the moving crowd. However there is one group of lonely individuals within the station that are not only a permanent fixture but, vitally they are totally and completely unnoticed, even irrelevant. They are seen as part of the fabric of the building. To everyone else rushing past, intent on reaching their destination, trying to catch that earlier train, this particular group are insignificant. There is a single tribe of unique individuals that slowly, silently, shuffle through the station, picking up the detritus that is casually discarded and left behind. Each one of them moves ever so slowly as though burdened by a heavy weight, often pushing a battered dirty yellow rubbish cart, purposefully collecting the refuse. In general they are avoided if possible, as they are grubby and smell. Any direct contact is undesirable and, in the eyes of the vast majority of the human flow rushing through the station, they are unworthy of any attention. The other, often unnoticed characteristic about this silent tribe is that they are almost exclusively of Afro-Caribbean descent. Although active racial discrimination is now removed from modern intelligent society it is not completely extinct, normally now driven by necessity rather than discrimination. This combination of irrelevance and physical appearance was perfect for Will's requirements.

So at just after four o'clock in the afternoon he became the unseen shadow to one of these insignificant individuals as they slowly, as ever, returned to the service centre where Will had already observed they were based. As the cleaner laboriously pushed his heavy cart through the grimy plastic curtain that dangled heavily down to separate the general public from the refuse collection and processing zone, Will silently glided through with him, an unseen shadow. The cleaner was approaching his fifty-seventh birthday and he had trudged this path for the last forty-one years. He had arrived from Jamaica as a teenager with nothing save the clothes on his back and had considered himself lucky to be given stable employment. He had fulfilled his role with quiet personal pride and dignity, he had never been late for a single shift, he had always completed his allocated task with personal pride that was part of his persona, to complete his job as he said he would accomplish. His children and their children had benefited from his hard graft and the state education system in the UK, available and free of charge to all, and were now doctors and lawyers dispersed throughout the city, a fact that always brought a private smile to his lips. He had no reason to expect an assault, who in their right mind would attack a cleaner at work? What possible gain could there be in such a senseless act? Stealth was not really required as any sound of Will's approach was easily drowned out by the constant noise of the recycling of rubbish deposited in the collection zone. The elderly and strangely dignified man was completely unaware, he had no warning. Will had no intention of causing any permanent damage so he used the softer part of his outstretched rigid forearm, it descended at speed and collided with the cleaner's temple; he simply crumpled to the floor, instantly unconscious as Will knew he would be from previous experience. He rapidly scooped him up and pulled the unconscious man deeper into the recycling area, hidden from view behind mounds of decomposing rubbish, where no one was going to casually stroll through. He expertly bound him with some brown wrapping tape that he had purchased earlier from the gift shop in the main terminal, which when wrapped several times around the wrists and ankles was stronger than any rope or cable tie, and gently laid him down in the mounds of rubbish, covering him over so that any casual observer would see only discarded used cardboard coffee cups, sandwich wrappers and plastic bottles of all various varieties, the standard detritus discarded by the city dwellers on the move. This unknown and undeserving victim, just in the wrong place at the wrong time, would wake in a few hours rather confused and with a large bruise on the side of his head, but otherwise with no knowledge of his attacker and none the worse for wear. Even more perplexing would be the five thousand pounds that he would later discover stuffed securely into his jacket pocket that Will now placed there. He looked down on the weathered features of the unconscious older man and felt a fleeting pang of compassion. It did not last long, he was in the zone he needed to be!

Twelve and a half minutes after Will had ghosted through the industrial plastic drapes following one of the regular employees, a single lone individual re-emerged, slowly pushing aside the heavy fronds that separated the world of refuse collection from the far gentler, cleaner world of London society. He shuffled painfully slowly, weighed down by the unwieldy refuse cart, back along the long platform heading towards the centre of the station. He was now dressed in the grey grubby boiler suit of the station's cleaners, stained by the ground in dirt and grime from many day's labour. The slow man was tall, although it was difficult to tell this as he shuffled, stooped over his cart, hunched over his broom with which he laboriously and methodically began to sweep the platform, curled up over the ancient wooden handle. He moved at a pace commensurate with his position in life and the task in hand and, to all but the most perceptive observer, he appeared to be of an age beyond which he should reasonably be expected to be working. The illusion was finished with a grimy grey cap pulled down low over his downturned face, intent on only the concrete of one the stations many platforms. He had become insignificant.

Intermittently he moved the heavy grey cart forwards a couple of feet at a time, slowly, almost unnoticed, edging towards the centre of the station, creeping closer to that window of safety he had previously identified. Inside the cart, securely taped to the underside of its upper surface, were his weapons and the remaining cash he had decided earlier in the day to bring with him. In an instant, if he required them, he could access both. He now hoped with every fibre of his body that he would need neither in a hurry. Either way it always paid to be prepared, lessons hard learned from past experience and never forgotten. Not a soul noticed him as he inexorably shuffled forwards, no one paid him the slightest attention — ideal. The commuters and tourists alike simply walked around him as they would avoid a stationary pillar, although with a wider berth as pillars smell less than he did. Over the next ninety minutes he swept the platform, picked up rubbish and emptied bins as someone in his line of work should do, yet cautiously edged ever forwards, unnoticed, towards the central area of the station. He could observe the entire area but he fervently hoped that he was as yet unobserved. He had achieved his aim as best he possibly could, he was approaching the exchange zone and he had become insignificant.

CHAPTER THIRTY-ONE

It was approaching a quarter to six in the gathering evening, bright daylight giving way to the half-light of dusk, fifteen minutes until the previously agreed deadline. It was the beginning of the crazy rush hour in the capital and suddenly the entire station was being engulfed by a river of human traffic. Thousands and thousands of daily commuters were disgorging from the Tube, and entering the station, intent on catching the next available train, escaping from the heartless metropolis that sucked so much out of their lives both in time and content, intent on getting home. By six o'clock the rush hour would be in full swing and the station would be jammed, it was a good place for an exchange. The whole area was mobbed with lots, seriously lots of mobile people, among whom it would be easy to disappear and almost impossible to track a single individual. Also no one in their right mind would be interested in starting a firefight in such an environment. The disadvantage of the situation however was that any one of the myriad of individuals moving though the station could be part of the enemy team. Every situation cut both ways, there was always an upside and downside to any event, always a positive and a negative to any position.

Will had chosen the location and prepared as best as he possibly could in the time allocated. There was no going back now.

It was five fifty, ten minutes to go until the agreed time so Will did what he had intended. He continued to shuffle, ever so sedately, almost painfully up the platform towards the centre of the station, picking up rubbish, sweeping the platform, emptying bins, all in keeping with the role he had assumed. As he eventually began to enter the exchange arena he could feel the adrenaline begin to surge through his veins, the tension of pre-contact raising all of his senses. He had experienced this before, many times in different environments. He was the ruthless soldier he had been forced to be, and then trained further, refined into the weapon that he was. As he stooped over the ancient wooden broom, he was, to the outside world, an elderly broken-spirited nobody simply cleaning the harsh concrete platforms. That was the perception he wished to project. However, from under the peak of the dark cap he had borrowed earlier his eyes scanned the area with laser-like precision. He was looking for something out of the ordinary, something that was just not right. He needed to identify the team that Jarrett would inevitably have in place before he arrived. Will was under no illusion that Jarrett would come alone. He would have as many assets in place to protect him as possible, any rational individual would and Jarrett struck him as completely, totally and coldly rational. Having said that Jarret had only had less than ten hours to mobilise. While Will did not really know yet the resources available to Jarrett and M&C, he did not expect them to be able to raise a significantly large and highly trained team at such short notice. So as he painfully shuffled forwards into the central part of the station his eyes raked the entire area, looking for something, no matter how small a detail, but something that was out of place.

He spotted the first asset easily. At the top of the concourse, naturally in high ground, just where he would have placed a controller there was a lone man. There was nothing out of the ordinary, just a businessman simply having a quiet drink before catching the next train, but everything about him was wrong, it screamed out of place. He was sitting alone at a table pushed just too far forwards, the table was abutting the clear Perspex barrier that protected the high balcony. The table and the man were just a fraction further forwards than would be naturally expected, a fraction further forwards than would normally be comfortable for any normal individual forty metres above the central platform of Paddington station, he was too close to the edge so that he struggled to sit comfortably, his legs bent back in an awkward position. The lone man had a beer on his table but, despite it being almost six o'clock, the end of the working day, he had not drunk a single drop, it just could have been recently purchased but there was no white head of a freshly poured pint and the fizz of the drink had already faded over time

— minor details, but of major importance. More obvious however than these subtle incongruities was the man's unwavering focus on the central area of the station, the arena of exchange. If there had been any doubt Will observed that every three minutes this supposedly innocent commuter uttered a single sentence. Will could not hear the words and they were spoken as though he was speaking to himself, but he was in no doubt that this overseer was communicating by a hidden comms device with a team. This meant that there was a team in place. Not only had the command position revealed himself, he had shown Will that there was a team, numbers unknown as yet, currently on location, well-organised and in regular communication. He had expected this scenario but the confirmation of the professional nature of his current adversary and their ability to mount a well organised and structured team at short notice was not encouraging. It did not deter him for a second, he had been started on a rollercoaster path that was running and there was no getting off and he had decided to see it through. Rather than worrying him it warned him, emphasising the seriousness of the current and imminent situation and served only to increase his level of awareness.

As he carefully emptied another black bin liner taken out of one of the refuse bins at the end of the platform into his partially filled refuse cart, he checked his weapons that were carefully taped to the underside of the lid of the cart, immediately available if required; their proximity provided some small comfort. As he looked up from emptying the rubbish bag he spotted the second and third members of the team he was facing. They were a young couple, just sitting among many others at the bar of the sushi restaurant in the centre of the ground floor of the station's main concourse. To the casual observer they were simply a twenty-something couple having a drink at a bar. But they were not. Both were well dressed in keeping with London commuters, both were clearly physically fit and the woman was extremely attractive in a figure-hugging expensive grey flannel work suit, yet despite this neither were in the least bit interested in each other. They did not talk, there was no eye contact, rather both were focusing their entire attention directly away from each other, directly at the centre of the main station, the designated arena of exchange. In addition in the last few minutes since Will had noticed them neither had taken a single one of the micro-plates of delicately prepared raw fish that slowly rotated past them on the revolving conveyor belt, nor had they ordered a single drink. They were clearly not there to socialise and they were not there for the food, they were an attractive young couple uninterested in each other and uninterested in eating at a restaurant, they were incongruous, they were wrong, they were there for him. Next to both of these inconsistent individuals was a moderate-sized bag. The attractive woman had a designer holdall, on the surface consistent with a business executive on an overnight trip. The slightly younger man had a rucksack of types, or more a laptop bag cum travel rucksack. Either way both could and probably did contain some significant weaponry. Will's level of alertness suddenly rose another two dozen notches. There was clearly an organised team already in place. He continued, slowly sweeping his way forwards into a potential killing ground, significantly outnumbered and unaware of his enemy's potential or strength. Despite this he kept sedately, painfully slowly moving forwards, keeping the large solid information screens between himself and the obscured scaffolding tower he had identified earlier. Whilst Jarrett's team may or may not stretch to a sniper he did not want to find out the hard way. While he had a chance against the ground team a distant sniper was a threat that he could not possibly influence or control, so he was careful to remain in the relative protection of the virtual shadow of the solid information screens.

At one minute to six in the evening three men emerged from the depths of the London underground, cresting the top of the constantly revolving escalator and entered the station. Although they did not communicate to each other it was obvious to Will that they were a single unit. From the metres that now separated them it appeared that Jarrett was in the centre flanked by the two other slightly younger men, both instinctively taking up protective positions on his right and left just three paces ahead of him. To his trained eye they had assumed a classical triangulated position and were almost certainly ex-military. They moved in the way that only special forces do; they were well muscled but not overly so like the unrealistic bodybuilders popular on reality-style television shows and they moved fluidly, purposefully, confidently but at all times their eyes were constantly roaming, scanning the area for any potential threats, controlling their allocated vectors. It was time for the exchange. Time to be rid of these discs that he had never wanted or known about, time to move on with his life, whatever it may become. Despite the situation he was not afraid. Fear was an emotion that had long ago left him forever, even as a young boy in the jungle he had very quickly learnt that it was a useless emotion. Fear served only to cloud one's judgement and uncontrolled fear led only to panic, panic only ever led to disaster. He was ready.

Will was now directly under the main information screens and in plain sight in the centre of the station. He was now vulnerable and he felt it. The problem with any exchange was that you had to physically be at the exchange in order to make it work. As the trio of men approached, they stopped and stood stationary. He could now finally see them clearly. Suddenly he knew in the pit of his stomach that something was wrong, terribly wrong. None of these three was Jarrett. Jarrett was in his mid-fifties, these three were all at least twenty years younger, if not more. Suddenly each had one of their hands concealed in a pocket, clutching an object. This was not a normal pose and it did not take much imagination to work out that each had his hands on a concealed firearm of sorts. Suddenly as he glanced up and around him there appeared to be a stationary well-built man at each of the immediate exit points that he could see. In rush hour people do not stand still, they either rush into the station to catch a train or leave, entering into London for the evening entertainment. At each of the immediate exits there was now a lone individual, not moving and looking for someone. Each also had a hand obscured from vision in a variety of ways. With sickening realisation Will knew that he had made a terrible mistake. This was a trap! There was to be no exchange. All around him there was a team and they were here for one purpose only, either to take him or to finish him. Neither was an attractive prospect.

As one, all of the members of this offensive team started to converge towards the centre of the station, towards Will. The couple from the sushi bar were now mobile, both clutching their bags across their chests, military style. The individual men, previously stationary at the exits began to converge forwards moving aggressively and with controlled purpose. The only two individuals not moving were Will and the executive businessman high up in the lounge overlooking the entire area, although he was now clearly barking orders through his personal comms gear, poorly disguised by a newspaper held upwards partially obscuring his mouth. The strands of a net were rapidly closing down about Will like a fly trapped in a spider's web. He was about to be taken. Neither panic nor despair entered his mind for a single second, neither were of any constructive use. With each passing second this well-coordinated team drew closer, decreasing any room that he had for manoeuvre, closing the net on their intended prey, him! Calmly but rapidly, he appraised his options — there were two. He could reach into the rubbish cart, grasp his weapons and fight his way out. He calculated that with the element of surprise he had a reasonable chance of creating enough panic within the packed station to be able to escape in the stampede that gunfire would surely create, with the added bonus of eliminating several members of this team currently trying to eliminate him. However this was a high risk strategy in which he could easily come off worse, a single well-aimed bullet from any of the members of this team closing in on him would be enough to end his journey and, as of now, the range of only a few metres was not in his favour. In addition this course of action would almost inevitable result in the death of some innocent civilian bystanders just going about their daily business. While this was clearly undesirable it would also lead to some serious unwanted attention from the city's highly effective police force and this he currently needed like a hole in the head. The second option, the far more difficult one, required seriously large kahunas and it was to tough it out, to remain undetected while surrounded, to try to evade and escape. There was always an alternative option to all-out violence and it was often tactically the better choice. Yet often it was the most difficult to achieve, requiring the sternest of resolve. So he continued doing what he had done for the last ninety minutes. He swept, hunched over the old wooden broom, laboriously pushing the dirty heavy grime-encrusted cart. He continued to clean, desperately hoping to remain insignificant. While every sinew of his steel-hard body wanted to run, to be out of the kill zone that had now been created for him, he knew that any rapid movement would immediately betray him and bring down a serious shit storm of trouble. Outnumbered and in such close proximity with little room to manoeuvre, the odds were not in his favour. So he shuffled, he shuffled forwards, close enough to actually brush against the coat of the right flank man of the central trio, making no attempt to be anything else than the refuse cleaner, insignificant.

He edged one metre past the trio and hoped beyond reasonable hope that he would remain undetected. An interminably slow five seconds ticked past and another three metres clear. Fifteen seconds and now it was almost ten metres and at least four bustling commuters interrupted the direct line of sight between him and the central trio sent to capture or kill. With each passing second that he remained undetected, with each metre further he managed to shuffle out of the kill zone and, with each of the many rush-hour commuters that were now filling the crammed space between him and the central platform, his confidence grew. It was only one minute past six in the evening, it was only sixty seconds after the allocated time for exchange and the station was rammed; in his peripheral vision he could now see the core team of five converging together at the base of the screens. He did not dare to look up to risk any direct eye contact, but he saw them clearly. They had converged and were now obviously coming to the rapid conclusion that either their target, him, was either not coming, or worse the target was alert to their presence. The need for any subterfuge or disguise was now redundant so they openly, roughly pushed any male of appropriate age around so they could see his face, so they could confirm what they already expected. Their target was not in the kill zone, he had either not arrived or had slipped under their radar.

As confusion turned to anger and recrimination in the group behind him, Will shuffled further away, moving slightly faster now and with more purpose, and approached the south-west exit. This corner of the station was not gated but rather just opened out into a steeply slopping road that led upwards and spilled out directly into central London. Once out and buried in the throngs of thousands of closely packed moving people rushing through the city centre, he would be safe, impossible to track. However blocking his path was one of the solitary stationary men he had spotted earlier. He was standing still, right in the middle of the exit, not blocking it completely but still monitoring the flow of humanity through the narrow exit and he was actively looking for someone — actively looking for him. As Will drew closer he could now easily see the now obvious earpiece and realised that this sentry would now be alerted that he had neither been captured nor neutralised as planned in the kill zone. This man's level of alertness would be high and he would be expecting Will's arrival. Also ominously, predictably based on the body positions of the other members of this team, his right hand was obscured from view, buried in the deep side pocket of his heavy navy-grey street coat, no doubt clutching a weapon of some sort, most likely a handgun. A further three paces and Will was almost at the exit yet, as he moved into almost touching distance, he suddenly saw a spark of recognition in the sentry's eyes, almost like an internal alarm clock being ignited. Whether he had moved too fast and was no longer the stooped old man sweeping the platform, whether he had stood too tall or whether the man had simply looked past the grimy boiler suit and dust cart and recognized him it did not matter. Will's luck had finally run out and he had been compromised. His reaction was instant. He could not allow this sentry to communicate with the rest of his team. While one against one was unfair odds, on his opponent, one against six was a different prospect. Will reacted first and reacted decisively. He could have reached into the dust cart for the pistol that was securely taped to the underside of the lid but this would have been too slow, it would have allowed enough time for several words of warning to be spat out from the sentry, bringing the entire team rushing to their location. Instead he reacted instinctively knowing that he had to both incapacitate this man and allow him to pass through him and escape, as well as silence him before he could utter a single syllable of warning. So, with blurring speed and unbridled aggression Will leaped forwards, closing the three metres that separated them in less than half a second, less time than it took to draw breath, no longer the slow tired old man shuffling over the concrete with a refuse cart. As he lunged forwards with unreal speed, he extended both arms, locked out in front of him, rigid and between them clasped in his vice-like grip was the wooden handle of the ancient broom, now horizontal and taut as a metal bar. Will's aim was perfect, as ever, and the thin horizontal beam struck directly as intended with sickening force. The impact of such a small rigid surface area moving at serious speed, driven with force was catastrophic. The wooden bar slipped just under the man's chin, exactly as intended and crashed directly into his throat. The main force landed squarely onto the larynx and then the cricoid cartilage, the only two semi-rigid parts of the throat, normally known as the Adam's apple, immediately shattering them. As the solid wooden bar struck the sentry's head was snapped forwards and downwards with sickening speed and the sound of collapsing cartilage was audible to the two of them, similar to the sound of an apple being struck and shattered into a dozen pieces. Predictably when receiving such a savage blow this man who had been sent to take him began to collapse, clutching his now shattered airway, fighting to breathe. As he fell Will continued to move forwards with him using his speed, his full weight and the momentum of both of them to drive the rigid wooden rod further down on the victim's already shattered throat and, as they landed on the unyielding pavement, he forced the wooden bar further backwards and felt it crunch as it ground against the cervical vertebrae at the back of the nameless man's neck, his airway completely destroyed. The prostrate man did not as yet realise that he had been struck a mortal blow. How could one single strike delivered in less than half a second be fatal? He tried to shout for help, to alert the team, but no sound filtered through the broken vestiges of his shattered cartilaginous airway, it was impossible to speak with such an injury. He made all the actions of one trying to speak but not a single sound escaped. This was one of the main reasons that Will had attacked in such a brutal manner, not only had he taken him down, neutralising the threat and allowing him to pass, he had taken away the ability of this unfortunate soul to alert the other members of his team to his location. Survival instinct had taken over. Another enemy had died so that he could survive.

Will knelt at the side of the dying man gasping for breath through his broken airway and slipped his hand inside the pocket of his grey overcoat, removing the weapon he had suspected was there out of his grasp. While it was clear that he was mortally wounded and would soon be dead, he was still able to discharge his firearm if he wished. Will expertly relieved the dying man of a high-tech mini radio that was linked to his earpiece which he also removed. To the outside world he appeared as a though he was a concerned passer-by attending to a member of the public in distress. However this man's airway had been shattered by the single vicious blow, the cartilage fractured and crushed beyond recognition by the ferocity of the attack and now, fifteen seconds later, the soft tissue swelling that accompanied such an injury was contributing to an irreversible process. The man had lost his airway. He could not physically get any air in or out of his body. The Emergency medical teams train to resuscitate trauma victims using a simple algorithm of ABC: airway, breathing, circulation. The reason behind this is straightforward; the loss of an individual's airway is by far the fastest way to lose life, after this is the inability to breathe properly and surprisingly third is circulation, as it takes several minutes if not up to an hour to bleed out, to exsanguinate from a knife or gunshot wound. The medics know this and train accordingly. Unfortunately for this horizontal man his airway had been irreversibly destroyed and, as Will gently laid him down on the cold smooth concrete of the station floor, he could already see the light fading from his eyes as they slowly glassed over and he slipped into a final unconsciousness from which he would never wake. Regret and compassion would come later, to a degree, but there was no place for such emotions currently, the reality was that this man had been here to either take him or kill him, and he had responded in kind.

Right now he had opened up a window of opportunity, a possible avenue of escape and he needed to move fast. The time for subtlety and disguise had passed. He reached into the refuse cart and ripped out his rucksack containing his carefully wrapped bundles of cash that he would need and the phones he required, now deactivated. Then he grabbed the weapons that had been securely taped to the underside of the lid of the cart and, unobserved, stashed them in the holdall. While every part of him wanted to sprint up the exit road, out of the station and away from danger as fast as possible. He knew that such behaviour would draw immediate attention. A running man would be immediately obvious to all around him, so coldly, calmly controlled as ever he crouched, hidden by the throngs of commuters he shook off the dirty, grey, stained boiler suit he had been wearing, under which was a very plain grey business suit and then he did what his mind was telling him but his body did not want to do, he stood up, stood tall and made no attempt to hide. Trying now to be unobserved would be very out of the ordinary for a normal commuter. As he stood he had his rucksack over his shoulder, just as so many others carried laptop bags and overnight holdalls and briskly walked out of the station, up the steeply slopping road. He now just joined the flow of thousands and thousands of commuters, almost as a drop of water slipping into a river and then he was gone. Reaching the top of a short, steeply-sloping road, he was immediately bathed in the gentlewarmth of the dying rays of the evening sun. He risked a casual glance back over his shoulder and could see the chaos that he had left behind just a few seconds earlier; there was a man down in the middle of the exit and a crowd was beginning to gather around him. Several individuals were on their mobiles, presumably alerting the emergency services of the situation. On the periphery of this cluster of concerned commuters however there were four men and a single woman acting differently, in contrast to all the others they were looking outwards, away from the injured man, looking for him. Will did not wait for a second look. He turned, merged with the tireless flow of human traffic and, at a moderate unhurried pace, simply walked away.

CHAPTER THIRTY-TWO

As he crested the road leading out of the station Will turned right for no other reason than the majority of the crowd turned right also and he simply followed the motion of the majority. He moved forwards, keeping pace with the others around him, putting as much distance and as many people between himself and the team left behind, the team that had clearly come to take him. With each minute that passed and with each turning of a street corner, he moved further away from the immediate danger he had just left behind in confusion. As he turned yet another corner moving steadily further away from danger, he was suddenly faced with an entirely different and not unwelcome challenge. He found himself square in front of the elaborately gilded main exit gates of Lord's cricket ground. Even Will, who had never understood the intricacies of cricket, knew that Lord's was the homeland of the game. He had never been able to fathom how a game that can take twenty-two men five days could still end in a draw. Either way this was currently irrelevant as there were now suddenly thousands of well-dressed fans disgorging from the holy land of cricket at the end of a day's play, heading for the upmarket wine bars and restaurants of north-west London. Will needed to evade and escape, to remain anonymous and untraceable and the anonymity that such a large moving tightly packed crowd provided was an opportunity that he was not going to pass up. So as the jovial crowd, if not well intoxicated by a hard day's drinking in the sun, flowed forwards he incorporated himself into it, becoming an indistinguishable part of this river of humanity. Within fifteen minutes he was almost two and a half miles away from Paddington Station and securely ensconced in the back of a London pub among several dozen rowdy cricket supporters. In the darkness of the depths of a crowded London pub, a unique environment on so many levels, unreproducible anywhere else in the world, he slowly, ever so slowly allowed himself to relax. The adrenaline of such close contact began to ebb with each heartbeat and while cocooned in the security of an unfamiliar crowd, holding a pint of ale in order to blend in with his environment he began to logically break down the events of the evening, he began to surgically dissect the situation.

He was currently safe. The brutal fact was that he had narrowly evaded a potential lethal situation where he could easily have been taken or terminated. If his liberty had required the death of one of his opponents — so be it, he felt no remorse for the man who had died, he had come to kill him after all. Kill or be killed, it was as it had always been and Will had never hesitated in the past, he knew he would not in the future. In addition to this he now knew several other facts that he had not known earlier in the day, none of them were pleasing. Firstly and most importantly he had underestimated Jarrett. He had foolishly thought that Jarret was simply the lead for a moderate IT security firm that would logically opt to pay out to achieve closure and endeavour to avoid direct conflict. He had been wrong. Jarrett was not only well resourced, he was able to plan and manage an efficient and capable team at short notice. More pertinent to the future was that he was quite prepared to commit highly illegal actions, he was quite prepared to take and most likely eliminate him given the chance. Jarrett's resolve was far more sinister than Will had given him credit for, he would not make that mistake twice. Secondly, was that whatever information, personal data or programs were stored on those discs was of significantly more value than he had anticipated. They were important enough for Jarrett, or for whoever was pushing Jarrett's buttons and signing his pay cheque, to commit not only highly illegal and publicly visible actions they were important enough to kill for — to kill him! None of this information that he now sifted through in a cold logical manner gave him any comfort. On the positive side he still had the discs, or at least was the only person who knew where they were in the secure lockers in the underground levels of Paddington station. In addition and vitally he remained free, a situation that clearly needed to continue to ensure his continued survival.

As calm continued and the minutes ticked past and turned into hours, the extreme arousal of lethal contact slowly pulsed out of him. Immediate critical analysis and self-reflection of acute situations was part of his training, embedded into him by his years in the special forces, reflecting on actions, always looking to improve, always looking to remove random chance, and always looking to draw out any information available. It was crystal clear. It was time to take back the initiative. He took out the mobile phone that he had liberated from his original assailants on *Amnesia*, reinserted the battery and SIM card, reactivated the device and pressed redial. He had to wait for less than two cycles of the monotonous ring tone for a two-word answer.

"Major James."

Will paused, temporarily thrown by the very correct usage of his name and rank. Clearly they had now done their research and would know all the basics about his past career. The had used their time well yet they would know nothing of the lethal man-child he had been in his previous life.

"You made a mistake," Will replied.

There was no answer, just silence. Will had made a simple statement, not a question or comment and no answer was required. It was a measure of the control and experience of Jarrett that none was offered. Despite himself reluctantly Will was impressed.

"The cost has escalated significantly, the terms of the agreement remain the same. I will contact you in the future."

And with that single and unequivocal statement he severed the connection, there was nothing further to discuss. Out of habit he immediately deactivated the phone, removing the battery and SIM card. While he did not believe that Jarrett would have access to mobile tracking facilities. He had underestimated him once before, almost to his ultimate cost, he would not do it again.

With the clarity of decision making that he had always possessed Will now knew exactly what he would have to ultimately achieve. Right now, his most pressing need was to buy some time. He needed to disappear, he needed to create some breathing space, some room for manoeuvre. With every passing day that he remained free and unaccounted for the pressure on Jarrett would mount. The longer he remained at liberty and an unknown variable the more anxious, the more stressed Jarrett and his team would become and the more likely they would be to make irrational decisions and, when individuals or teams behaved irrationally, they would make mistakes. As always the seminal decisions in Will's life had been relatively easy, black and white in their nature. These decisions were in reality straightforward and binary, it was the practicality of turning those decisions into reality that was the difficult part. Now however it was time to leave, he had lingered in the relative anonymity of the back of this crowded London pub for too long. Now it was time to disappear.

CHAPTER THIRTY-THREE

To simply drop off the grid completely was not as difficult as it may seem in a large, densely populated city such as London if one adheres to some simple rules. However it depends more on the resources and determination of the team tracking you. While Will calculated that Jarrett was well financed, clearly ruthless and certainly not afraid of breaking a few laws, he did not expect that he would have access to all the CCTV footage that criss-crosses any modern city. While the secret services, whom he had worked with previously and the domestic police could tap into this live footage and archived data at any time, forming a blanket of surveillance and imagery that it was virtually impossible to avoid, Jarrett and his team were a privately operated company and Will seriously doubted that they would have access to any of this information, in fact he was banking on it. In addition he was convinced that even if they did have an opportunity to access this image tracking they would not wish the appropriate authorities of the United Kingdom to be either involved or aware of their current activities. The capture or kidnapping at best or simply the murder of a serving British naval officer was not an act that any individual or organisation would wish to advertise or have recorded. With this basic premise formed on sound logic Will knew that he would be able to fade away into obscurity for some considerable time of his choosing and remain undetected in the human jungle of the city of London.

As the rather attractive young woman dressed in a fantastically inappropriate figure-hugging top that revealed the majority of her ample cleavage to the customers called "Time at the bar" and started to gently encourage the last few inebriated clients to leave, Will calmly collected his rucksack and strolled out from the bar, appearing to the outside world as though he had not a care in the world. He mingled with the happy late night crowd of revellers as they exited but his eyes were constantly scanning for any sign of threat, anything that was out of place, out of the ordinary. He saw nothing that raised alarm and so, as the crowd dispersed, he headed north-east from Lord's towards the groomed splendour of the London parks. He skirted around the large and famous Regent's Park and then moved to the north for just two minutes at a brisk pace. He found himself at the gates of Primrose Hill Park, a far more beautiful and much less well-known area and significantly more secluded. He had been here before, sitting in conversation on summer evenings with Chris in a life gone past and now lost for ever and, just a few days previously, this park had offered him shelter. While all the parks were swept and cleared early each morning he knew that he would find shelter and vitally, anonymity, in one for the night. Spending a night sleeping rough in the open was hardly a daunting prospect for him, he had spent the majority of his youth in this way and so, with a single vault, using his toned and powerful body Will was over the glossed black railings, landing perfectly balanced and ready. As he lay, looking out at the stunningly lit backdrop of the city from under the cover of a densely packed bank of rhododendron bushes he began to evaluate his options. He could still run. He had enough money for a short period of time. But how long would they hunt for him? How long would there be a constant threat of unseen violence at every turn of every corner? He dismissed the idea, he knew he could not live in fear, he had always known this. The option of a future exchange, the discs with whatever information they contained for money and freedom had been his original plan. The events of the last twelve hours had made it evident that Jarrett and his team had not entertained this as a viable option. The brief conversation on escalating cost had been a smoke screen, designed to make Jarrett think he would be stupid and greedy enough to try again for more financial gain, to give them another opportunity to take him. He knew that this would never happen and the option of any exchange was firmly closed.

In the quiet calm of the night he continued to evaluate, to calculate, working through potential scenarios, it was part of his training that had been drilled into him in the special forces. There was always another way, another option, and another action you could take to alter the outcome. That was the mantra that had been ingrained into him during his training. When exhausted both mentally and physically by the never-ending onslaught of fatigue and mental stress, intentionally heaped upon him by his instructors, they had always forced him to find a third option. An unexpected unpredictable action that would change the eventual outcome. This had served him well in the past in various conflict zones around the world. Stopping, thinking, finding a third option, even if it was to withdraw to safety had saved Will's life and that of his comrades many times in the past. Now however he was alone and it was becoming clear that he would have to personally force the situation in order to take back control. In order to be free of constant persecution, in order to be able to start his life again on a clean slate, he needed to find an effective third option.

CHAPTER THIRTY-FOUR

At ten to five in the morning, just before the park keepers swept through the meticulously groomed park, Will once again vaulted the gilded railings and, undetected, strolled away from Primrose Hill. Each morning at five a.m. the park keepers would trawl through, clearing the park of any left-over detritus from the previous day; removing any lingering refuse, both normal waste and human alike. Sanitising the entire area before any of the so-called normal people of the smarter, more affluent parts of London might be there. In general, the younger Londoners would frequent the parks first in the early morning in their hundreds as Lycra-clad runners and joggers, attempted to maintain a degree of physical fitness within the confines of an enclosed city. Slightly later would come the elderly, often walking small dogs accustomed to a brief period of exercise to relieve their pent-up frustration from being shut up in flats and town houses. While the autumn days retained some warmth, it was now cold and Will shivered in the half-light of dawn of an early October morning.

He had remained undetected and at large now for twelve hours since last contact. With each passing hour, with each passing day that this current situation held up the pressure on Jarrett would gradually mount. Yesterday Jarrett would have thought that he had a potentially awkward situation under control and that resolution would have been swift and complete. Today the opposite was true, he had lost control, and worse the information that he so desperately wanted to be permanent history was still available and in the hands of, from his perspective, an unknown quantity. Will now needed a safe place to rest, a place to plan. While on the face of it finding such a safe house while being actively hunted by a determined and well-equipped team would seem difficult, in reality it was not for Will had in his possession the single key that would unlock this immediate need — hard fluid cash. While he had left the majority of his current possessions, including the discs, safely locked away in the storage lockers of Paddington station he had taken with him three essential items; weapons, communications and money. He had the two handguns with several spare clips of ammunition that he had liberated from his original assailants on *Amnesia*, plus his old blade, strapped as always in the small of his back. He had two mobile phones, one his own and one again taken from his two now deceased attackers, both deactivated and untraceable and he had a significant amount of cash. The basic triad of any successful covert operation is weapons, comms and money and his willingness to spend significant amounts of untraceable cash would allow him to simply disappear. There would be no electronic record to be traced, no receipts or official bookings to be recorded. As the twilight of dawn marched into the slightly brighter grey mist of a typical late October morning in London, Will walked briskly eastwards. He moved as though he had a distinct purpose and was on a deadline, mirroring the migration of the city dwellers on their way from flats and houses to their offices. After just twenty minutes at a brisk walking pace he left the groomed affluent streets of North London and began to enter a considerably dirtier and definitely rougher area. Leaving the designer streets of Highgate and Hampstead behind, he moved through Archway and into the far less salubrious area of central East London. As if travelling from a first world country into a developing country suddenly, after only a twenty-minute walk, it was as if he was in an entirely different city. For anyone who has lived in and walked through any large city this is not so unusual, but the stark contrast between such extreme affluence and obvious poverty existing so close to each other is so obvious in London, it is almost bizarre and shocking to the uninitiated. Now he knew he was in an area where he could simply melt away and remain undetected for some time. Here no one cared who he was, no one cared what he did or where he was going, here only one thing was of any value, money.

As the morning passed he pushed deeper into this down-trodden area, his progress slowed by a street market rammed to capacity with desperate individuals doing anything they could to sell whatever goods they had on their stalls. In every alcove, on every street corner there were signs of the homeless sleeping rough in the city, gaining shelter wherever they could and from wherever they were not roughly evicted. This was not a kind and forgiving city for those of no financial means. Will briefly lingered at the window of one particularly grubby café squeezed in under the arches supporting a rail line, where trains thundered overhead packed with commuters. There were several adverts plastered to the inside of the window, some for manual labour but on the whole many more for local prostitutes and then a few for rooms to rent. As he memorised the addresses of three suitably low-level potential locations available for immediate occupation, he was suddenly struck by the pervading sadness of his new location. It was not just the stark polarity of the dirt and the poverty surrounding him that contrasted so obviously with the shiny affluence — constantly within vision but most definitely out of reach. It was the essence of pure despair that soaked through the air and soaked through all the people living here or even just those passing through. It was the scent of human despair, of people with no hope, no future and nowhere else to go. He had sensed it before, back in the jungle while a captive and then active member of the LPT. Then it had been accompanied by indiscriminate and brutal violence. The scent however, the scent of basic human desperation was no different here and, as it filtered through his olfactory plate into his brain, it filled him with a deep sense of sadness. There is a biological reason that the sense of smell is so evocative and that certain scents can evoke such strong emotions and it is the nerves that detect different scents that are hard-wired directly into the brain. Most senses, touch, sight, sound, even pain are linked to the brain by a network of interlocking nerve cells with multiple branching connections, points where the signal can be interrupted or modified. Scent however has none of these extra junctions, it is the only sense that runs directly into the central nervous system without interruption, directly into the brain through the fenestrated plate of bone called the cribriform fossa that lies at the top of the nostrils and the base of the brain. There are no junctions, no delays and the oldest of all senses flows directly into the cortex and as such certain scents can directly arouse associated strong emotions or memories. The scent of despair had been seared onto Will's cortex previously, it was rekindled here.

He had momentarily phased out, for a brief moment he had taken his eye off his immediate objective and he shook himself back to reality, angry with himself. He had a mission to accomplish. He needed his life back, or whatever life that may become in the future. Angry at this brief self-indulgent loss of focus he checked the three addresses and quickly moved on. By the end of the afternoon he was ensconced in one of the grubbiest, most deprived flats he had ever seen. It was damp, any wallpaper remaining was flaking off the grimy walls and in one corner there was a collection of needles and other paraphernalia left by the last occupant to signify their recreational pastime. However, on the upside there was running water and a bed. It was enough for now and most importantly no one would look for him here, it was safe. He had become just one of the many dropouts in a block of falling-down flats in one of the most deprived, roughest areas of East London. The owner had wanted only cash and Will had paid for a week in advance. To pay for any more would arouse at best suspicion and more likely robbery. If anyone knew the actual amount of cash that he was carrying the local gangs would have been sure to come calling. As the light of the day began to fade he knew that for the moment he was safe, that for the moment he would remain undetected and with this knowledge he allowed himself to slowly drift off to sleep. One of the handguns was next to him, loaded and ready, the second was carefully hidden, strapped to the inside of the toilet cistern, difficult to find but immediately available if required. However strapped to his back, as always, snug in its leather scabbard, remained his blade, almost like a child's security blanket it had never left him. He was still the natural trained combatant he had been forged into over many years. He slept but always ready, never fully relaxed.

CHAPTER THIRTY-FIVE

He woke at first light, as always immediately alert but remaining outwardly motionless. To any casual observer he was still asleep. His first waking actions were learned instinct and not just unusual but unique to him. Very slowly, almost imperceptibly, he oscillated his shoulder blades, first the left and then the right. This had been his personal early morning ritual that he had developed all those years previously in another life. He could feel the caress of the rough wooden handle of his blade against the skin of the inner aspects of each scapula and it gave him immediate comfort, almost as a security blanket would to a small child. He had subconsciously trained himself to do this first on wakening, prior to any other movement, before even opening his eyes and the action came instinctively to him. To the outside world he appeared to be still in deep slumber but, with this action, he knew that he was ready to face whatever challenge may be present. No other living soul knew he did this, it was his secret and he seriously doubted anyone else would ever know. He opened his eyes to the glare of the unshielded bare single light bulb that hung from the damp ceiling of his grimy one-bedroom flat.

He was still safe and woke refreshed after several hours' uninterrupted sleep. It was time to find his third option.

A simple exchange, the discs with whatever information they held for money, was now quite clearly out of the question. He had never really thought that in reality this was a viable or realistic option. This was not the boy scouts or a Marvel comic, it was real, harsh life. Why would they simply let him walk away with no guarantee that he no longer possessed the data on those discs? The natural assumption would be that he would have accessed the discs and saved the data, either in hard copy or in a secure location in the cloud, probably both, as a guarantee of his future personal safety. The logical move therefore would be to take him out of the equation, to eliminate him once the discs had been retrieved. Deep down he had always realised this and perhaps that was why he had been so hesitant, so cautious, in his approach just twenty-four hours previously. He had always really known that they would try to take him. Running, leaving, disappearing forever was still an option that was available, it was not however a realistic one. He had already decided he could not live a half-life in constant fear, under constant threat and besides, he had already crossed well over any point of turning back after his actions on *Amnesia*. He was fully committed.

He could however take out Jarrett. This was definitely one viable option and probably the simplest one. It would not be difficult for a man with Will's specific skill set, he knew he could with relative ease eliminate Jarrett and never be caught. They would not see him, there would be no warning and Jarrett would never even be aware of what had happened. In addition there was no moral dilemma here, Jarrett and his team had already tried to kill Will, twice, and had failed. Unfortunately, several weeks previously, in Chris's case, they had been more successful. He owed Jarrett no sympathy, and felt none. In fact, he would take considerable personal satisfaction from ending his miserable life. He knew that Chris, and in his turn Father Wilhelm, would disapprove but the hardened fighter, the soldier, had never left and his instinct was to remove any immediate threat with extreme prejudice. There was a problem however with this potential avenue and it was a pretty big one; while eliminating Jarrett would not be without personal pleasure, it would not result in achieving his ultimate goal — to be free, to be allowed to live in peace, without constant threat. While Jarrett appeared to be currently in charge of this offensive operation against Will he was also part of a much, much larger organisation. If Will was to simply remove him another would come; by cutting off one head of the beast, like the hydra it would just grow another, just as vicious and this time they would be an unknown quantity. The issue of the discs, the information they held and any potential knowledge Will had of this data would unfortunately not be resolved simply by Jarrett's demise. His organisation, M&C, had already demonstrated its resolve to go far beyond the law, they would not just quietly go away. Another team leader would be appointed, another team would come and this time Will would not know who they were. He currently had a name and a face to work against so he reluctantly discarded the appetising option of taking out Jarrett.

He needed to find that "third option" his drill instructors had talked, or more accurately shouted about, so often. He needed to convince Jarrett, his team and his superiors that this particular case was closed. They needed to believe beyond any doubt that all the information on those discs was both secure and also no longer of any use and, hence, Will was no longer of any concern. This was the third option he was looking for. He needed to convince them, force them, to believe that this issue was totally and completely locked down and that more importantly the he, Will James was therefore to them completely and totally irrelevant and of no consequence. He needed to be so completely irrelevant to the corporation of M&C that the risk of removing him, the risk of breaking the law to eliminate him, simply did not justify the benefit. He now needed to become insignificant.

Once again decisions were straightforward, it was the practicality of making them reality that was significantly more difficult. Will knew he had found his way out, a potential third option; he needed to become irrelevant, but he would need some significant leverage to convince Jarrett. It was time to get it. Over the last few weeks his life had been turned upside down and inside out. His career as a soldier in the British special forces was irrevocably over. His brief period of financial luxury had been stripped from him, although it had never been his in the first place. More importantly the only living person who he had trusted had been murdered and taken from him, just as his father, Father Wilhelm, had been in the Mission of St Xavier many years before. And now the individual and the organisation behind all of this personal loss were zeroed in on him. They were desperately searching, seeking him with all their considerable might and if they found him they would surely kill him, there would be no polite conversation or warning. He was fighting for his life just as if he were in hand to hand combat and he knew it. However all of his previous life experiences, all of his training up to now had equipped him with many skills with which to survive. Jarrett and his team would have no idea of his lethal skill set and of what he was capable of. He was angry. He wanted to strike back for what had been taken from him and he wanted his life back. It was time to get it.

CHAPTER THIRY-SIX

By the end of the day he had amassed the basics that he required. It was remarkable what could be purchased on the downtrodden streets of inner-city London for pure hard cash. No receipts had been issued, no identification had been asked for or offered and certainly there had been no digital trail of a credit card or digital transfer that could easily be traced by a banking organisation such as M&C. In the street markets of Camden Town, he had found a digital camera with a highly powerful x 2,000 optical zoom lens. It was certainly second hand, probably fourth or fifth hand and almost certainly stolen, it did not bother him, the basic optical capabilities, particularly the ability to observe form a significant distance combined with a new SD memory card would suffice. The second essential item had taken the majority of the rest of the day to source. He needed to be mobile. Under the ancient brick arches hidden from sight and just beyond Smithfield's meat markets there are always used cars for sale. These were all most definitely stolen, again it did not matter and in the current circumstances was an advantage. There was no users' manual, no guarantee or service contract nor was any identification or proof of insurance required on Will's part. It was just a simple exchange, untraceable cash for an untraceable car. By the end of the day he was the latest owner of a non-descript dark blue VW Golf, or at least it was once dark blue in colour, now it was more just coated in grime and dirt and marked with various dents and scrapes. It was completely forgettable and melted into the London traffic, it was ideal. He was mobile and had the equipment for distant observation. It was time to take back the initiative and start getting into Jarrett's life. He needed leverage, significant leverage to convince Jarrett to close his file. He needed to make him call off the team that no doubt was right now combing through London frantically searching for him. He needed the case to be permanently closed and, with each day that passed that he remained free and at large, the pressure would slowly mount on Jarrett and his team.

The following evening, he picked Jarrett up as he left the impressive glass-clad offices of M&C just off Fleet Street. He was not difficult to follow as there are not that many chauffeur-driven limousines with reinforced glass, even in central London. He kept a safe distance back, safely obscured in the chaos of normal inner city traffic. Just barely fifteen minutes later, which is no distance at all when moving at the pace of gridlocked traffic, the limo turned out of the main stream and entered a very luxurious gated, security-guarded complex in upper Westminster, close to the Houses of Parliament. Will drove on, not looking either way as here was danger, here there were armed security guards, here there were sophisticated security cameras looking for any potential threat to the high-paying occupants of the privileged protected complex. This was a virtual fortress, an area of strength and safety for Jarrett and all of Will's previous training and life experience in combat had taught him to find the enemy's areas of weakness, their vulnerabilities and to exploit these ruthlessly and if possible, avoid their areas of strength. This current situation was neither weak nor vulnerable and Will did not wish to linger for a second longer, so he simply moved forwards in turn in the never-ending traffic, leaving this zone of danger behind.

By the end of the first week's dedicated surveillance it was startling quite how much information Will had gathered on Jarrett's daily routine. On the surface, from the outside, he was a straightforward hard-working family man. He left his security-guarded gated complex by seven fifteen each morning and travelled directly to the central offices of M&C. Shortly afterwards the chauffeur would return home and then re-emerge, again checked carefully by the security each way, with what Will presumed was Jarrett's two daughters. They both went to school at the fifteen thousand pounds a term elite private school of Westminster School for Girls. While they could easily have walked as it was less than a kilometre, this was clearly not the daily routine they had become accustomed to. They were dropped together from the stretched black reinforced limo at the school's entrance which shared a communal driveway with the historic Westminster Abbey itself at eight forty, in time for the start of school. Their privileged mode of transport was not altogether unusual for this school that catered for the children of the financial elite of central London as theirs was not the only chauffeur-driven vehicle to deposit its cosseted wards at the school gates. It was not difficult for Will to remain unobserved by mingling with the large crowds of tourists and some true pilgrims that had come to visit Westminster Abbey and hence to obtain close images of both girls as they came and went from the school. He felt a very brief pang of guilt in setting them up to be used as bargaining chips in his future negotiations. He dismissed this transient frailty with contempt, no harm would come to them; they were just extra leverage that he may require.

Most days the chauffeur would once again retrace his steps and, once again, later in the morning exit through the security checks with a single woman. She was in her late thirties or early forties and of Nordic origin with striking, almost white-blond hair and angular features. She was elegant, she was attractive, well dressed and confident and had clearly become used to the comforts of a lifestyle of luxury that only serious wealth could provide. Most days she would go to an exclusive gym and personal grooming boutique and then return home, on others she would meet friends in expensive trendy restaurants, the lifestyle of ladies who lunch. Such was the daily routine of the Jarrett family and Jarrett himself would remain in the offices until later in the evening when once again the hard-working chauffeur would deposit him back into the safety of his security-guarded complex. To gather this information and remain unobserved had not been difficult, after all he had received extensive training in these techniques by the British special forces and he had just melted in to the busy streets of London. In general he stationed himself on street corners alongside the homeless and the occasional better-dressed beggar who was tolerated in direct view on the affluent streets. Jarrett, his privileged family and his security team paid no attention to such individuals and so Will remained firmly in the realms of those unfortunate souls who were there, present and just about tolerated but in reality not really seen at all, almost invisible in the minds of those he was watching and in the minds of those watching for him. He remained of no consequence, irrelevant.

After two weeks of reconnaissance and information gathering he was building an accurate picture of the daily routine. On day fifteen he decided to move from his squalid flat to another equally unpleasant location to ensure that there was no chance of any familiarity being built up around his comings and goings. Once again no ID was required, just hard cash which he still had in abundance. By the end of the fourth week he had become confident in the pattern of Jarrett's normal routine. While on most days he would return home around seven o'clock in the evening to the protected complex criss-crossed with surveillance cameras on a Tuesday and Thursday evening he would take a detour that would delay him. It seemed that his attractive wife was not quite fulfilling all of the aspects that he needed to satisfy. Twice each week on the way home he would stop for two to three hours at an elegant building in Mayfair divided into expensive flats. Here he would go in alone and then emerge several hours later freshly showered. On the third occasion he saw the reason for this detour and she was truly stunning. She was in her early twenties with a body that screamed sexuality. She was beautifully tanned with unblemished silk like olive skin. Her long dark auburn hair flowed behind her reaching down to her waist. She moved with the ease and the grace of youth and oozed sensuality and a deafening aura of sexuality, carefully presented to appear as though it was just kept almost hidden, simmering hot bubbling under her designer clothes that clung to all the right places. She was instantly desirable even from a distance and it was clear that she was not afraid or ashamed of her obvious sex appeal. This was not a business meeting or a stop at the gym. It took only a few more days of discrete observation to realise that Jarrett was not the only gentleman that called at this address on a regular basis. There were never any women callers and all of the men were well dressed, entered and exited alone and would characteristically stay for between one and three hours. It had become clear that this was a fee-paying establishment and that the oldest trade known to women was still going strong in central

London, albeit with an extremely high price tag and at a sophisticated level. Here at this Mayfair address there was no significant security, there were neither external guards nor cameras. The clientele here would demand discretion and complete anonymity above all else and would never come if they were recorded. Here Jarrett would be alone, unguarded for several hours and this was clearly not a party for three, no others would be invited! This need to satiate his carnal longings had given Will an opportunity. Here was an area where Jarrett was alone and unguarded and the regularity of his appointments was predictable and hence could be exploited in a planned and prepared manner. Here was a point of vulnerability Will could use.

CHAPTER THIRTY-SEVEN

He returned to his grimy dwelling on the outskirts of Newham, the poorest and roughest part of London that had the unwanted distinction of leading the country as the borough with the highest level of gun crime in the land. Here no one cared who he was or what he was doing, in fact the residents of this particularly downtrodden and forgotten borough of inner London had learnt never to ask. They knew that to pry into the business of any individual of this neighbourhood was always met with at least hostility but more often violence. Here gang culture ruled and to disrespect this system was not good for one's short-term longevity. It had now been almost two months since his escape from capture at Paddington and there had been no contact of any sort. With each passing day Jarrett and his team would be becoming increasingly anxious, increasingly desperate and as their level of anxiety rose the more likely they would be to make rash decisions, the more likely they would be to rush to any possible contact with less preparation than would be prudent. Any small weakness in his opposition could be exploited and he would use any opportunity without hesitation. Will looked at himself in the unframed chipped mirror of his one-bedroom flat; he looked dreadful. His recent existence, mainly outside on the unforgiving cold streets for the last two months, had taken its toll. He looked, and smelt, like a vagrant; drawn, tired, unkempt and general highly undesirable. This had been intentional but his altered appearance now staring directly back at him caught by surprise. Despite his outward appearance his steely grey-blue eyes, inherited from his German father still burned bright, staring right back at him and filled with cold hard rage. He shifted his shoulder blades almost imperceptibly and felt the comforting presence of the rough blade, as always nestled in the small of his back. It was almost time, he had prepared well and almost had all he required. There was one more piece however to this puzzle that he required and that was the information on those discs. He needed to know what information they contained and to understand why it was so vital to Jarrett and his masters. Whatever information they held was apparently worth killing for, it was worth killing him for!

There was no option, he needed to reacquire the discs that he had left in the secure lockers in Paddington station. However with this there was an element of risk. Currently he was relatively safe, hidden in the depths of human despair, residing in the inner-city suburbs amongst the poor and homeless. However as Paddington was the last concrete point of contact with Will it was possible that Jarrett had it under continued surveillance. It would be standard practice once the trail had gone cold to go back to the last point of confirmed contact and then wait. However it had been two months and to mount any form of effective surveillance on such a large area with so many people passing through would require an enormous team dedicated to observation alone. Will doubted seriously if this was even possible and more seriously that Jarrett would have the resources to mount such an operation and continue for two months. Yet it remained a possibility and so he would have to take care. He considered paying an intermediary to go in his place. It would minimise his initial personal risk but was not without other problems. Any individual he could currently recruit would have none of the skills that he possessed and would be easily taken if there was a trap in place. It would then be simple to extract Will's location from them and then he would run the risk of being taken by a better prepared superior force than before. Also there was the outside possibility that once any other individual had the discs they might just have the streetwise gutter instincts to try to use them themselves. Both situations were to be avoided so he would have to go himself. So at seven thirty the following morning, at the peak of commuter rush hour, a tall, clean-shaven man, elegantly dressed in a dark navy three-piece pinstripe suit, carrying a polished black briefcase strode positively out from the steps leading up from the London Underground and moved directly into the station, moving as if in a hurry and with a place to go to. He was now just one of the many thousands of commuters, one of the smarter ones, but one among many. Hidden in plain sight yet obscured by the crowd. He walked purposefully and with an air of confidence and familiarity as though he did this journey every day. He rapidly reached the stairs leading down to the secure lockers and as yet had detected nothing out of place. Yet once he descended, he would be effectively trapped, there was no other exit than the narrow stairs back up again. Every one of his highly attuned senses were on high alert, seeking out any clue of an observer left behind, anything out of place, anything or anyone who was just not right. There was nothing out of the ordinary, just normal people going about their normal daily lives and so he committed and took the stairs two at a time and, within seconds, was at the lockers. There was no one waiting for him, there was no unusual activity, there was no one out of place, just normal people going about their daily business. He swiftly walked to the small combination locker where he had left the discs two months earlier, opened it, scooped up the discs and just calmly tucked them into his breast pocket as though he did this most days. With that he turned and retraced his steps and, in under six minutes, he was back on the Tube heading away from Paddington and any potential danger, confident that he had been undetected and was not being followed. He had anticipated that this would be the outcome of the day but had also been mindful of the potential threat, for once it had been easier than anticipated. He did not think this was likely to occur again.

Later ensconced in his low-quality room he downloaded the data to the laptop he had previously purchased, once again for untraceable cash on the streets of London, and sat down to examine what precisely was so important, what was worth killing for. While he was no computer genius he had a rudimentary understanding of programming, bizarrely it had been one of his obligatory courses while with the special forces. The rationale had been that if he were required to access complex weapons systems and deploy them or if he needed at any time the use of encrypted data, either for instructions or data protection, he needed a basic working knowledge of these systems, as always nothing done in the special forces was without sound logic and a sensible underlying reason, no time was ever wasted unnecessarily. So within a couple of silent hours he understood and it was genius. Chris's program was simplicity itself but in its simplicity was its beauty. Essentially he had created a program that once uploaded would integrate itself into the main servers of the financial exchange network, the mechanism by which money was sent between institutions. It was a digital worm that would burrow into its host, just like any other biological parasite, except this particular worm once incorporated into the host system became part of that system and was as such undetectable as foreign. Each time any transaction of over £100,000 pounds sterling occurred the embedded system simply siphoned off £1, one pound only. It did not seem like a lot to start with but Will began to do the maths. In any given working day there were approximately two million different individual transfers of funds between the several International offices of M&C, particularly focused around the options trading departments where the high-stakes financial exchanges took place. Approximately half of these, one million transactions a day were over one hundred thousand pounds. That made roughly on any given working day one million transactions from which Chris's program would siphon off an unnoticed one pound. That made in effect one million pounds sterling a day, or five million a week, twenty million a month and so on. The figures were simply incredible! And in essence who would ever notice? One pound taken from a transfer of over one hundred thousand, that was just so insignificant no one would ever even notice. It was in fact 0.00001% of any financial exchange, such a small inaccuracy would not even be detected. However, it was the fact that there were so many of these transactions buzzing across the Internet superhighways every second that led to the very rapid accumulation of undetected illegal wealth. As far as Will could decipher the funds, once creamed off, any transfer would then rotate through multiple different coded accounts across the world, mainly based in countries with more relaxed legal requirements for taxation and financial accountability and then eventually fall into a single, central account, This was the account he had temporarily inherited on Chris's death, the final end point for each of those token one pounds extracted, highly illegally, from the business transactions running through the several international offices of M&C. It had been worth over one hundred million pounds, for a short time anyway, and it was not difficult to see how Chris could have amassed this vast fortune at the rate his software removed it.

The problem however was that there appeared to be two more facets built into this poorly conceived idea, as far as Will could work out, that Chris had added to his final brainchild, like a vicious extra kicker. It was likely that it was the last of these two that had got him killed. It was not the money that was the real problem. In fact the money was all gone, it was long gone. It had been reclaimed by its rightful owner through the digital networks where the press of a button means the transfer of enormous wealth, instantaneously to pretty much anywhere in the world with Internet access. Will had always found this bizarre, probably due to his childhood in the jungles when one could be killed over possession of a simple gun or a blade or just for enough food to feed one's family, let alone millions of pounds. The main issue Will realised lay in the extra subtly hidden aspects of the system, as always the devil was in the detail. The first part was the ability of Chris's program to essentially piggy back onto the financial operating systems of all large multinational financial conglomerates and remain undetected. In essence the transfer of money and assets across the globe required a set of systems that all talked to each other in a rapid and efficient manner, time is money. Basically they all used the same underlying system to communicate and to do business and Chris had used this fact to integrate his worm. His system simply became part of the host system and thus would not be recognised as foreign, thus simply bypassing all of the in-built cyber security mechanisms. All the firewalls, all the anti-virus programs were designed to recognise foreign programs and prevent breeches of the system. They were not designed to act against the host server and so Chris's system would remain undetected, integrated into the host software, seen as friendly, remaining digitally unchallenged and therefore free to continue taking 0.00001% of the funds without any warnings being raised.

While this was a significant issue it was not as major as the final part of his program. For some unfathomable reason he had built in a data collection facility. He had stored within the hard drive of his system all the details of each transfer from which he had removed a single £1. Here was the true danger. Within these discs was enough information to cause real harm. He had recorded as a matter of process all the details of each exchange worth over one hundred thousand pounds. He had the details of exactly who was dealing with whom, what had been sold, what had been bought and by whom and for how much. Here there was real danger. There was the hard data of transfers, the amounts and the personally identified back accounts; there were high court judges who had suddenly bought holiday homes in Barbados using so-called charitable gifts from dubious offshore accounts, there were politicians and world leaders who had received hundreds of thousands in apparent consultancy fees from many different business enterprises for no demonstrable input on their behalf. This was bad enough but there was worse. There was also the identifiable records of the business transactions of several Italian-American families with multiple business interests, in effect the Mafia. They would not take kindly to this information being readily available. Worse still was the exact details of the billion-dollar transactions that occurred on a not irregular basis between the major international conglomerates, the banks and the trading houses of the world of finance. This kind of data was seriously bad for the health of the owner for, as sure as eggs are eggs, only a fraction of these major deals would show up on their tax returns. The harsh reality of the situation was that when it came down to it the life of one criminal was not worth the public humiliation of an important public figure, it was not worth the discrediting of a regime or political party and that life was certainly not worth a major corporation losing millions or even billions of dollars. That was reality and the reason Chris had been killed.

Will now finally understood what was so valuable, why Jarrett was so desperate to reacquire the discs and eliminate anyone who could possibly have accessed them, why it was worth killing for. Why Chris had built this data collection platform into his program he would never know, perhaps it was as a misguided protection mechanism where he foolishly thought that if he possessed this data he could use it to protect himself. As it turned out the opposite was true. But with this he also now had a weapon he could use. Not a conventional weapon like a gun or a knife but a highly significant virtual weapon all the same. Jarrett and his team would be desperate to regain these discs and he could use them as a bargaining chip, a form of leverage against Jarrett and his superiors. He downloaded all the data and stored it in two separate compressed files, one with the system files including the ability to integrate into any of the large financial networks and remain undetected, the other with the personal data and transfer records and exported it to his personal encrypted storage files in the cloud. He then spent the next two hours adding a further word document attached to the system file and then logged off.

He had what he needed. It was time.

CHAPTER THIRTY-EIGHT

It was three o'clock in the afternoon on Thursday in late December, Christmas was fast approaching and it was almost dark, the street lights were already on piercing the winter gloom in the city. Will took the mobile phone that had lain dormant for the last two months, the one he had liberated from his would-be killers all those weeks previously on *Amnesia* and reactivated it. He replaced the battery and SIM card and allowed it to register on the network for a few moments. He pressed redial. Six cycles of monotonous and repetitive dialling chimes later a familiar voice answered, yet this time the tone was different, less assured, less forceful.

"Major James, I was not sure if we would ever hear from you again. We have been looking for you."

Will waited, saying nothing, giving nothing, allowing the silence to stretch out and hang uncomfortably. Jarrett and his team would have been waiting, monitoring this line, hoping for contact of any sort, desperate to glean any information on his location and that of their precious discs. For this brief moment he had control, he had a degree of dominance in this brief conversation, the opposite to their previous exchange and he could hear it in Jarrett's voice.

"Mr Jarrett, does our original deal still remain open?" Will replied succinctly in a calm and level tone. He knew that they would never let him simply walk away, there would never be a simple exchange for money, the information on those discs was too sensitive, too dangerous to rich and unscrupulous men and corporations. However he wanted them, Jarrett and his team, to believe that he was still after the money, that he was so stupid to believe that he could make a profit and walk out alive. He was banking on the fact that the pressure that had built up over the last two months with no contact, no information, no resolution of the situation would have made Jarret too desperate to get him, too keen to arrange a location for exchange. He was using their desperation to make them careless, to have no choice but to agree in haste and hopefully, from Will's point of view, to regret at leisure. Pressure creates stress and stress leads to poor judgement, this was the situation he had imposed on Jarrett.

"Of course," came the too-rapid reply, almost choked out from Jarrett struggling to hide his surprise and satisfaction. Struggling to hide his disbelief that this soldier he had never met but had been desperately seeking would be stupid enough, greedy enough to allow him another opportunity to take him, to silence him permanently and close the current situation.

"Tomorrow 0800, same location as before, same terms as before." And with that short sentence Will terminated the call. He switched off the mobile and removed the battery and SIM. He could almost visualise the panicked situation in the offices in the security section of M&C. He could almost hear the commands being issued, the teams being assembled and deployed around Paddington. There would be a frenzy of activity and the timeline he had allowed them was short. This time he was in no doubt that they would prepare a welcoming committee that no one would possibly be able to evade. There would be so many M&C personnel on the ground waiting for him the station would be practically flooded by them. For the rest of the day and night Jarrett's team would be fully occupied with preparation, preparing to take him again.

He had already packed all that he needed earlier in the day, everything fitted into a single rucksack. He carried all he required, weapons, money and leverage. He turned and left his damp one bedroom flat in Newham for the last time. It was time to take back his life.

CHAPTER THIRTY-NINE

As dusk fell that evening, approximately twelve hours before the allocated time of exchange, Will ghosted through the back entrance of a specific high-rise exclusive apartment block in Mayfair. It was on the second day of reconnaissance of this particular area that he had noticed that only either the well-groomed and clearly affluent customers of the various but always stunning female residents of this particular establishment passed through the front entrance. However the mere mortals, the normal people that served and maintained the building and its occupants, the cleaners, plumbers, food deliveries, rubbish removal and all the rest that was required for a normal existence in the twenty-first century entered and exited through the back door, a true tradesman's entrance. Here, as in the front, there were no CCTV cameras and importantly here, unlike the front entrance, there were neither guards nor significant security, not even a doorman. It had taken only forty-five minutes of patient, unobserved waiting for one of these service personnel to enter, slightly longer than when he had rehearsed this uninvited entry over the previous few days. As the delivery man entered, as it happened this time with an armful of pizza boxes, Will silently ghosted in behind him, as always unheard and unobserved. Now he was installed in a small cramped room on the third floor just opposite Jarrett's mistress's apartment. He had found it on his last visit and it was normally used for the storage of cleaning and maintenance equipment, however this evening it housed Will. He was in touching distance of Jarrett and he was back, back in the warrior state he had grown to be as a man-child, the unfeeling, remorseless soldier he had been refined into in the special forces. He was close and he was definitely ready.

He had made the initial contact just three hours previously and he was confident that Jarrett and his team would have spent every precious second of the available time planning exactly how to remove him from the equation, permanently, running multiple scenarios, all with the same eventual terminal outcome. They would not make the same mistakes they made three months previously. However today was Thursday, it was the usual evening for Jarrett to visit his young professional lady and if nothing he was certainly a creature of habit, he had not missed a single Tuesday or Thursday evening over the last few months. Will was betting on this fact, combined with the recently increased stress, imposed by Will, of a potentially lethal contact the following morning would encourage Jarrett to keep his regular appointment. If for nothing else but for a brief few hours to relieve his personal level of anxiety. And so Will waited, alone, in a store cupboard, his muscled form squeezed between brooms, mops and cleaning detergents. In the silence he allowed his mind to wander back into the past, to his beginnings. This had happened to him before in the past, in the brief silent moments before decisive action, this private reminiscing served to reinforce the ruthless, self-preserving zone that he needed to exist in in order to survive. It had worked for the past two decades, he hoped it would work again. He was born from nothing and with nothing save the love of his only surviving parent. That was all too soon stripped from him and his harsh education in the fields of combat began. He had excelled. Then chance and Chris had taken him on a different and unexpected path, however yet again those whom he trusted were once again taken, violently stripped away. Now here he was, totally alone and totally ready to take vengeance against all that had befallen him. He knew that tonight, the here and now, was not about vengeance, it was about freedom, a small chance to live free. How many more would have to suffer and die for that to be achieved, he wondered? He hoped it would be none, or perhaps one, deep down he suspected his hope was misplaced. The high-pitched ping of the lift arriving cut through his reverie like a knife. As he had predicted Jarrett was right on time. He allowed himself the calculated risk of squinting through the smallest of cracks left by the door to his service cupboard being just a fraction of a millimetre open, undetectable from the outside. Jarrett moved rapidly and smoothly for an older man along the corridor, as expected and as he was previously he was alone, this was not a party for three to which his guard would be invited. He heard the soft padding of his footfalls of polished shoes on the plush thick carpet of the corridor and, as he approached, the door to the apartment opposite was flung open. Whether he was always this punctual or more likely she had been notified by the doorman, she glided out of her apartment with the rustling of expensive silk that was wrapped around her firm and beautifully formed body and moved forwards sensually to greet him. She was stunning, she was thirty years younger than him and she wrapped her toned arms around his slightly sagging frame. They turned, still in the forced embrace and wobbled together in the entrance. It was time to move and there was no hesitation, there never was. As they turned away he silently moved forwards, rapidly but unrushed and with the speed and aggression he had always known he did what came instinctively. His arm descended at speed holding his blade inverted, the wooden shaft aimed precisely at the posterolateral aspect of Jarrett's skull. He had done this before and the result was predictable, what should have happened was that the blow should have landed precisely as intended and Jarrett would have simply crumpled to the beautifully carpeted ground, unconscious but otherwise not permanently harmed. However what actually happened was the unexpected, it often did. From somewhere in her consciousness she became aware of his presence, she had somehow noticed him and had reacted. Whether it was the rapid movement, an incongruous sound or his scent that had alerted her just as he was about to deliver that incapacitating strike, she had sensed his movement and had moved, fast. She had reared backwards, instinctively moving away from danger. The problem was that she had been wrapped around Jarrett at the time so that her lightning-fast movement of self-preservation had unintended consequences. As she dived backwards she dragged Jarret with her so that the wooden shaft of the blade, instead of taking Jarret on the skull as intended, landed on the soft fleshy part of his shoulder, the deltoid muscles. The blow was painful but not as intended incapacitating. The really negative aspect was that the unexpected angle of attack had forced the blade out of Will's hand, the forceful rebound from the massive muscle complex had thrown the blade viciously upwards and as he was grasping the razor-sharp blade he could not effectively control the recoil. It spiralled away from them both and clattered as it ricocheted off the polished wall of the corridor and then landed two metres away, embedding itself into the thick cream carpet of the corridor. Jarrett reacted with surprising speed for an older man, he was not a stranger to violence and he had not survived in his world of conflict for so long without considerable personal skills. Rather than resisting the force of the impact of Will's strike he rolled forwards with it, absorbing its energy and using the momentum of the blow to circle around 180 degrees. Immediately, and without any thought for her welfare, dropped the beautiful girl from his arms who a millisecond before had been straddling him and whose acute reflex actions had unintentionally saved him. He now turned in a trained fighter's stance, crouched with a low centre of gravity, one foot slightly in front of the other, leading with his non-dominant arm and his head and torso rotated to minimise exposure. In an instant he was facing Will, up close, less than a metre apart, his eyes narrowed to vicious slits, his body weaving back and forth as a cobra standing erect. Alert. Searching for a target.

"You!"

It was the only word that Jarrett uttered and it was spat out in surprise but also with total vehemence, there was nothing held back.

"Me," replied Will.

He wasted no further time or effort on useless dialogue. He needed to take Jarrett. He needed to take him now, he needed to take him down rapidly and without any significant disturbance that would alert the porters in the lobby below or his bodyguard waiting outside. He moved forwards without hesitation. Perhaps it was his desire to end this fight before it really got started that made Will move too close too quickly, perhaps it was his mistaken impression of Jarrett as an old man who sat behind a desk ordering others into harm's way that made him overconfident. Either way Will moved too close without adequate caution and suffered the consequence. As he approached the shorter older man expecting to take him down in seconds, Jarrett crouched lower, taking advantage of his shorter stature and unexpectedly lunged forwards himself, instantly closing the two metres between them to just thirty centimetres. At this range he unleashed a volley of powerful and accurately aimed short punches into Will's torso which drove the breath from him, his abdominal muscles reflexing contracting to protect his abdominal organs. As now Will recoiled under the impacts of these unexpectedly powerful blows Jarrett moved forwards again, a street fighter sensing a small advantage and pushing forwards, forcing the advantage further, and crouching lower still he used all of his advancing momentum and strength and hit accurately and with real force into the inside of Will's knee. The impact of the well-aimed and powerful punch jarred through Will's body like a sledge-hammer, the impact of the vicious blow reverberating up his femur and into his pelvis temporarily throwing him off balance. More importantly than the pain that was searing up Will's lower limb was the fact that the medial ligaments of his left knee had been stretched to almost breaking point by the combination of the force and accuracy of the blow. Now his left leg was not only totally numb from the knee down it was no longer responding to his mind's commands. Will was limping, he was moving slowly and he was vulnerable from that side. It was immediately clear that he was now facing a powerful and skilled opponent who was unafraid. This was now a real one on one confrontation that he had engineered and could not afford to lose and they both knew it. Will rapidly appraised the situation. The woman had been thrown into the blind end of the corridor by their initial contact and had simply backed away, she had nowhere to go. There was no other exit so she moved as far away as possible and plastered her stunning frame to the end wall of the corridor. He was facing the crouched and ready Jarrett and was now between him and the only exit from the luxurious corridor that accessed the plush apartment, while he could not run and escape Jarrett was still dangerous and needed to be neutralised, right now. However, Will needed him alive for his eventual aim, dead he was no use to anyone and could serve no future purpose. Will knew that his leg was not broken so he used sheer mental resolve to ignore the pain that was shooting down his limb each time he moved it or placed any weight through it and, more carefully this time, advanced on his now cornered prey.

This time he advanced expecting to take some blows, expecting to absorb some punishment in order to manoeuvre himself into a dominating position, this was a pure street fight between two experienced opponents. As they exchanged body hits, blocking the more savage thrusts that would cause significant damage Will glimpsed a potential weapon. There was always something you could use as a weapon, whether it be a rock or sharpened branch in the forest or the most advanced sniper rifle ever built, capable of putting a bullet accurately through an eye socket at a thousand paces. As he closed on Jarrett he allowed himself to absorb several direct body blows but, in doing so, he reached into the breast pocket of Jarrett's expensive pinstripe suit and his palm closed on the weapon he had seen. He blocked the next three punches and two kicks that were aimed at his kidneys and jumped back away from flailing arms, but now clutched in his fist was Jarrett's very expensive fountain pen. Will flipped off the lid and inverted the pen, now it was a weapon. As he now moved forward once again but with more purpose, he parried Jarrett's striking arm and, moving forward under the outstretched limb now held painfully rigid and twisted to one side, he embedded the short blade of the pen deeply into Jarrett's thorax. He was fast, lightning fast and holding Jarrett in this vulnerable position he was able to pierce his chest wall cavity four times in rapid succession before lunging back. It was done. He had taken some punishment but he was not incapacitated, now, from past experience he knew what was about to occur. He had pierced Jarrett's chest cavity in four places with a small blade. Each time he took a breath in the negative pressure created in order to suck air into his lungs would now also suck air in through those pinpoint wounds. Unfortunately for Jarrett, as they were such small injuries as his chest wall contracted to automatically exhale, the wounds would close up and consequently trap the air within his chest cavity. With each breath the volume of trapped air would increase, with each breath the increasing trapped air would squash his delicate lungs and compromise his ability to breathe. The lungs are just like a delicate sponge contained in an air-proof plastic bag and, with each breath, the pressure compressing them would increase, with each breath the functional lung volume would decrease and with each breath Jarrett would slowly die. Emergency department doctors call this condition a tension pneumothorax and it is a swift killer that they train to resolve, rapidly. As it happened Will only had to wait for twelve seconds, twelve seconds standing two metres away from a man who had tried to kill him on several occasions in the last three months, twelve seconds or three complete breaths. As Jarrett took his fourth breath the pressure that had built up within his chest cavity was enough to compress his lungs to a degree that he felt he could not breathe and, as he took his fourth breath, the oxygen levels in his bloodstream dropped below 90% and he fell to his knees, his muscles starved of oxygen no longer able to support his weight. As he took his fifth breath it increased the pressure further, squashing the delicate foamy lung tissue almost flat and Jarrett's oxygen levels began to plummet. The pain in his chest was excruciating and he fell to the luxuriously carpeted floor, clutching his failing chest. He took his sixth breath and it would have normally been his last, the sixth sucked in enough air through his puncture wounds to completely crush his lungs, his gas exchange ability was now zero and he was about to die. The sensation is horrendous, being crushed from within and unable to even utter a scream of protest as there is no air to scream with! He lay on the carpet in the corridor of the exclusive apartment block and looked up at Will's unrepentant emotionless face, looked into his steely eyes and found no mercy.

It was over. The contact had lasted for less than two minutes but the outcome had been lethal. Timothy Jarrett lay at Will's feet dying. He could no longer breathe and was beginning to turn blue as the oxygen levels in his body dropped even lower. There was a problem however. Will needed Jarrett alive. For a moment he paused above the prostate incapacitated body. Here lying at his feet was the man responsible for killing Chris. Here was the man who had sent an active kill team after him, not once but twice, and all he had to do was to watch. If he did nothing in the next thirty seconds this man would go into respiratory driven cardiac arrest and die. God knew he deserved it for his actions. For a brief half of a second Will paused. It would be so easy just to do nothing and watch him die. Then logic kicked in, it always did. Will needed Jarret alive, as unfortunate and unjust as it seemed he needed him to live. Will had been well trained by the Marines in battlefield resuscitation and he knew what to do. He knew the simple treatment that was required to relieve the lethal pressure within Jarrett's chest that had now permanently stopped his breathing. He turned away from the dying man and walked back towards the girl. She was standing still at the blind end of the corridor. There was nowhere for her to go but she was not cowering in fear as he would have expected having witnessed the events of the last few minutes. Instead she was standing tall, stationary and silent and just looked directly at him. He stopped three paces away from the truly beautiful woman, bent down and grasped his blade from out of the carpet where it had embedded itself previously. He turned away from her, although reluctant to do so as she was so captivating in her beauty and brave silence and returned to the almost dead Jarrett.

In order to relive the tension pneumothorax, the crushing pressure in Jarrett's chest, the trapped air had to be let out. Will had seen this done before to one of his former comrades in arms in the once-lush green fields of Afghanistan. So he took his blade and calmly inserted into the front wall of the now unconscious and dying Jarrett's chest wall, higher than you would anticipate, just under the collar bone and twisted as he inserted the razor-sharp blade. As he did so he opened a channel of escape, a route that the trapped air under high pressure could escape. He heard the loud hiss of escaping air, just like a tyre under pressure suddenly deflating and as the air escaped Jarrett's compressed lung re-expanded and he unfortunately, returned to the living.

Will turned away from the totally incapacitated Jarrett and faced the woman. She had uttered not a single sound, there was no scream, no shout of alarm and instead her eyes were level, calm and cold, looking directly at Will, rapidly appraising the situation and calculating whether she herself was in imminent personal danger. It was immediately clear that she was a professional. She was without doubt young, perhaps twenty and she was certainly breathtakingly beautiful but it was clear that such situations, that violence was not a stranger to her. This was not the first time she had been close to lethal conflict, it was not the first time she had been under threat. Will recognised the rapid and calm appraisal of the situation, unconcerned by the prostrate unconscious man at her feet. He was impressed despite himself and she had the presence of mind to make no noise, to scream or at least call out for help would be the normal reaction, however that would only draw immediate unwanted attention to herself and force him to act to neutralise her as in doing so she would become a new threat, she knew this and so kept silent. She stared right back. She was not afraid, she was not intimidated by his size nor his close proximity and sudden appearance and the presence of the unconscious man crumpled at her feet from the ever so rapid and unexpected violence did not appear to faze her. He was impressed although he tried not to show it, his face the emotionless mask it always was. She simply stood in silence and stared right back at him, unafraid and defiant.

"I have no wish to hurt you," he said slowly and calmly, just loud enough for her to hear but so that none others would be aware of his presence

"I have come for him, not you, remain silent, cooperate and you will be unharmed."

Again she said nothing, just met his gaze directly and without fear. He was suddenly struck at how truly beautiful she was. He suddenly found himself wondering what events had occurred in her life to lead her to this particular situation. How had her path been trodden? She was young, stunning unrepentant and unafraid. He suddenly saw echoes of himself reflected in her direct deep dark eyes. It did not help that she was exceedingly attractive. The moment was broken as she slowly and clearly nodded and said one word only in a soft, educated European accent.

"Yes." It was clear that despite her tender age she was a professional and not unaccustomed to violence. She was not going to put herself at direct risk for Jarrett. So she silently glided backwards into her apartment, stepping over the prostate body with no concern for the unconscious man and sat down. She placed her ever so elegant arms along the sides of a plush armchair with her palms open and facing upwards, signifying compliance and to show that they were empty. She had made her decision, it was rational and she understood that self-preservation for her now required silent cooperation.

This entire interaction had taken only a few minutes. Jarrett was unconscious on the plush thick carpet of the entrance hall of the apartment and Will and the girl were both inside, the door was shut, they were alone and his entry had been undetected. He had achieved the first part of the evening's mission but for a brief moment he found himself side-tracked by the woman sitting silently, palms upwards in front of him. He recognised in her eyes and in the way she had immediately responded to a threat the knowledge of one who had experienced great hostility in the past and had survived. He saw a woman who depended on no one but herself, someone who would not apologise for who they were or what they did in order to survive. Despite her stunning beauty that was breathtaking, emphasised by their now close proximity, underneath he could see the steely determination and self-assuredness. He saw a reflection of himself in her lithe petite frame and her enchanting eyes. He saw it in her and she recognised it in him. As he moved forwards over Jarrett's unconscious form into the main part of the apartment she held her hands out, ready to be bound, she understood what was to come. Despite how affected Will was by her skilled reaction to the situation coupled with her beauty, he was not deterred for a single second. He took her arms and gently but firmly tied her so she was totally incapacitated. He lifted her slight firm body with ease and placed her in one of the large armchairs in the apartment, turning the chair and her to face away. He stooped and bent over her from behind and quietly spoke into her ear. As he placed his head against hers his nostrils filled with her scent — rich, fragrant and like her, alluring. He spoke quietly and succinctly to her alone.

"Be quiet, stay calm. I will free you when it is over. Nothing here is of your concern." She simply nodded and remained motionless, she had understood that cooperation was her best avenue in the current situation. He placed her so she could see nothing save one of the walls of the apartment. It was time to go to work.

CHAPTER FORTY

As the ice-cold water splashed into his face Jarrett woke, coughing and spluttering his way back to consciousness. As he opened his confused eyes the first and only thing that filled his clearing vision was Will's face, only millimetres away from him. Will knelt, almost touching Jarrett's pale and sweaty visage so that the only object that Jarrett could see or sense was him. As Jarrett began to focus Will rocked back on his heels and stood up to his full six feet and seven inches, towering over the confined Jarrett, constrained into a small rigid-backed chair. He looked down into the bleary eyes, one with a trace of dried blood still adhering to the lid from where he had been struck earlier, and said:

"My name is Major Will James, you have been looking for me. It is time we had a talk.

"I know you had Chris murdered. I know you tried to take and to kill me. I know it was driven by the information on those discs, which I now possess. What I need to know is how much further you are able to go?"

With that sentence calmly spoken just inches from Jarrett's face, Will waited. As Jarrett began to speak Will struck him, a firm but glancing blow with the back of his hand square across his face. It was not significantly forceful but it served to remind Jarrett of his current situation. Will waited for an answer. He waited for what seemed like minutes but in reality was only a few seconds. Then Jarrett looked up into his piercing stone cold eyes and recognised the unrepentant, unfeeling fire within them. Will saw the uncertainty ebb into his captive and saw his resolve beginning to crumble. It was time to demonstrate the consequences of his actions over the last few months.

"Do not speak, just look and listen." And with that Will took out three A4-sized photographs that he had brought with him.

"I am showing you these to demonstrate what may happen in the future. If this comes to pass it will be of your making, yours alone and then, afterwards I will visit you."

He uttered these words quietly, slowly and in a completely neutral tone. He was once again and without any doubt the cold, merciless guerrilla fighter he had once been and had never really been forgotten.

"The first image is your wife. I will visit her, just once, and she will breathe no more. It may be close, or more likely from a distance. She will have no warning, no chance, no knowledge, but what is without doubt, what is totally certain is that her life will end." As Will placed the image down in front of Jarrett and said these words without any trace of emotion he knew that he was losing another small part of his remaining humanity. The untouchable part of his soul that Chris had tried so hard to preserve what was left of it. At the same time he knew that this was the only way he could conceive of to give him, Will James any form of a future.

The second image he put down was of a young girl, perhaps fourteen years old, the third was of a twelve-year-old girl. Both were in school uniform arriving at Westminster school.

"You know who these are," he said. "I will wait longer for them but the same fate will befall them.

"Once I have visited them I will then visit you. Once you have lost them, felt the pain of their passing, then and only then I will terminate you."

As Will placed the images of Jarrett's two daughters in front of him he knew that he had won. While he had remained defiant when his wife's image was produced the risk of harm to his children was too much, it was for almost all sane people. Will could sense the capitulation in Jarrett, he had seen it before, yet to his credit Jarrett tried to maintain the offensive.

"You would not dare," he blurted out with a degree of forced bravado that he clearly did not entirely believe.

"I represent a powerful organisation. We will hunt you down and…"

That was as far as he got. Will knew that it was time for definitive action, a demonstration of his resolve. He did not hesitate. He never did and this was probably one of the main reasons he was still alive. As Jarrett continued his verbal diarrhoea Will reached behind his back with a speed that defied reality. As he had so many times before his open palm flowed in an automatic movement as if magnetized and closed instinctively around the smooth wooden handle of his blade. In a blur of practised motion created by the muscle memory born of repetitive action the razor-sharp long black blade appeared instantaneously before Jarrett's eyes. Powerless he saw it rise and then before he was even able to utter a single syllable of protest it descended in a blur of speed, impaling him to the seat of his wooden chair. As Will had intended it passed directly vertically downwards passing through the wide muscular part of his thigh and fixing him to the seat of the chair. It had tracked through the medial, or inner part of the quadriceps, the group of four muscles that form the large muscular part of the thigh, missing the vital structures of the femoral artery and nerve and exiting, just missing the sciatic nerve, the main nerve controlling all function of the lower limb. It was an injury that was not life-threatening and could easily be recoverable from, yet not only was it exquisitely painful, passing so close to the major neural structures, the rapidity and degree of unfettered aggression combined with now being impaled to his chair had achieved its aim. Now, Jarrett was silent.

Will moved further forward, his face now millimetres from Jarrett's which was covered with cold perspiration from a combination of pain and fear.

"Look at me," Will said. "No, just look at me. There is nothing else. I come from nothing, from nowhere you could ever possibly know or even imagine. I was born in terror. I was taken by force and trained in all aspects of human suffering and despair, from all angles. I survived. I excelled. I do not recognise pity, I do not know mercy but I do know you."

He waited, observing dispassionately as the last of Jarrett's reserve dissolved in front of his eyes. He clearly had no further resistance to offer.

"Look at me now, look closely and you will see what is before you. It is not pretty, it is ugly, it is basic, it is wild and it will do anything and everything in order to survive, there are no limits. Your actions have brought me back to the misery from where I grew. Look at me now, stripped back, naked. Look at me, just me and there will be no doubt what will occur."

As Will spoke these few words in the luxury apartment in Mayfair, central London, so far away from the jungles where he began there were two very different individuals to hear them, one man and one woman. He provided Jarrett with a brief synopsis of his past, just enough so that he would truly appreciate the gravity of his current situation and to reinforce the fact that he would, without any compunction or second thought, carry out the actions he had spelled out earlier in the evening, without the slightest hesitation. There was one other person in the room who now knew his background, who now knew who he was, where he had come from. She said nothing, she did nothing.

Jarrett slumped forwards, or at least as far as the blade fixing him to the seat would allow, all signs of resistance gone. He appreciated that there was no option for him now, no means of escape, and no avenue for negotiation. His only remaining bargaining chip available to him was the sensitivity of the information on those discs.

"But the discs!" he spat out through cracked and swollen lips.

"Ah, those," Will replied, emotionlessly.

"Were they worth it? Was the information on them so valuable? Was it worth the money? Was it worth the lives of so many to protect?"

As Jarrett started to compose a reply Will struck him again, harder than previously and with real conviction, he could not help himself. Here in front of him was the pathetic excuse for a man attempting to justify the taking of innocent life to protect the finances and personal embarrassment of those who had so much already. It was obscene. He had realised some time previously that this process could and would never end while this so-called important information contained in these discs remained at large. He knew that Jarrett, or the next Jarrett, or the next corporation involved would just keep coming for him as long as he held that information they desperately wanted. So he took out his iPhone and stared directly into the defeated eyes and pressed "send".

"I have just sent all the information you so desperately wanted, so desperately wanted to remain hidden. I have sent it to the five largest financial corporations in London. It has gone to the financial editors' desks of *The Times*, *The Telegraph* and *The Sun* newspapers. It has gone to the main news desks of the BBC and CNN and it has now arrived in the in-box of the Metropolitan Police's fraud office. Each of these have direct email addresses readily available on-line to anyone who wishes to look. Every organisation I just mentioned are now in possession of all of your data, all of it. Not only do they have the complete files they also have your name. Piggy backed to each file is an attachment stating that you, Timothy Jarrett are the man who discovered this fraudulent system. That you, and you alone decided that in order to prevent this fraud from continuing to threaten public service you, and you alone disseminated the information. In this you are the hero, you have prevented any further loss of finances and prevented the use of this illegal system ever again. You Mr T Jarrett are irrevocably linked to the discovery of this system and the dissemination of the information and I do mean all the information, identities, transactions, dates, amounts, everything. All the data is now out there and you are responsible for this action!"

Will had long ago decided upon this course of action. The data in Chris's discs had always been the key. Knowing what they contained had brought serious danger and the only way to neutralise that threat was to make the information public. By widely broadcasting all the data Will was no longer the only individual capable of using it and by disseminating the information Will was no longer a threat. There was now no logical requirement to reclaim the discs as the data was now out there for all to see. By openly linking Jarrett personally to the information leak it made him publicly the hero who had discovered and stopped the fraud. Privately it directly linked him to the dissemination of all the data, highly sensitive information about very sensitive individuals and organisations, placing him in a very personally awkward situation. This was the third option he had needed, the third option his drill sergeants had drummed into him in the past. Now Will was no longer of interest to any serious parties. The tables were turned and the one person responsible for this data breach was a Mr T Jarrett. Will had had plenty of time over the last few weeks to download all the data to his personal storage in the iCloud and attach specific files detailing Jarrett's contribution. He had already preprogramed all the email addresses ready for delivery and the simple SMS message from his phone was all that was required to trigger a cascade of messages to be sent with their attached files. With this he had removed the last vestiges of direct threat against himself. He no longer possessed anything of unique value. He turned back to Jarrett's spent form.

"There is nothing left for you save disaster. The information has gone. Very soon I will be gone, permanently. It is time now for you to make a choice between logic and emotion. I am now of no value or risk to you or your organisation and will disappear for ever. You may choose to come for me, to hunt me but it will serve no purpose save vengeance. If you choose to pursue me however rather than forgetting, rather than closing the file I will visit in turn all those I promised to visit, and then at the end, when more innocent lives are wasted on your account I will visit you. If you have any lingering doubt, any last desire for closure, stop and look deep into my eyes, see the blackness of my soul. There is no place for confusion, no place for mercy, it was forged out of me in my past life. You will understand."

As he quietly uttered these terrible words he slowly and painfully withdrew his blade from Jarrett's thigh, twisting it as he gradually withdrew the steel from the sinew of his leg and silently slid it back into its leather sheath, turned and walked away. He paused to cut the bonds wrapped around the wrists of the only other person in the room. The young beautiful woman had said nothing, she had uttered not a single syllable, had made no protest or plea for safety. Will cut her free and turned her round to face him. Once again almost physically struck by her beauty so close to him, he spoke in a hushed tone directly to her so that they could not be overheard.

"You now are the only other person in the world who knows who I am and where I came from. I am going to leave and I will leave you unharmed. What you do now is your choice and yours alone. I am sorry, you did not ask for this interruption to your life and you have done nothing to deserve it, this was my conflict that you have been caught in. You may stay and deal with the consequences of my actions tonight or you may leave, it is your decision."

As he finished this brief yet intimate interaction between just the two of them he bent down and took from his rucksack half of the cash that he was carrying and placed it on the floor in front of her. It was not an enormous sum but it is was a few hundred thousand pounds, enough to start again in a new life.

"You did not ask for me to disturb your life, you did nothing to deserve this interruption and I am sorry. This is all I have to give you in return. I think you and I are not so dissimilar, our backgrounds not so far apart. Take this money, leave, start again, go and be free."

Will then turned, gathered his belongings into a single rucksack and left.

It was not perfect, nothing in real life ever was but it was the best he could do with the deal he had been dealt. He was no longer a threat to anyone. The information and all the data was now readily publicly available and the discs themselves were now of no value. Jarrett was linked to the dissemination of the data, publicly as the hero who had prevented the loss of further capital, privately he would have serious worries of his own; there would be a number of seriously unpleasant individuals and corporations who would be seriously pissed off with the widespread availability of this information. There would be consequences for being responsible for the release of all that unwanted information being out there for all to see, including Her Majesty's Inland Revenue service who would now be chasing a number of very affluent, very angry and soon to be less affluent individuals and organisations for their unpaid tax returns. Nothing was perfect but this was the best he could do, his best chance of being able to simply move on, a chance of a new life free from persecution, free from the constant threat of recrimination. Free from the violence he had known for almost all of his life. Free from those who had most recently threatened him. Free to move on, alone.

CHAPTER FORTY-ONE

It had been three months. Three months ago Will had left two people in a luxury apartment in an exclusive building in the centre of Mayfair. One a semi-conscious defeated man with a significant but not -life-threatening leg wound and a treated, major chest injury, the other a beautiful and intriguing young woman who he had never met before and who he was highly unlikely to ever meet again. He had constantly migrated from various low-class locations, hostels, downtrodden and unnoticed bed and breakfast houses, unoccupied flats and occasionally had just slept rough, mixed in with the many homeless on the cold and unfeeling streets of London. He had done as he had promised and simply disappeared into the ether of obscurity afforded to the homeless and poorest parts of society of inner city London. For all its glittering wealth, so obviously on public display there is another layer common to all great cities. There are those that dwell, not normally by choice, in the realms of poverty and homelessness and it was here that Will had taken refuge. Here in this society of undesirables he was able to remain unnoticed and unobserved, principally as in this particular world no one cared. No one was the slightest bit interested in him, in his actions or what became of him. No one had the luxury of caring for one more lost soul. Everyone else was just focused on making it through the next day and long, cold night, one day at a time. It suited Will perfectly. He was anonymous and had readily available cash, the only commodity of any worth in this situation and so he was able to move untraced from one seedy undesirable location to another with no questions being asked nor any need for formal identification.

Three months had now passed with him existing in this world of poverty and nothing had happened. Nothing at all! There had been an ever so brief mention on the national news that a financial fraud within the trading sector had been discovered and "appropriate measures" had been taken to control it. There had even been a still image of Jarrett's smiling face attached to the report as the upstanding and honest man responsible for discovering and dismantling this potential threat to the wealthy's already considerable assets and now the one man able to protect them for the future. He came over well, dependable, reliable, trustworthy, someone who would be a suitable safe guard for your assets. However twenty-four hours later there was a terrorist attack in Paris. A lunatic had driven a truck into a crowd of innocent shoppers, just visiting the shops in the middle of the day over the New Year holidays, in the name of some deluded religious group or cult who thought that their way was the only way, who somehow mistakenly thought that this demonstration of senseless violence would persuade others to follow their cause. And as the saying goes, today's news is tomorrow's chip paper and so the story of a few very rich people losing some money faded into insignificance, as it rightfully should.

In truth Will was now bored. Boredom was a state of mind and body that he had never known in his life. Although he was now twenty-eight years old he had lived his entire life at full throttle. There had been danger at every turn, life-threatening situations normally not of his own choice or creation. Now, after three months of inactivity, of essentially doing nothing except remaining obscure and insignificant, he was officially bored. As he munched through yet another plate of greasy eggs on toast at yet another nondescript grimy London café he reflected on his new-found state of boredom. In truth, in reality being bored was great. He, Will James, was for the first time in his living memory able to do just nothing of any consequence. There was no one shouting at him to go faster, push harder or be stronger. As far as he could tell there was no one actively trying to kill him at this precise moment in time and he was not now in a conflict zone that could erupt into lethal violence without warning. He was just sitting quietly in a London cafe, bored. His biggest decision of the morning was whether to have ketchup or brown sauce on his eggs. Once he had understood this state of inactivity, once he had been able to get his head around this passive existence that he had been so unused to, he had begun to realise that boredom in fact was not such a bad thing after all.

Will had decided to wait for a minimum of three months before resurfacing. He figured that if anything was going to happen, if there was going to be any direct retribution from Jarrett, or the next Jarrett or his team it would happen sooner rather than later. He figured that if there was to be an attack on him it would be for reasons of emotion rather than logic and the longer he left it, the faster the emotions would fade and the stronger reason would become. With time as he rationalised the situation the more confident he became that they would not come for him. The main reason was that he was no longer of any consequence. The money had long gone. The one hundred million that he had briefly possessed, the money that Chris had stolen, was back where it belonged with its original owners. Chris, for all his excellent qualities, despite everything he had done for Will, had ended with a big mistake. He had taken something that was not his from those who were not prepared to lose it. If he had just taken one million pounds, an enormous amount to most people, he would probably have been fine, such a relatively small amount could be overlooked, but one hundred million, it was too much and those in financial power could not tolerate this loss. They had sent Jarrett to resolve the issue and to all intents and purposes he had been highly successful. He had retrieved the money, the primary objective. He had neutralised the system that had defrauded the money, the secondary objective and the data on the discs was no longer as sensitive as it once was now it was public knowledge. How this had occurred was known only to three people, two men and one woman, none of whom were ever likely to discuss the finer details of the process. The money was gone, the mechanism was gone and the data was now irrelevant. All that remained was Jarrett's pride, could he put it aside and let him go? Of course he could, he did not really have a viable choice and there were three very good reasons why Jarrett would not counter-attack. To come after him would serve no purpose, save self-satisfaction and revenge. It would require a significant team to take him down and this would be expensive, really expensive and Will doubted that personal satisfaction came above material loss in Jarrett's priorities. However, and most importantly, was the simple fact that to come after him would risk triggering the actions of their private discussion three months previously. The more time he spent working through his current situation the more he became convinced that it was now relatively safe for him to resurface. On the balance of probabilities he, Will James, was now of no consequence, irrelevant. No one should care what happened to him or what he did, there was no reason for them to do so. Irrelevant was an ideal state to be in. It was time to move on.

CHAPTER FORTY-TWO

The Marines. The Royal Marines had given him a second opportunity in life, it had been his family of sorts for almost a decade. They had not cared who he originally was, they had not cared what his background had been or where he had come from and there had been no prejudice or bias. They had welcomed him, trained him and embraced all that he was and harnessed and refined his considerable skills. He had spent the best part of a decade living, breathing, fighting as a Marine and he figured that he owed them at least an explanation for his absence. It had been a little over six months, half a year, that he had been away without any reason or notification. He was officially AWOL and this was an unacceptable end to his career both for him and the Marines and he knew it. He had decided that now was the time to return to the Marine training camp at Lympstone, his former base of operations. His reasons were not purely altruistic as he had decided that if retribution was to come, if there was to be any direct recrimination for his actions over the last six months there were only two solid points for any hostile team to reacquire contact. The first and by far the least likely was *Amnesia*, although he doubted if anyone knew about her.

His yacht was his only significant personal possession. To most it represented a luxury, a plaything of the rich, but to him it was home, the only home he had ever known since being taken as a boy all those years ago from the sanctuary of St Xavier's. Even if a hostile team had found out about his ownership of a yacht he seriously doubted that they would have been able to locate her. Last seen, *Amnesia* was anchored safely in the middle of Batson Creek in Salcombe harbour on the south coast of Devon. However, he had left her alone on a swing mooring in a deepwater pool halfway up the deserted Avon River, isolated and unknown. Even if his yacht had registered on their search patterns and if it had then been located in Salcombe Harbour he was confident that she would have remained undetected and unobserved on her lonely mooring on the isolated estuary. The second point of reference in Will's life however was far more concrete. The Marine base at Lympstone, Exeter, had been his official base of operations for almost ten years and was the point to which he would have to return if he wished to regain any vestiges of his former life. It was here that any team wishing to take him out would wait, it was the only realistic option that they would have available to them of reacquiring contact. All logic, all common sense told Will to never return, to leave, to run as far and fast as he could while he still had the chance. However there were two more pressing reasons for him to return, two reasons that outweighed the need to run. The first, and least important, was that he figured he owed it to the Royal Marines to explain his absence, although this could be overridden if there was no other benefit to returning. The second and significantly more important reason for his return was that it was about time to find out whether or not he was free to move on, whether he would be able to create a new life, or if Jarrett had been unable to let go, unable to let logic win over emotion. It was time to discover if there remained a continued personal threat that he would have to neutralise, whether more would have to die for him to be free. Despite the obvious personal risk of returning to Lympstone the benefit of knowing this one fact, knowing whether he was able to move on without persecution, outweighed the risk. It was time to find out which way the cards were going to fall.

So now as spring was pushing back the cold and damp tail of winter he found himself shivering high above the Marine base at Lympstone looking through the lenses of a powerful pair of shielded binoculars. He was hidden from sight in a hide that rose just thirty centimetres above the irregular ground that surrounded him. He had built it himself in darkness overnight from the bracken and foliage that was lying freely on the ground, it was undetectable from the surroundings, the silhouette of the hide blended in perfectly with the rough terrain. He was just over 100 metres away from a very rarely used rough car park of sorts known by locals as Four Firs for obvious reasons, namely the four large individual conifers that dominated each corner of this clearing and were visible on the skyline from below. Will however was completely hidden and you would have had to step on top of him before being aware of his presence. This little-known spot at the top of Woodbury Common was frequented only by the occasional group of mountain bikers who profit from the criss-crossing stony trails that cut through the shrubs and gorse of this large area of common land that towers over the city of Exeter and the estuary below. This location had other significant benefits, apart from its ready access to mountain biking trails, it was easily accessed from different directions and, if required, very rapidly vacated from any given angle. Also the primary reason for Will's presence at this location was from this high point he had a panoramic view over the marine base and all of its entry and exit points. He had first discovered this isolated spot as a recruit being beasted over the exposed gorse land by his physical instructors in basic training. Now he had been here for three days. Each day he would arrive before dawn and remain motionless, hidden in his hide and then steal away undetected under cover of darkness. He had silently and unmoving observed everything that was unfolding below him at the front of the marine base over the last seventy-two hours. He was looking for anything that was not quite right, anything that was out of place, incongruous or without specific function. Anything or anyone who lingered longer than necessary and without a good reason. After three days of observation he was confident that the area was clean, there was nothing out of the ordinary, nothing that did not fit in to the normal routine he had known so well for almost a decade, nothing that aroused suspicion. While he owed the Royal Marines an explanation he was not simply going to walk right up to the gate without preparation. If he was still a target it was here that a team would be waiting and it always paid to be careful. His natural cautiousness, hardwired into his makeup, made him wait a further two days and now, after a week of lonely reconnaissance with absolutely nothing out of the ordinary, he was satisfied it was as safe as it could possibly be expected to be. It was time to find out if Jarrett and his organisation, M&C had been able to walk away, able to close his case and let logic win over blind emotion. It was time to find out if he, Will James was still a target.

He walked forwards, slowly and alone and approached the barrier in front of the marine base. He stood still, a lone individual in the centre of the smooth tarmacked approach just five metres from the barrier. To the casual observer this was just a single horizontal wooden coloured bar that could be easily raised or lowered or shattered if required with minimal force. To the uninitiated there was nothing else to prevent unwanted entry. To those who knew however this ten-metre area was far more. As he stood stationary in front of the feeble barrier he knew that there were no fewer than six cameras trained on him and his immediate surroundings, including three highly efficient and lethal tripod-mounted automatic rotating-barrel machine guns that, with the press of a single button would instantly literally incinerate anything in this specific ten by ten metre kill box. Hidden below the simple wooden horizontal barrier, embedded in the smooth concrete, were four rows of steel claws ready to fly out and rip the belly from any vehicle that tried foolishly to force entry. They were called crocodile teeth as the impact they had on any vehicle was phenomenal and permanently disabling, they used its own momentum to just rip it apart. If that were not enough behind the seemingly innocuous office windows just seven metres to the left and right of this gated area were four further XM rotating-barrel machine guns, each trained over a specific overlapping arc of fire that created a kill zone that nothing could survive if they were activated. Knowing all of this made it far easier for Will to stand still, motionless, arms outstretched and palms open and obviously empty in plain view. He clearly stated his name when challenged from the guardhouse.

"Major William James, previous active commando of 43 Squadron"

As he stood there, almost crucifix-like in his stationary pose, completely exposed with no cover at all, every fibre of his body was strained with adrenaline-fuelled alertness. Each hair on the back of his neck was erect, he was tense with anxiety but totally self-controlled as ever and remained motionless. He knew that if it were to happen, now was the moment. He had considered running, disappearing for ever, but then he would never know if it was over. That nagging doubt of potential lethal threat would always be there. He figured that on the balance of probability the odds were slightly better than even, perhaps sixty to forty in his favour, he had taken worse in the past and survived. Over the last five days he had seen no evidence of any threat and he was good at detecting anything out of place, he had done it many times before.

He was stationary, alone, completely exposed, out in the open in broad daylight. He would have no warning. He would not hear the shot. He would not feel the impact of the high-velocity round ripping through his torso or even shattering his cranium as it exited his skull, if the shooter was good enough. If they wanted to terminate him, if the risk was viable for M&C. It was not the formidable hidden arsenal in front of him he was waiting for, that could be predicted and controlled, it was the single unannounced high-velocity round that would finish him without his awareness that might now arrive. Nothing! Nothing happened, as if time were standing still the seconds and then minutes ticked by. Here he was totally defenceless, motionless and out in the open, exposed. Nothing! As each precious second passed, as each cycle of his heart continued, continued beating uninterruptedly a tiny bit of relief crept into his mind. Maybe, just maybe he was free to move on.

Eventually the computers had churned and his name had been spat out with his details. His AWOL status was flashing in bold red print across the front of the screen with instructions to "Detain with extreme prejudice". Suddenly there were six armed professional marine commandos all on high alert and all training their weapons directly at Will. The command to remain still was shouted out clearly with the customary loud and direct confidence that it would be instantly obeyed, it was the manner of the armed forces that Will was used to. With at least six weapons zeroed in directly on him from less than a ten-metre range it was not a difficult command to follow and he remained motionless as stone. In moments he found himself bound securely by his wrists, his arms behind him, with two cable ties. It was the technique he had been taught and had used many times in the past. These ties were easy to apply and could be closed in less than a second, far faster and far stronger than any rope and, with no fatigue or capability for stretching, almost impossible to break free from. As in everything they did in the special forces two ties were used in case, for whatever bizarre reason, one broke, there was always a backup if possible. The manner of his detainment almost drew a grin from his characteristically stony emotionless visage. It had been done in a textbook manner, the way he had been taught and then in turn had taught others. He was then taken firmly but efficiently and placed in a holding pen just inside the guardhouse. He was now out of public view, protected from the outside. He now belonged once again to the Marines. He was corralled by four armed soldiers, all of them young, in their late teens or early twenties. He had not met them before and he knew that earlier in the day they would have been grumbling to each other that they had been allocated to guardhouse duty, normally the most boring and slowest of all grinds on the base, the one most in the public limelight and the session most disliked by all the base's resident soldiers. There were no bored faces now. Will did not care whether they had been bored five minutes previously or now fully alert, he knew that they were professionals. The fact that he was still alive, still breathing, heart still beating meant only one thing. Jarrett, his team, his organisation M&C were now with a following wind a thing of the past. He, Major W. James was clearly not important enough for them to take any action, simply put killing him was not worth the risk, he was just not worth it. He had won! He had become irrelevant. As he stood in stationary silence, surrounded by armed professional soldiers with their weapons trained directly on him he allowed himself for the first time in just over six months to relax just by the smallest of amounts. In a situation that would seem on the outside to be extremely hostile to all but the very few he found a surge of hope beginning to creep into his soul. Facing four rifle barrels pointed directly at him he allowed himself for the very first time in what seemed like forever to perhaps consider a life in the future. A life of his own making, a life free of conflict.

CHAPTER FORTY-THREE

He was rapidly moved deeper into the base, further away from any public vision or hearing. He was taken from the initial holding pen and placed in a secure windowless, featureless square box of a room, officially known as the decontamination area, in essence a containment cell. Once his details had been registered and he had been identified the gate patrol knew enough to politely but effectively detain him. He sat now essentially a captive, in a cell, alone and content. He had made it through into the marine base, he was still alive. He sat in silence in a prison cell finally safe.

Several hours passed and he was given water and some basic food. He waited. He was aware that he was now under constant CCTV surveillance so he simply sat and waited in silence, there was nothing else that he could do. The hours slid by and as they did he had a fairly accurate idea of the actions taking place outside his detention cell. One could not simply up and leave the British special forces without notice, without any prior warning or explanation and the harsh plain truth was that he had been AWOL for just over six months. The Royal Marines had invested a considerable amount of time, effort and not inconsiderable finances in his specific training and to them the current situation was unacceptable. To add to this the simple fact was that he was an incredibly valuable asset. His specific skill set both in personal survival and destruction on an individual and more major scale had been demonstrated and harnessed time and time again, he knew he excelled. Added to this was his physical qualities, his multiple languages, his knowledge of Africa and his ability to pass as either European or African as the situation required. He was fluent in English, French, German and several African dialects. He was fluent in the art of combat and this combination was very, very rare indeed. Will was aware of this, he had never hidden from reality and he knew what he was worth and he knew that the Marines would want him back. However he also knew that the Marines and all the special forces were built on certain rules, they relied on a chain of command that was sacrosanct and these rules were not for breaking. Being AWOL, even for someone of Will's qualities and value, was not acceptable. With these thoughts roaming around his consciousness he continued to sit stationary in silence in a cell. There was a single desk in the centre of the featureless room, secured to the smooth vinyl floor with screws, set into the floor so that they could not easily be removed without a specific tool and made into a makeshift weapon. The Navy never stinted even when it came to the finer details. The chairs were made of light plywood, just strong enough to support a man's weight but not solid enough to be formed into any significant weapon. There was a single semi-circular bulge in the ceiling with non-breakable reinforced glass that contained cameras for recording both vision and sound to document and archive any information that may be gained. The room was specifically designed for interrogation and Will knew all of this as he himself had interrogated others in similar rooms with almost identical structures. So he sat and waited.

Several slow hours passed and his mind began to drift to past experiences, his previous life in a distant continent and as the hours stretched further he began to lose track of time. This of course was the intention of the long delay in this featureless room with no access to the outside world, no indicator of day or night, and then without warning the door opened. Unannounced two officers entered, both of whom he immediately recognised. The first was Lieutenant Commander Wilson, he was the base commander and Will had known him for a little over five years; he had trained with him and he had been deployed on several missions by him. This officer had sent him in to harm's way on active missions several times in the past and he respected him greatly. Will knew that he had gained his rank, his elevated position the hard way. He had served his time on active duty and understood what it was to be in a combat zone, under constant threat and he was unafraid to send others into the same situation if the reasons were good enough. The second man surprised Will. He had only met him once before at a regimental parade, in fact it was this man who had pinned his silver wings onto his green beret at his passing-out parade all those years previously, the physical sign of his acceptance into the Marines. His name was General G. M. Campbell and he was responsible for the entire special forces of the UK. As would be expected for someone in his position he was tough, intelligent, logical, uncompromising and in complete control and it was his presence that probably accounted for the long delay. His presence also indicated to Will the importance of this meeting, if he was here there was to be no mucking around, no provocation and no room for miscommunication.

"Where the fuck have you been?" was the first question they asked. It was a fair question that deserved a fair answer. As always in the forces there was no time or space for any ambiguity or delay, straight to the point. He had already decided to tell them the truth, or as much of the truth as he possibly could without directly incriminating himself in any serious criminal acts that might lead to any further or more permanent detention. So Will started at the beginning, telling them how he had discovered that a one Mr Christopher James, his guardian, had been murdered and the reason why. He told them how he had come to be in possession of the critical information held on those fated discs, although he omitted any of the details of the incident on *Amnesia* where he had been forced to neutralise his two assailants. He then went on to describe how he had been threatened and how he had responded in kind, just as he had been trained to do so, removing and retaking the initiative, neutralising the threat. He explained how he had taken Jarrett and then released all the information publicly, again omitting the finer details of their discussion and the exact technique he had employed in order to change Jarrett's viewpoint and persuade him to close the file. There was no need for these specific details, these were intelligent experienced commanders of the special forces, not boy scouts and they were well aware of what Will was capable of, they had trained him. They could read between the lines. Neither were naive and both could assume the tactics and direct techniques that Will would have used. There was one other detail that Will held back, he was not quite sure why but he mentioned nothing of the beautiful young woman who had been present for his conversation with Jarrett. He mentioned nothing of the only other living person who now knew his true background, where he had come from. He was not overly sure why he decided for her to remain anonymous, whether it was out of a feeling of protection or more likely guilt, guilt for turning her life upside down in the process of restoring his. Either way he saw no positive purpose in involving her any further. And so after several hours interspersed with the occasional question he had told his tale to his previous commanding officers. He had laid himself bare leaving only a very few details out. He had spelled out the highly illegal activities that he had willingly undertaken over the last months and had kept very little back. He was well aware that if this was a civilian case, if he was currently sitting in a police cell, being interrogated by a police department, he would be facing a not inconsiderable amount of jail time. His actions had hardly been what would be considered normal for modern-day society. This however was not a civilian case, he was still currently an officer in the British special forces and he had served his time over the last decade, he had paid his dues and more in active combat zones and this was most definitely a military matter.

Now after the telling and in this relatively safe environment he suddenly felt emotionally spent. After six months on constant alert without any support he had little mental reserves left. What had been left of his mental strength had been further depleted by the processes of the last few hours, mainly by the moments when he simply stood still, out in the open, in front of the marine base, the moment when retribution could have come and fortunately did not, he had little left to hold together. Despite his inner mental exhaustion, as always, his external appearance was unchanged, neutral. His years in the jungle as a boy, experiencing countless acts of human misery had created this unmoving façade. His facial features always remained motionless, showing no emotion whatever the situation and today was no exception. It was a trait common to all who have experienced such hardship, showing any external sign of weakness only lead to potential exploitation and his steely ice-blue eyes showed no weakness, they never did. As he finished silence fell on the room. Both the commander and the general were in no doubt of the truthfulness of his testimony. There was no reason at all to fabricate such a complex tale and the absolute conviction in his voice was enough for them. They knew when they were hearing the truth. They passed no judgement, offered no acceptance, showed neither reassurance nor disappointment, they simply closed their files, confirmed the time and date for the cessation of recording, rose and left. After all both men were battle hardened marines, emotion was not a big part of their makeup. The door closed and Will was left alone to wait.

As it happened the wait took four days. He was transferred to holding quarters, slightly larger and slightly more comfortable than the interrogation cell but still locked and guarded. He was in reality held in a military detention prison, he had expected nothing less and in fact this was the best that he was hoping for. It was not possible to be AWOL and have no consequences and it could have been so much worse in a permanent way. Ninety-six hours later, almost to the minute he was securely escorted back to the same interrogation room, cameras rolling. This time there were four men facing him, all senior, all in formal uniform, a military tribunal panel. The exact configuration of the panel and the location of this hearing were unimportant. The decision, their decision, the decision of the Royal Navy had been taken, it was final, there was no room for any negotiation or an appeal. He stood upright and to attention as he had been trained to do and stood waiting to hear their decision as many had done in the past, it was the tradition that had been continued for several centuries and now, as his verdict was about to be delivered, he understood why. He wanted to be standing tall, standing alone as a man, to hear the decision that would shape his immediate future.

"This closed military panel has taken all the evidence placed in front of them into account and have placed particular emphasis on the testimony of the defendant. We have come to a final decision from which there will be no opportunity for appeal. The actions of Major James over the period concerned can be in no way recognised by Her Majesty's Naval Forces. During this period of absence without leave he has acted independently and as such all of his actions have been taken by his own personal volition and as such he will now accept both responsibility for them, and the consequences of them, in keeping with his position as an officer of the Royal Marines. On the first point of civil criminal charges, having carefully considered all the information placed in front of this panel we cannot find any firm evidence of any civil crime being committed and as such there is no statutory requirement to involve any of the other authorities of the UK law-enforcement services. However you have left your post of active service without any notification or authorisation and this is unacceptable, even if your personal reasons appear to be morally just. The statutory punishment for this action, the act of desertion, is a maximum of ten years in military detention. While we would be entirely justified in levying this sentence upon you we would also wish to balance the service you have paid to your country and this armed force in the past. Therefore, despite the evidence presented over the last week, in recognition of Major W. James exemplary and long combat service in many arenas of conflict over the last ten years there will be no military charges for his prolonged absence without organised leave."

As Will stood ramrod still and listened to their verdict begin to unfold, he became aware that they had decided that his actions over the last six months should be dealt with within the military and remain an internal matter.

"However, your persistent absence, unauthorised and not negotiated, remains unacceptable and cannot be tolerated. The Royal Navy's rules are created for a purpose and cannot be disregarded under any circumstances, however extreme they may be. Therefore our considered and final decision is to grant you a Dishonourable Discharge from her Majesty's Royal Naval Service with immediate effect. All previous benefits, funding, pension rights and any rank or privilege are now withdrawn, active immediately."

Will stood motionless in silence and absorbed their decision delivered in the military monotone he had grown to know so well over the last ten years. In essence he was free to go! His life in the special forces was now over, he was not surprised by this decision, his actions had given them little other option. He was discharged with immediate effect. He looked directly at each of the four men present who had decided his future and each met his gaze with a level unflinching stare. These were all men who had experienced conflict and lived through it, none were afraid and he respected them all. He was patently aware that they were letting him go. If they had wished they would have been justified in keeping him in a military detention facility on an indefinite basis due to his actions of the past six months. They had chosen a different path, they were letting him leave. He had served his time, he had paid his dues over the last ten years putting himself in harm's way for the Navy's purposes time and time again and he figured that this was the reason that they had shown such leniency. He looked directly at them all, slowly, individually, one by one and then replied with one word only.

"Thank you."

He turned and left, leaving another chapter of his life behind.

CHAPTER FORTY-FOUR

As the late spring sun rose through the early morning mist, turning the mirror-flat waters of the Avon estuary from featureless inky black to the dazzling sight of a million individually oscillating interlinked shimmering lights, a single black neoprene-clad figure in a dark wetsuit slipped into the water without creating a single ripple. Will had made his way from the marine base at Lympstone to Averton Gifford, a tiny picture postcard perfect Devon hamlet at the head of the Avon River. This village, if one is being generous for it was more a collection of a few dozen houses and of course a traditional pub, the heart and soul of the village, was centred on an imposing 200 year-old multi-arched stone bridge that forges the head of the river and in generations gone by had served as a point of access and as a trading post that the village grew around. Now it was mainly just photographed by tourists as an iconic image of a Devonian village and occasionally used by the locals who fish this particular stretch of the river chasing after the sea bass that migrate upstream to spawn their young and then died in the effort. This particular morning there were two lone anglers, revelling in the silent early morning solitude and natural beauty, casting their lines across the river and hoping that a fish may be fooled by their lures. Neither noticed the single swimmer as he silently glided by, pushed past them by the outward flowing ebb tide.

The thick white blanket of early morning mist slowly began to lift off the surrounding countryside as the heat of the rising sun warmed it by a few degrees. Yet as always at this time of year it lingered over the colder waters of the river, slower to heat up in the morning sun. Will had entered the icy cold water just above the bridge on the turn of the tide. This was the upper limit of the tidal reach of the Avon River, upstream the river soon turned into marshlands and then rich arable lands, beautifully cultivated for generations and generations, downstream the river grew and lead eventually to Bantham and the Bigbury estuary. However, before that, three quarters of the way to the sea lay *Amnesia*, he hoped, undiscovered and waiting for his return.

He half swam, half floated and half scrambled, when it became shallow, down the estuary, pulled downstream by the outgoing tide. As he silently slid by mile after mile he drank in the scenery and wildlife that he floated past and it was truly spectacular. The lush green of the Devon pastureland with cattle grazing undisturbed and serene, the unthreatened wildlife of the river that paid him no attention as, to them, he was no threat and the icy cold water of the flowing river; the combination invigorated him, made him feel alive. As he slowly rounded a particularly wide and meandering bend of the river the throwaway comments of his Marine guards came back to him. As he was escorted out of the marine base at Lympstone for the very last time, now in effect a free civilian, one of the four soldiers assigned to escort him on his way had flippantly asked:

"What next then, mate?"

He had replied without thinking, which was abnormal for him and almost as flippantly.

"Hopefully nothing. Hopefully boredom, unemployment."

All four of his guards looked at him, none removed any of his bindings, but all of them just laughed. The more talkative one of the quartet replied though his convulsions of laughter.

"Boredom, unemployment! Not fucking likely mate. Not for someone like you."

These were the last words he had heard uttered from them as he was set free at the gates of the marine base and now they replayed through his mind. Could he move on to carve out a new life? Would he be allowed to move on? Was that in fact a possibility for someone like him, someone with the specific skill set he had developed, someone with the mental alertness he had always had? Yes, of course he could, given the opportunity he was now the master of his own destiny, a situation that had never occurred in the past, a basic human liberty taken so lightly by those who possessed it and craved after so desperately by those who did not. This ability to do simply as he wished was liberating and he revelled in it as the icy cold water pulsed around him.

He had been in the water now for almost two hours and was beginning to shiver. It did not bother him as he knew that all of his physical faculties were still working perfectly, in fact the reflex contractions of his spinal muscles caused his skin to rub against the blade still snuggled in the small of his back, his comfort blanket, ever present. More importantly he was 100 per cent certain that he had not been followed, there was no one else bobbing down the deserted estuary, there was no overhead or even satellite surveillance that could follow him here; he was alone. As the strengthening tide floated him round the next bend in the enlarging river he saw her. His home. *Amnesia* was right where he had left her. This was the only other firm contact that he had and the only other location that a hostile team could possibly be waiting to take him. It was unlikely as he had passed through Lympstone without any contact but *unlikely* was just not good enough, he was well aware that he was entering a zone of potential threat. As he floated closer his mind, his body and all of his senses became fully alert, suddenly he was not aware of the cold anymore. As he approached his beloved yacht he could see that there had been some expected superficial external damage caused by the winter season and a few dozen zealous seagulls, but otherwise on first inspection all seemed to be in order. Superficially, from his angle of vision from the water, she was as he would have expected, weathered but pretty much just as he had left her. Slowly and silently he slid by her letting the ebb tide take him further on downstream. He did not make any attempt to approach or board her. To any observer, if there was one, he would simply be a rather deranged estuary swimmer and of no threat. He let himself be carried around the next bend in the river and *Amnesia* slipped out of sight. As she did so he swiftly swam to the near shore with strong underarm strokes, nothing breaking the surface, no sound, no splashes or ripples to alert an observer and hauled himself out of the water. He wriggled across the ten metres of thick black estuary mud on his abdomen, maximising his surface area in contact with the mud so he did not sink into the energy-sapping slime and pulled himself under the roots of a massive ancient tree that rose majestically out of the estuary, its roots forming a latticework that he was sheltered below. He was caked in black estuary mud, he was hidden from sight by the hollow of the tree roots, he was virtually undetectable and a perfect location to watch. From this location he was now dry and could observe *Amnesia* undetected. It had paid many, many times over in the past to be cautious and old habits die hard. He had arrived at a potential area of conflict and he was not going to simply barrel in unprepared. *Amnesia* looked deserted, but he needed to be sure.

The tide fell away from him converting the huge expanse of water into a small mud-flanked stream full of wading birds. He remained motionless, hidden, watching and waiting. Six hours later the water rose once again as it always did, covering the thick clinging estuary mud with cleansing clear seawater, filling the estuary, he watched and waited. As the tide turned for a third time and began to flow out once more there had been no activity at all. He was satisfied that he was alone. There had been no change of shift of any hostile team, he had not detected any observer waiting for him to appear, as expected *Amnesia* remained anonymous and isolated, just as he liked it. He slid back into the water and with strong strokes was soon at the side of his yacht. The cleansing clear water ridding him of his coating of black estuary slime that had served as such excellent camouflage. He pulled down the boarding ladder with a thrill of excitement and with some trepidation clambered aboard. He was cold, he could not feel the extremities of his body, his fingers and toes were numb from the combination of the cold and inactivity, but he forced them to work by sheer mental will power, they were not broken so his mind told them to grip and to function, despite the lack of sensation after being in the water and mud for so long. Swiftly he climbed the boarding ladder, hauling himself on board. He lay down flat on the teak-clad deck so as not to create a silhouette in the moonlight, for it was now dark and he waited. Nothing! Nothing had happened. There had been no frenzied activity from belowdecks and there was no sign that any human had placed a foot aboard since he left almost nine months previously. He turned over and lay still on the familiar deck, looking up at the unmistakable sights of the South Coast's night sky and waited. Nothing, mercifully nothing. His arrival had not triggered an explosion that would have ripped both him and *Amnesia* apart, this was the other possibility that he had considered, the possibility that an explosive device could have been placed aboard to greet him on his return, a vey unfriendly welcome home present. He had been aware of this possibility as he arrived but had seen no signs of tripwires or any trigger. He waited, lying still for a further thirty minutes and still there was no signs of any activity at all, he was alone. He had arrived back where he had left off nine months previously, his yacht had remained undetected and in general unharmed by the winter season. He was alive. He was home. It was enough.

CHAPTER FORTY-FIVE

The mainsail was already set and as *Amnesia* moved out of the estuary and into the open ocean Will cut the engine. The sudden lack of any man-made noise as the last vibrations of the diesel engine faded was always relaxing, peaceful. As the gentle swell began to massage the boat's sleek smooth hull she rose and fell to its natural rhythm. The wind came from the south-west as it generally did on the South Coast and it began to freshen as he moved out of the shadow of the land. He knew from previous experience that it would take between eight to ten hours if the conditions remained the same to cross the Channel and arrive in France. From there he would hug the coast, staying anchored in small deserted protected inlets or private harbours, never remaining in the same place for long, just drifting aimlessly along. He had enough supplies aboard to last for several months and certainly enough finance to last for at least half a year. After that he would just work it out as it came, day by day. He had no fixed itinerary and could go as he pleased, where he pleased when he pleased.

As the coastline shrank behind him he unfurled the jib, the large triangular shaped sail at the bow of the boat. It was mounted on a roller mechanism which allowed him to unfurl the huge sail single-handed with just the pull of a single rope from the cockpit. As he did the wind caught the relaxed flaccid material and filled it with life. The loud, unmistakeably crisp snap as the material transformed from a hanging curtain to a taught stretched canvas, raising the bows of the boat upwards and even out of the crests of the waves as its inexhaustible energy propelled it forward, was a sound like no other. As the sail snapped taut the crystallised salt from last year that had clung to its surface from its previous outing was jettisoned in a fine mist which floated down and covered Will. This fine powder, combined with the freshening south-west wind and the salt spray that flew up each time the bows plunged down and through an oncoming roller filled his lungs. He breathed in deeply, slowly savouring the moment for this, for him, was the scent of freedom.

Will closed his eyes, lost in the moment and despite himself was plunged back to his beginnings. In his mind, as vivid as it had been then he was a child once more, stood in a village square surrounded by death, destruction and human despair. The thick, almost sweet stench of death, fear, flames and cordite fumes mixed together had been seared into his soul for ever. He stood alone, surrounded by it all, alone on the red-stained mud where it had all begun. Sight, sound, touch, taste, they had all been there but for Will it had always been the scent that he could never forget, could never shake off. Occasionally in his dreams he would return to those terrible violence-filled days of his youth, but it was in such rare still moments that the memories became more vivid, more real. He realised now that they would never leave him, they were a part of his past, a part of him he could not ignore or relinquish. He now understood that each and every event, mainly based around human pain and suffering, that he had experienced, the good and bad had led him to be who he was; he had to accept it. Chris had temporarily dragged him out of that life, for a brief period but it was not to be. His actions over the last few months and in reality the life he had lead over the last ten years in the Marines had never strayed far from the path of violence. He knew what he was, he knew how he had become the individual he was, the things he had done and those that he was capable of. Now he had the opportunity to move on, to make his own decisions and determine his own path. Now he had to live with it.

As *Amnesia*'s smooth bow cut through a cresting wave, the spray it generated caressed Will's face and brought him out of his reverie and back to the present. He was here, now. He was alone, he was on *Amnesia*, his home. He was beholden to no one, for once, at this exact moment in time he was completely free! He breathed deeply once more, taking in the salt, the spray, the silence and the clean moving air. This was the scent of freedom.

He hoped it would last.